Self-Portrait

Fr. Tom #4

A Novel

By Jim Sano

Full Quiver Publishing
Pakenham, Ontario

Self-Portrait
copyright 2023
by James G. Sano

Published by Full Quiver Publishing
PO Box 244
Pakenham, Ontario K0A 2X0

ISBN Number: 978-1-987970-50-0
Printed and bound in the USA

Cover design: James Hrkach and Jim Sano

NATIONAL LIBRARY OF CANADA
CATALOGUING IN PUBLICATION
ALL RIGHTS RESERVED

Copyright 2023 James G. Sano
Published by FQ Publishing
A Division of Innate Productions

One of the great blessings of writing stories of faith has been the number of inspiring readers I have met and friends I have made along this humbling journey. Their support and comments have meant more than they may know. One example is Father Mike Coleman, chaplain at Tolton Catholic in St. Louis, who says he has been a happy priest for 40 years. A few years back, he found out that he had a softball-sized cancerous tumor in his chest; his only response was trusting and saying, "God's got this." Through a miracle, he is still here, calling sporting events at Tolton Catholic, being a great example of faith, and still smiling. I want to dedicate this book to his encouraging example and vocation to serve God and each person he meets. Thank you.

Chapter 1

The runner's high had passed at mile four, and she began to feel tired, her pace slowing as she took a shortcut through an unfamiliar alleyway in the South End of Boston, a turn that suddenly seemed longer and darker than she had anticipated. She stopped to see if she'd only imagined the sound of footsteps behind her, but the pounding of her heart made it difficult to tell. Normally, she wasn't nervous running at night, but at that moment, there was an overwhelming sense of dread as her mouth felt dry and her stomach nauseated. Heart pounding, she started to run again, counting her long strides. The reek of urine rose from the wet pavement, and she panicked as her foot turned on an empty beer can that screeched loudly through the narrowing alleyway. Quickly glancing back into the pitch black, she started to hyperventilate, sure there was someone else there. Her feet and heart sped up, and then, abruptly, her breathing stopped as she lashed out at the dark frame of a man who had stopped her with his strong arms.

Beads of sweat running into her eyes and the panting of her short breaths made it challenging to make out what was happening.

"It's okay. It's okay," he crooned.

As they stepped out of the alley, she could see the street light shining off of the gold "BPD" on his collar.

"What's a young girl like you doing in a dark alley like this?"

His face, with its pink cheeks and kind eyes, was friendly and gave her a sense of relief as she continued to shake, taking deep breaths as her hand rested on her chest to keep her heart from busting out. "Sorry. I thought—I don't know what I thought. I don't normally panic like that," she responded, noticing the name "Quinn" on the badge of his dark blue jacket that sported a bright blue-and-gold patch emblem on his shoulder that read, "Boston Police, A.D. 1630."

"If I had a young daughter, I wouldn't want her running alone in the dark of these streets."

"I know. My dad keeps telling me the same thing."

"Where do you live?"

"I have a studio in Beacon Hill."

"Studio?"

She laughed. "It's a small studio apartment, not an art studio, although I do paint."

"That's nice. So why are you running in the South End?"

"I haven't before. It's a little busy with Halloween, so I picked another route."

Officer Quinn shook his head. "Tell you what. Let me walk with you a bit."

She felt a little embarrassed but relieved. "You know what's funny?" she said as they made their way down the busy sidewalk. "I love this time of year, with the winter holidays coming and its coziness, but I dread it at the same time. It's getting dark before I leave work, and I like to run."

"Hmm. What's your name?"

"Jessica."

"Well, Jessica, my name's Quinn—William Patrick Quinn, if you'd have asked my mother; God rest her soul."

"I guess I've only met police officers who were giving me a ticket. This is a nice change."

"Jessica, there're many men around who you wouldn't want to be runnin' into in an alley like that. You probably know this, but you're an attractive girl, and there are some—let's just say lonely and dangerous – men out there."

"I can't live my life hiding in my apartment."

"I know. And I know it's not fair, but I'm just sayin', you've gotta be smart." Officer Quinn tapped the side of his forehead with his finger.

"I do know that." As they reached Charles Street at the base of Beacon Hill, filled with its historic brick buildings and charm, Jessica stopped. "I think I'm good now. I appreciate the company on the way back. Thanks."

Quinn tipped his cap. Several groups of young kids dressed in various Halloween costumes passed them on the street corner with moms and dads close behind. Old-fashioned lamps lit the street, and most businesses were open for the trick-or-treaters who were out in droves now that it was almost seven o'clock.

As Jessica made her way down the busy sidewalk, she turned and waved to Quinn as he got into the police cruiser that had pulled up alongside him.

* * * *

"You can't protect them all, Billy," joked his partner driving the cruiser.

"I know, Sean. I know," replied Billy as he watched Jessica disappear around the corner, wondering what it would have been like to have a daughter like her.

Sean O'Donnell had been on the force for only five years, and Billy knew that Sean was more than happy to be patrolling the streets as his partner.

"I'm going to grab a coffee. You want one?"

Billy waved his hand no.

"Sure? You don't want to fall asleep after that double shift yesterday, do ya?"

"Doin' a little extra detail duty for a World Series parade ain't goin' to wear me out. I think you're just spoiled. I had to wait fifty-seven years for my first one in 2004, and the parade for this one was just as sweet."

"No complaints here. Just offering to buy a cup of coffee for my partner."

Billy watched Sean climb out of the car—all six foot one of him—and disappear into the crowded Starbucks on the corner of Charles and Beacon Streets. Sean reminded Billy of his departed son with his short black hair, athletic build, and handsome face, but no one could fill the hole left by his only son's demise. Billy had never regretted taking Sean in as a teenager. He shook his head as he watched his grinning partner return with two large coffees and a bag of pastries. "I told you I didn't need one."

Sean smirked. "Who said one's for you?" He radioed in their location before heading back to their normal patrol route of the Back Bay Fens area, which included Fenway Park, the Emerald Necklace Greenway, several colleges and museums, and then onto the tougher sections of the South End and Roxbury, where the gang activities would heighten their vigilance. "How's she doing today?"

Billy knew Sean was inquiring about Mary, his wife, and in many ways, Sean's adoptive mother.

Billy sighed. "She's okay. Tired a lot and dizzy at times, ya know. I worry about her fallin' on those stairs. Her appetite has been kind of erratic—I think she feels nauseated more than she admits. On her good days, things are gettin' better, but then there are days I can tell she's strugglin'." He paused, staring out the window. "Of course, she never complains about it. You know how she is. She does get to Mass most mornings. I think that gives her some peace, but—"

"But you said she's going to need that operation and some nicer winters than she's getting around here."

"I know, Sean. I can't let her down. I don't want—" Billy's throat tightened as he struggled to keep his emotions in check.

"We'll take care of her." Sean put his hand on his partner's shoulder. "You've got a lot of brothers in blue in your family too. You aren't going to lose that just because you're retiring soon. You know that, right?"

Clearing his throat, Billy said, "Yeah, I know that. And I know you're not goin' anywhere."

The night was fairly quiet as they made their rounds up and down the streets. One call came in for a gunshot heard near Lenox Street, another for a few drunk kids still partying near Fenway, and then a domestic dispute at one of the project apartments. Their shift ended at midnight.

Sean dropped Billy off at his apartment in the South End, down the street from St. Francis Church. Billy and his wife, Mary, had lived in the upstairs apartment of the two-family home for all thirty-five years of married life. Billy always tried to avoid the creakier wooden stairs as he ascended to their apartment and quietly got ready for bed. Still, Mary never failed to make a point of greeting him with a hug and a kiss, even if she had been sound asleep when he lifted the covers and eased into bed.

"Good to have my hero home safe and sound."

"No place I'd rather be, Mrs. Quinn." Billy leaned over and kissed her cheek.

Chapter 2

For decades, the Eastside Café had been a favorite neighborhood breakfast stop for locals. Despite the basic breakfast menu, so-so coffee, and a cranky waitress named Linda, something about the atmosphere and personality of the locals made it work. Billy was already sitting at the usual table when several other guys came in for their regular get-together. Billy Quinn, Sean O'Donnell, Butchy Doherty, Matt Connelly, Eddy "Sully" Sullivan, and Tom Collins had all grown up in Dorchester or the South End, were all Irish, and now all Boston police officers, who felt more like brothers. Most of their grandparents and parents had received the brunt of the harsh anti-Catholic, anti-Irish bigotry, and nativism from a hostile Protestant majority. Still, nowadays, Boston was much more of an Irish enclave, making up almost a quarter of the population and fully entrenched in Boston politics and law enforcement.

Billy enjoyed the lively conversation, even more so when Linda tried her best to give every one of them as hard a time with their orders as they gave to her. By the time she finished, she walked away with her hands in the air and her head shaking back and forth. "Who knows what you boys'll end up with 'cause I don't even know!"

As they talked and drank their coffees, two men entered through the front doorway and stopped at their table. "Talk about a celebration of diversity," exclaimed Father Tom, adding a hint of an Irish accent to his broad grin. The other man, David Kelly, stood quietly beside him.

"Oh, wouldn't that be a Fitzpatrick and a Kelly callin' the kettle black?" responded Billy.

Father Tom Fitzpatrick placed his hands on Billy's shoulders. "Mr. Kelly here's half-Italian, so there's no comparison a-tall, Billy. It was good to see Mary at Mass this morning. She seemed well."

Billy glanced up. "She puts on a good front."

"We'll keep praying for her."

"Thanks. We need all we can get," replied Billy as he caught Sean empathetically staring right at him. Billy and Father Tom knew most of the people in the diner. Mike Carbone and his crew were there, despite the tragic loss of his friend and brother-in-law, Gus Busbi. Tom told him he was meeting today with David Kelly, with whom he had become very close five years earlier. Being a parish priest allowed Father Tom to share the ups and downs of life with many who lived in these South End neighborhoods, and he often let Billy know he wouldn't trade his parish for anything.

After breakfast, many of the patrons extended their goodbyes on the corner sidewalk in front of the Eastside in a patch of warm November sunshine.

Father Tom accompanied Billy back home since St. Francis Church was just around the corner. "So, Officer Quinn is going to hang up his badge this year?"

"I'll be sixty in the spring, and I have a feelin' Mary's going to need me around more."

"So, what's the latest prognosis on her kidney and liver?"

"Nothin' good to report. She's a candidate for dialysis, but the doctor said a double transplant is her best bet. Right now, her quality of life isn't what she deserves."

"Definitely not," replied Tom as they turned a corner and felt a warm breeze.

"Tell me this. Why doesn't God care for the people who've been nothin' but the kind of people He wants? Always good, always devout, and never complainin'. Hasn't she endured enough sufferin' in her life to let her play out these years with a better deck of cards?"

"I know how you feel. But she's a great example of offering that suffering back to God."

Billy shifted his weight from one foot to the other.

"What I mean is that we don't always know how many people we impact and the good that can come from the suffering we endure."

His head down, Billy scoffed. "Good? What's good about this?"

"Look, Billy, I know it doesn't seem fair, but God always takes care of us. We just need to trust God to take care of her."

Billy stopped and stared at the cracks in the sidewalk, shaking his head. "Why couldn't it be me instead of her?"

"Billy, there's a plan for you in this, and there's a plan for Mary. You're both some of the best people I know."

With a deep breath, Billy exhaled. "I'm not that good. You might be surprised."

"Hey, your award dinner is coming up on Saturday, and a lot of people think you are more than a good man. You'd better be; it's in my speech."

As he continued to stare downward, Billy's insides felt unsettled and empty. "I don't know why they even have these things. I told them I wasn't goin' to show up."

"Recognizing a career and life of accomplishment of a very good man is always worth doing," replied Tom as he leaned down to look Billy in the eyes.

"Yeah, yeah. Thanks for the company, Father."

"Anytime for a friend. Take care of that girl of yours."

Billy nodded as he headed home, and Tom made his way to his rectory.

Billy spent the morning with his wife, had a late lunch, and then took a nap before Sean picked him up for their evening shift.

Sean grabbed his cap off of the passenger seat. "Ready for another exciting tour of duty?"

"Always ready. With only a few months to go, it feels almost sad to think about not doing this anymore."

"That's because you'll miss your great partner."

"Sean, you know you're much more than a partner."

A dispatch call came in on the scanner. "Attention units in SB. We have a reported 10-57. Shots just fired at 906 Albany Street. Repeat, shots fired at 906 Albany Street, Orchard Park. Any units in two or less?"

Sean responded, "316 in 2."

Then he heard Butchy's voice on the scanner. "This is 1183 in three. 1183 in three."

The dispatcher said, "316, 1183, respond to a 57. Be careful entering Albany."

"316. Always am. 906 up ahead. There's a crowd gathering."

"1183. Coming in behind you. Approach with caution."

Sean and Billy stepped out of their car and pushed through the circle of people surrounding a man on the ground who apparently had been hit by a gunshot to the side of his torso, which he was holding. Billy scanned the crowd around the scene and then knelt to apply some pressure to the wound with a clean cloth bandage from the first aid kit he'd carried from the patrol car. "What's your name?"

The man grimaced. "Kenny. Kenny Green."

"We have an ambulance on the way. You're goin' to be okay."

Kenny squeezed his eyes tight. "Am I gonna die?"

"We're goin' to try to make sure that doesn't happen. Do you know who did this?"

Kenny glanced at Billy but didn't respond.

"Street code isn't going to stop them from killin' someone, you know," said Billy.

Sean continued to scan the crowd and neighborhood windows before squatting down and asking, "That's a lot of blood. What's your blood type, Green?"

Kenny furrowed his brow. "What?"

"You might need some blood. Do you know what type you have?"

"I don't know—wait, it's, ahh O something, O negative. Is that good?"

"Sort of. You're a universal donor, but you can only get blood from someone with O negative," responded Sean as Billy continued to apply pressure. Finally, the ambulance turned the corner screeching, and soon the EMTs jumped out to attend to Kenny.

In vain, Sean, Butchy, and Sully tried to get at least one of the neighbors to provide some information. Too many kids in these poorer black neighborhoods never made it out of their youth due to this reluctance to snitch on a brother to the cops, never mind four lily-white Irish cops. It wasn't a code that helped the police do their job or the neighborhood to become safer. Part of Billy understood it, but the rest of him raged with frustration, one thought screaming through his mind: *We're on your side!*

With no identification of the shooters, all they could do was patrol each of the streets in the area to see if anything appeared suspicious. Billy would sometimes get flashbacks as they slowly patrolled the streets with old cars parked on both sides and worn-down apartments and abandoned buildings these neighbors called home. It looked nothing like the villages in Vietnam during that endless war, but the same hunted feeling, the sensation that a sniper might be aiming from a window, was a constant reality.

Officer Sam Willow had been laid to rest just three weeks earlier after being shot by a dealer he tried to stop on the street. Sam had pulled alongside a suspicious dealer, and before Sam could even ask a question, the dealer pulled a chrome-handled pistol from the back of his jeans and shot him point-blank in the face. The officer riding with him was stunned as the shooter quickly made his escape down a tight alley, never to be found.

There were times when Billy would become quiet and distant as he carefully studied each window, car, and pedestrian along the way. He never brought up the war, and Sean never asked about it, but it was clear he was still haunted by it.

Just as they loaded Kenny into the ambulance, Billy said to the EMTs, "Let me ride with you." Sean's eyebrows rose as Billy added, "I'm O-negative, in case they're runnin' short and don't have time to find a donor."

Sean nodded, staying with the others to finish up the interviews before heading to the hospital to pick up Billy.

Two hours later in the cruiser, Billy told Sean that they had taken a pint of his blood for Kenny, but he was okay to ride patrol.

Sean smiled. "Huh, good thing we asked."

Around seven-thirty, they cruised by St. Francis Church as a few parishioners were climbing the granite steps to the All Saints' Day Mass entrance. Billy had gone to Mass with Mary in the morning before breakfast.

Sean asked, "What's going on tonight at the church?"

Billy smiled. "All those years, and you still don't know when it's a holy day."

"I don't go anymore."

"It wouldn't hurt you to go once in a while. It'd make 'you know who' very happy."

"I know." He shrugged. "I'm going to head up to Fens and see how things look around the ballpark, and then we can stop for a bite?"

Billy laughed. "I'm surprised you've made it this far without a stop."

Sean drove the cruiser around Fenway Park. Some younger fans were still celebrating the championship win, but nothing to warrant stopping them. Sweepers continued to clean up the streets, brightened by the floodlights outside the park. He drove down Jersey Street, took a right turn, and crossed over the Back Bay Fens greenway. Turning left, they passed several quiet streets only livened by the college girls strolling together in front of Emmanuel College and then Simmons.

Suddenly, there was a call on the radio. "Attention units in SB. Burglary in progress at 280 Fenway—the Gardner. Any units—"

Billy picked up the receiver. "316. We're one block away and will respond. Did you say the Gardner?"

The dispatcher replied, "Yes, the Isabella Stewart Gardner. Thank you, 316. Back-up units requested."

"This is 1183. Confirmed back-up. We'll be there in a few minutes."

The dispatcher responded, "Thank you, 1183. We don't know if they're armed. Exercise caution. Repeat, we don't know if they're armed."

Sean pulled up in front of the four-story, pale-brick Isabella Stewart Gardner Museum. The streets were lit only by the old street lamps, which cast a glow on the modest entrance doors no more than ten feet from the sidewalk. Sean and Billy got out of the cruiser, and as they approached, the front door sprang open with two people darting out from the building and running into them.

Billy placed his hands on the young women's shoulders. "Whoa, whoa, hold on."

The college-aged woman looked up at him with her dark-brown, shocked eyes as she panted to catch her breath. "There's a robbery—inside!" She pointed toward the door.

Sean lifted his hand to hold up the young man. He had dark, curly hair, horn-rimmed glasses, and an equally panicked expression on his face. "Billy, can you get their names? I'll see what's happening inside."

"We're goin' in together." Billy squinted, looking each of the students in the eye. "Stay here until this is over. We may need your help."

They both nodded as Sean opened the first of the double doors and cautiously entered the lobby area. The museum was normally closed at five o'clock, except for Thursday nights when it was open until nine p.m. Sean glanced up at the clock over the front desk that read 8:20. There was no one at the ticket desk and no guard in the lobby, only the CCTV camera overhead to greet them and the sound of security sirens and commotion around the corner. Billy nodded to Sean as they approached the opening to what was no normal museum room but a magnificent Renaissance Venetian-style courtyard garden that soared four stories in height. The Roman sculpture garden, green grass, flowers, palms, shrubs, statues, and Venetian architecture were breathtaking works of art.

Billy had never visited this captivating space, but he couldn't take the time to admire all of the surroundings as a shout rang out, "He's over here!"

Several security guards were in pursuit of the thief running through the garden and up the grand marble stairs in black sweatpants, a black hooded sweatshirt, and large sunglasses. Billy couldn't make out much in terms of details, other than he appeared to have black skin and was extremely athletic. The thief dodged each security guard who attempted to grab him. He held a small framed painting under his left arm and used his right to fend off his pursuers.

One guard shouted, "He has to come back this way!"

Sean yelled out to Billy, "I'll chase, and you can catch him if he comes back down these stairs!"

Sean sprinted up the stairs, two at a time, as he caught up to the guards in pursuit through the series of rooms on the second floor. If Billy were twenty years younger, the thief wouldn't have had a chance, but he could only hear the shouting guards and then a series of multiple alarms going off before he saw the thief and at least seven exhausted guards behind him, heading back down the marble stairs toward the waiting arms of Billy Quinn.

The thief stopped halfway and began swinging the painting at the guards like a weapon to keep them at a distance. A blow from the solid frame would hurt, but there was the obvious concern about damaging the work of art the guards were dedicated to protecting.

Billy called up the marble stairs. "Son, things'll go a lot better for all of us if you put that paintin' down and give yourself up." Just as Billy spoke, Butchy and Sully appeared behind him, and the thief slowly began to raise his hands into the air, one empty and the other still holding the painting.

As one of the guards began to approach, the thief turned quickly and sent the guard backing up the stairs in noticeable fear. The black ski mask he wore added to the tension as he slowly descended the long set of stairs, one step at a time. To the guards' relief, the excitement and danger to the painting seemed to be almost over as the masked thief reached the bottom step and lowered his arm with the masterpiece intact.

Just as Billy extended his hand to retrieve it, another masked man came sprinting down the staircase with a large painting under his arm. Billy couldn't make out the portrait as he reached out in an attempt to stop him, but the thief had too much momentum, brushing Billy back and knocking over Butchy on his way to the front door. Billy regained his footing, surprised as the first thief reached out and handed him the smaller painting before pushing his way past Sully and swiftly following the other man out the main entrance doors.

* * * *

Sean reached the landing and made sure Butchy was all right before racing out the door with Sully in pursuit of the two masked men. They headed across the street and into the Back Bay Fens, part of the Emerald Necklace park system. In the pitch-black darkness of the night, it was difficult to keep an eye on the thieves as they sprinted the park path that ran along this tributary of the Charles River. As they ran full speed, Sean and Sully dodged the branches and were almost hit by someone riding a bike heading in their direction. They reached a fork where one path went over a bridge, and the other proceeded along the Fenway. Sean took the bridge, and Sully ran straight ahead before eventually doubling back. The bridge path emptied onto a lit soccer field where some kids were playing. Beyond were two basketball courts illuminated for night games. With it being a warm night, a full-court game was in progress, and no sight of the men in black sweats and masks. They had lost their trail and hoped the backup units might catch them exiting the park with the stolen painting, which was too large not to be noticed.

Sean and Sully both stood bent over, their hands on their knees to catch their breaths. Sean finally stood to wipe the sweat from his brow as he studied each player in the game in front of him. None of them were wearing black sweats or a black hooded sweatshirt. He motioned to Sully to move closer as they scanned the ground and benches for any articles of clothing they might recognize. Nothing seemed to match. They stood and watched until there was a break in the game. One of the players, holding the ball and wearing long shorts and his baseball hat on backward, walked over and stared at Sean for several seconds.

Sean nodded. "What's goin' on, Trevon?"

"Just playin' ball. You two want in?"

Sean smiled. "We got our run in already. You didn't happen to see any brothers racing through here a few minutes ago, did ya?"

"Nope, but I was focused on the game, you know what I mean?"

"We know what you mean. Anyone join your game just before we showed up?" asked Sully.

Trevon smiled. "We've been here all night. What you lookin' for?"

"A painting."

Trevon laughed. "A painting? The only art goin' on here is my play. Ya know what I'm sayin'?"

Sean walked over and took a long look at each of the players. There were no black sweats but plenty of sweat dripping down their foreheads as they took a breather. "You guys see anyone sprinting through the park here while you were playin'? Anyone holding a large painting?"

They all laughed and shook their heads.

Backup units continued to circle the perimeter while others helped to scour the park with floodlights to see if anyone was hiding in the park's many shrubs, bushes, and garden flowers. The only thing they found was one pair of black sweatpants tossed under some bushes close to the Gardner Museum. One of the thieves must have gotten rid of them early in their escape route—but where was the painting?

Chapter 3

Billy gathered evidence with Butchy, and they interviewed the guards and visitors at the museum. When they returned to the station, Sean approached him, sighing as he spoke, "We lost 'em in the park."

Billy raised his head to the ceiling. "We had four officers inside blocking the door, a crapload of security guards chasin' them, and we let them stroll out the front door with a valuable paintin'. We're goin' to take some heat for this one."

Sean wiped his brow with the back of his hand. "What'd they take?"

"For some reason, the first guy handed me the Giotto painting, which is probably worth a lot of money and a lot easier to run with than the big one they took. It's odd," he replied. "It looks like they took a Rembrandt self-portrait."

"Is it worth a lot?"

"Could be ten to fifty million, from what I heard, maybe a lot more."

"Jeez. We are going to take a load of crap for this."

Detective Sergeant Tony Brooks waved them over to an open area down the hall. His cool demeanor was heightened by an unlit cigarette dangling from his lips as he waited for them to gather. "Billy, Sean, Butch, and Sully, right? We've worked together before, so you know I like to make sure we get all the details documented. That's where we'll solve or lose this case."

Everyone nodded.

Brooks continued. "I don't know who might be involved in this besides the two that fled. Could be one of the guards, a customer, one of you, or even me. Don't assume anything until we've officially ruled them out. From what I've heard, it appears the first guy was creating a diversion for the second guy, and the target was the Rembrandt. I'm not hearing that anything else went missing, but we have to confirm. Sean, I heard you ran after him up that staircase with several of the guards."

Sean nodded. "Yeah. He was pretty fast and agile."

Brooks pointed upward, moving his finger along the path of the upper rooms. "And he took you through each of those rooms in a circle and came back down this same staircase?"

"He did stop in the room with all those rugs on the walls."

"The Tapestry Room?"

"Yeah, tapestry rugs. He ran us around that room, dodging us, then through the door and into the last room."

"I guess they call that the Dutch Room. That one had the Rembrandt painting they took."

"Oh, okay. I don't know Rembrandt paintings, so I'll take your word for it. The guy started pulling on the frames of several paintings in that Dutch room, setting off the alarms, then went out that door up there."

Brooks was quickly writing notes as he listened. "We can do a few walk-throughs. So, the first guy came down these steps and was there for a while until the second one came running out of the Dutch Room with the painting and with you in pursuit."

"I almost got him from behind," responded Sean.

"Was he in the Dutch Room when you chased the first guy?"

Sean paused for a second, scratching his scalp. "I don't think so. We were moving fast, but then I spotted one of the museum security guards on the floor. I stopped to see if she was all right, and I noticed a rag on the floor next to her."

"Chloroform?"

"Makes sense. She was out cold. There were tools on the ground—an old hammer, a spray can with a rod, and a large frame too. Before I could get up, I was whacked on the side of my head. When I shook it off, I saw this guy running out the doorway, so I went after him."

"Did you see where he came from?"

Sean shrugged. "Ahh—I don't know. I was facing the door we ran out, so he must have been somewhere behind me. I never saw him coming."

"All right," said Brooks. "Um—we have the CCTV video ready. I wanted to watch it with you and the guards to see if anything stands out. Okay?"

Billy, Sean, Sully, and Butchy nodded as they followed Brooks, who pulled out a piece of chewing gum from his pocket as they huddled into the security camera room.

Except for Mattie Everett, the guard assigned to the Dutch Room, all of the other guards were there to watch as the chief guard, Bob Touhey, took them through the somewhat grainy recording. "This is where the two men entered and bought their tickets—with cash," Touhey said as he glimpsed at Brooks.

Brooks said, "We'll need the tapes for the past several months to review. Did you see anything suspicious before this point? Anything in the Dutch Room?"

"Nothing unusual. The crowd was heaviest from five to seven, but I didn't see anything strange. When they entered the museum, the two thieves looked like art students carrying sketch pads and pencils. I guess the goatees and sunglasses look odd now, but art students in this area are a pretty diverse and motley crew. Most of the time, these two were in rooms and hallways that were out of direct sight of the camera angles—almost as if they knew where they were all placed."

Brooks continued to watch the tape. "Have any of your guards ever seen these two before? They must have come in a few times beforehand to get the lay of the land."

Each guard approached and made a closer examination, but none of them remembered seeing the suspects before.

"Are there any cameras on the staircase?"

The chief guard scratched his head. "I never saw him go upstairs, but here we can see the other one entering the Gothic Room on the third floor with his mask on, taking the painting. There was no hesitation on which one he wanted. Giotto's *The Presentation of the Christ Child in the Temple.* He tripped the alarms for that room."

"So, he knows what painting he wants, but he leaves it behind?" grumbled Brooks.

"That's what it looks like." Touhey continued, "And this was where Simon tried to stop him, and he got pushed to the ground."

The guard, Simon, stared at his feet, appearing a bit embarrassed.

"Here, he ran down two flights of stairs and then out into the courtyard area, where we were all trying to catch him. It almost looks like he wanted everyone to chase him."

Brooks squinted as he studied the video. "That's exactly what he wanted, to create a commotion and pull the guards off of their positions."

"Well, he certainly did that. We called the police immediately, and you guys were at the front entrance within a few minutes. Looks like 8:20 p.m."

Brooks asked, "What was going on in the Dutch Room at this time?"

Touhey responded, "I thought you might ask that. Take a look at this other monitor. While the first guy was in the courtyard, the second guy entered the Dutch Room from the hallway here and appeared to ask the guard, Mattie, something about the Rembrandt painting. When she started to point to the painting, he pressed a cloth to her nose and mouth, and she collapsed. Then he pulled out a canister and an extendable rod."

Sean asked, "What was that for?"

Touhey replied, "Spray paint. It's one of those rods you can extend and operate a paint spray from fifteen feet away. He sprayed both of the security cameras mounted high on the walls with black paint. I was too busy watching the other guy running around and calling the police to even notice. When all I saw was a black screen, I thought there was a malfunction."

Pursing his lips for a moment, Brooks said, "Okay, back to the other guy."

Touhey pointed to the courtyard. "I think you saw this part as he dodged and weaved around everyone trying to catch him, and then he took off up the staircase to the second floor. Everyone chased him up and through the Early Italian Room, the Raphael Room, and the large and darker Tapestry Room. He must have known his partner needed more time because he started running around the large table several times, pushing Simon to the ground here before finally entering the Dutch Room and back to the staircase with everyone following."

Sean pointed to the screen. "This is where I noticed the security guard out cold in the corner and the painting frame on the ground with the tools. I didn't see anyone else in the room when I knelt down to make sure she was still breathing. When I called in for an ambulance, I noticed the old hammer and spray can, and I think there may have been some pliers. When I heard the commotion, I started to get up but was suddenly whacked pretty good on the side of my head. It took me a few seconds before I could shake it off and start after him out of the door and down the staircase."

Brooks interrupted him. "You said the frame was down on the ground?"

"Yep."

"And empty?"

Sean paused and then nodded.

Touhey narrowed his eyes at the screen. "It's odd they went after this particular painting."

Billy asked, "Why's that, Touhey? Not a good painting?"

"It's a masterpiece, but it's painted on oak panel, almost three feet in height. You know about the robbery in 1992, right?"

"I know it was big and is still unsolved."

"It's still the single largest art theft in history, thirteen pieces worth $500 million. They tried to take the Rembrandt self-portrait piece first in that robbery, but it was too much trouble. The other pieces were on canvases that they could cut from their frames and rollup. You've got to admit, a solid panel this size is a little awkward to be running around town with."

Brooks waved his hands. "Okay, enough history. Who left the museum before and after you guys showed up, Quinn?"

"Two college kids were running out when we arrived. We told them to wait. They seemed clean and did wait."

"Anyone else?"

"Only Sean and Sully, when they chased the thieves through the park and lost them."

Sully rolled his eyes. "Thanks, Billy."

Brooks said, "Seems like these two got by quite a few of you." He surveyed the group. "All right, I need all the guards to fill out the report that my partner, Detective Mullen, will provide. Contact information, everything you remember, and any contacts you've had that could be possible suspects. We will be interviewing each of you and the patrons who were in the museum this evening. Hopefully, we can piece this thing together."

Just as Brooks finished with the staff, the door swung open, and a man wearing a tuxedo with a white scarf strode in. His black hair, slicked back and parted in the middle, matched his waxed mustache. His accent sounded like an affected French academic. "Can someone tell *moi* what is 'appening? Why are all zeese people still here after hours?"

Brooks took a few steps toward the door. "And who might you be?"

The man was obviously taken aback, as he turned to find someone else to converse with. No one volunteered, so he pursed his lips and curled the end of his mustache. "Who am I? I am za one who should be asking, 'Who are you to be in my museum after hours?' Zat is who I am. What is 'appening here?"

"Tell me your name, and I'd be more than happy to catch you up, Mr. Frenchy."

He rolled his eyes in disbelief. "My name is Dr. Henri DuBois. I am in charge of management and security for za Isabella. Now, why are you 'ere? What is this commotion about? I must know."

Brooks glanced at Touhey, who gave him the nod. "You've been robbed, Henry."

"What?! Zis cannot be."

Bob Touhey stood up. "Doctor, the Rembrandt with the plumed beret has indeed been stolen."

DuBois swayed on his feet as if he was about to faint. "Zis is impossible! The painting cannot and 'as not been stolen! It must still be here."

Brooks responded, "Henry—"

"Dr. Henri DuBois," he insisted. "It is pronounced, *On-ree* and always proceeded by *Doctor.*"

"Everyone here saw the thief walk out the front door with that painting."

"*C'est impossible!*"

"Well, I *say* very possible. We'll need to close the museum until we finish our investigation," responded Brooks.

"Again, *c'est impossible,*" exclaimed DuBois.

Downstairs, Billy and the rest of the crew turned as Brooks waved them in. "Quinn, O'Donnell, Doherty, and Sullivan. We need to check with all the backup squads to see if they saw anyone leaving the park from either side, and keep scouring that park. I will need you here tomorrow morning. Can you do that?"

Billy replied, "We'll be here at nine o'clock, okay?"

"Perfect. Thanks, men."

Billy called out as Brooks turned to head up the stairs toward the Dutch Room. "Detective Brooks, we'll find these guys, or—"

Brooks turned back and squinted. "Or what?"

Billy's chest puffed with determination. "Or I'll delay my retirement until we do. That's what."

"Officer Quinn, that's quite a commitment for your last case, but I'd sleep on that. It's been twenty-five years since the first robbery, and they haven't solved that one yet."

Chapter 4

Darkness still permeated the room when Billy woke and sat on the edge of the bed.

His movement woke Mary. She rolled over and stared at him. "Hey, Mr. Quinn, what are you up thinking about so early in the morning? Are you going to breakfast with the boys?"

"Nope. I was just thinkin' about what I could make my beautiful bride for breakfast this fine mornin', Mrs. Quinn."

"You're the one who was working all night. I'll make us two cups, and maybe you can whip up some of that famous French toast of yours."

Billy laughed.

Mary gave Billy a light tap on the shoulder as she stood up. "What's so funny about French toast?"

"You reminded me about the flamboyant and irritated Dr. Henri DuBois at the museum last night."

Mary squinted at him.

"Okay, you make the coffee, and I'll tell you about my night while I make my internationally renowned *Fraunch toooast*."

Mary smiled and rubbed her hand through his hair. "It's a deal, Chef William."

Billy noticed Mary wince as she stepped toward her dresser. Dread and concern ran through him.

Well bundled in a thick robe, his wife sat at their small kitchen table with her hands wrapped around her steaming cup of coffee as Billy slid two thick slices of French toast onto each of their plates. "Well, we were called for a robbery last night," he said as he sat. "The Isabella Stewart—"

"Gardner? Did they rob the Isabella Stewart Gardner again? Did you catch them? What did they take?"

"Just one paintin'. A Rembrandt."

Mary leaned forward with interest.

He knew she was worried about him being a policeman, but he also knew that she loved mysteries as much as she loved art.

"Another Rembrandt. Which one?" She got up and then came back from the living room with a large hardcover book, flipping through the pages. It was a book on the Gardner Museum with high-quality photos of the mansion and all the works in the collection. She sat down and reached a two-page photo of the courtyard. "Isn't that so beautiful! I don't know any

23

other space in Boston like that one to captivate you. It feels like you're in Venice with the architecture, and seeing all those flowers and greenery, especially in the winter, makes me so happy." She started paging through the book again. "Which room was it in?"

"They called it the Dutch Room."

Mary turned the glossy-paged book toward Billy, her finger on a photo of the self-portrait of Rembrandt. "Don't tell me they stole his self-portrait."

Billy studied the photo of the masterpiece painting. The caption below read, *Rembrandt, Self-Portrait with Plumed Beret, Age 23, 1629*. He noted the sense of self-importance in the young man's expression, the expensive clothes he painted himself wearing, and the silvery-blue beret adorned with a large ostrich plume on his head. In the painting, the lighting shined on his shoulders and plumed hat but left much of his face and his eyes in the darkness. "I didn't get to see it, but I think that's the one we're lookin' for. I'm goin' back over this mornin' to meet with Detective Brooks."

Mary sighed. "Why do people do this? For the money? It makes me sad to think people will never see this work of art again." Mary sat back and gazed into the eyes of the young Rembrandt for several moments before commenting. "You never really know everything about someone from the outside, do you? What was he thinking? What secrets don't we know about him?" She finally glanced away from the captivating eyes. "I hope you find him."

Billy was still staring, almost hypnotized by Rembrandt's gaze. He mumbled, "I guess you never really do."

"I said, 'I hope you find him.'"

"Oh. There were *two* thieves."

Mary raised her eyebrows. "I meant that I hope you find Rembrandt. Who cares about the thieves?"

Billy was in front of the Isabella Stewart Gardner Museum early as he watched passersby trying to get to work or to their first classes at one of the several nearby colleges.

Sean arrived next and joked, "Officer, please. You must let me into the museum to do my daily sketches, or I'll—or I'll—oh, I'll just faint," before falling into Billy's arms.

"You're lucky I actually caught you."

Detective Brooks approached on the sidewalk to see Sean collapse in Billy's arms, only to shake his head. "This is no small robbery, boys. You can fool around when you're off duty."

Sean smiled. "But we are off our shift, Detective."

"Yeah, and I work eight-hour days too. Let's see if Dr. *DuBois* is here to let us in," said Brooks, exaggerating his name.

Before they could knock on the door, it opened, and there stood the one and only Dr. Henri DuBois. "*You* are early."

Brooks glanced down at the patent leather shoes DuBois was wearing and responded, "None of us are French, so you'll have to pardon our promptness. Can we come in?"

"If you must, but remember zat you are servants of ze public."

Brooks responded, "I'm sure you'll remind me often."

DuBois waved the officers in. "Please be careful of anything you must touch in your investigation. We have not touched anything from last night but 'ave done some inspection of our own." DuBois gave a disapproving look as Brooks reached into his worn jacket.

Brooks glanced up, holding a stick of gum. "Would you rather I smoke?"

To which DuBois pursed his lips, raised his eyebrows, and shook his head vigorously.

"What type of inspection?" asked Brooks.

They stood at the edge of the interior courtyard that Mary Quinn had marveled about over breakfast. Billy gazed up at the morning sun shining through the glass skylight ceiling of this four-story Venetian-style palazzo. He tried to view it through her eyes to better understand her captivation with this unique space. Each floor with arched Venetian windows, carved stone columns, and ornate balconies presented a classic backdrop for the garden below, which hosted flowers, palm trees, Italian statues, historic reliefs, and relics. On one crest plaque was a carved tablet inscribed with "*C'est mon plaisir.*"

* * * *

DuBois seemed to notice Billy's attentive appreciation for details, and Billy was grateful for that. "'*C'est mon plaisir.*' It was Madam Gardner's motto. 'It is my pleasure.'" DuBois raised his hand and pointed to the security room they were in the night before. "I wish I could say the same."

Billy and Brooks exchanged glances with raised eyebrows before following DuBois.

DuBois said that he had spent the evening with his security chief pouring through each tape and room of the museum. "Zeese two despicable men had obviously planned their steps. You can see 'ere zat they waited across the street until a larger crowd needed to be processed for tickets, avoiding being overly noticed. They tried to look like students of art with their sketch pads. Their gloves were the same color as their skin tone, so they were not very noticeable and would leave no fingerprints."

Sean frowned. "They almost look like twins with the same black sweats, goatees, and sunglasses. Didn't that raise any questions for the ticket counter?"

Billy noticed DuBois peering toward the ceiling and huffed, seemingly trying to find his patience. "Students tend to dress alike, and we try to encourage a diverse audience for our art. We are not 'ere to discriminate on the color of one's skin nor one's choice or personal style." He turned his attention back to the screen and pointed to the images. "Now 'ere they are seen sketching items in the courtyard and in several rooms, not unusual for students."

Brooks paused before asking, "Did you see them talking with anyone before the robbery? Any guards? Patrons?"

"No one. Most of ze time, they were out of sight of the camera angles, making me think that zey 'ad studied their locations. There is nothing unusual until ze first man enters the Gothic Room. He must 'ave waited until it was empty and then knew exactly which painting he wanted to remove." DuBois stopped and shook his head, putting his fingers to his lips.

Brooks broke the silence. "This is where he took the smaller piece?"

DuBois ran the video and showed the man, now with a ski mask covering his face, walking directly to a small table covered by a red cloth that held the painting. A larger portrait of Mrs. Gardner, painted by John Singer Sargent, hung in the corner overlooking the scene. The alarm immediately sounded, and the guard stepped back into the room to see the thief exiting before starting his pursuit and calling the other guards.

"Pause it," said Brooks. "Suspect One makes it all the way to the third floor—maybe because there were few people still there—takes a painting he never intends to steal and then sprints down to the first floor to run around the courtyard, drawing all but one of the guards in pursuit until he runs back to the second floor."

Touhey, the chief security guard, said, "Like you said last night, it looks like he was trying to create a diversion for his partner and the real target of the theft. He may have picked that painting because it was small and easy to grab. It wasn't bolted to a wall, but it sure looked like he knew which one he wanted to grab."

DuBois shivered at the description. "No civilized person *grabs* a Giotto. 'e must 'ave known it was one of our more valuable pieces. I don't believe in coincidences, even if he is a thief."

Sean asked, "Why would he care which one he grabbed?"

Brooks chewed his gum as he responded. "Because he knew the guards would have to be careful in trying to catch him, so they wouldn't damage the piece. Wouldn't you agree, Doc?"

DuBois closed his eyes and drew a deep breath before asking Touhey to continue the video. The thief ran through each room on the third floor and made enough noise on the second floor to draw as many guards as possible before sprinting down to the first-floor courtyard.

"Okay, how many guards are chasing him now?"

"Seven."

"How many guards are on duty?"

"Eight, plus Touhey in the security room."

Brooks paced the small room. "So, everyone except Touhey and the guard from the Dutch Room—"

"Mattie Everett."

"Mattie, right. He has everyone else on the first floor playing tag. What's going on in the other rooms at this same time?"

DuBois pointed to the multiple split screens. "You can plainly see that ze other rooms had nothing 'appening, except for ze Dutch Room. We saw this last night. The second thief uses, I imagine, chloroform to anesthetize Mrs. Everett, then, with an extension sprayer, covers the cameras with paint, so we see nothing."

Brooks stared at the black screen. "Can we shift back to the courtyard?"

They watched the circus atmosphere as the keystone cops chased the thief around the courtyard.

"And this is where you and Sean show up?" Brooks asked, glancing over at Billy, who nodded.

Brooks pointed to the screen. "It's not that odd he might go back upstairs to buy more time for his partner, but it *is* odd he would take them through the Dutch Room, where his partner was working. May I inspect the damage upstairs, Doc?"

DuBois closed his eyes a mere moment, then walked out of the security room to the grand marble staircase that led to the Dutch Room.

When everyone reached the doorway to the Dutch Room, Brooks' eyes rolled upward, fidgeting with the unlit cigarette in his hand. "No! Can someone please tell me that I am seeing a mirage?"

Crouched on the floor area, which was covered with a protective roll of brown packaging paper, two men were inspecting the large frame which had previously held the stolen Rembrandt painting.

Father Tom Fitzpatrick stood up with a broad grin on his face. "Detective Brooks, fancy meeting you here. I didn't take you as a man of the arts."

"Enough with the jokes. Exactly what are you doing standing in a crime scene—and what's *he* doing here?!"

Angelo, Father Tom's friend and all-around maintenance man at St. Francis, didn't bother to acknowledge Brooks as he continued to inspect the scene.

DuBois shuffled to the doorway entrance. "I am the one who asked zem here. Father Fitzpatrick is a good friend, and we both thought Mr. Salvato could provide some insights from, let's say, a different perspective."

Brooks stepped into the room, staying on the paper. "Yeah, a thief's perspective."

Tom shook Brooks' hand and added, "*Retired* thief. Think of him as a very observant and economical consultant."

Brooks replied, "We already have those. They're called detectives." He scanned the room to see a large gold ornate frame on the floor.

Angelo said, "They knew what tools they needed to pop this off the wall and release the painting from the frame. That old hammer could pry anything loose, and he must have known they would need those pliers. Did the video show any hesitation about knowing where the cameras were located?"

Touhey raised his hand and squeezed his jaw. "None at all. None of the tapes showed him in the room before he made his move on Miss Everett. And then he sprayed the two cameras as if he knew exactly where they'd be."

Tom turned to Brooks. "Dr. DuBois said they only took this one painting?"

Billy interjected, remembering, "For some reason, one of them handed me the smaller paintin' on the way out as his partner was headin' down those stairs with the Rembrandt."

"Diversion? What was the other painting?" inquired Tom.

DuBois wiped his brow and responded, "Thank God. It was Giotto di Bondone's *La Presentazione di Gesù Bambino al Tempio*. Luckily, despite him swinging it around like a croquette mallet, it was undamaged and is back where Madam Gardner had placed it."

Tom smiled. "I love that painting—*The Presentation of the Christ Child in the Temple*. 1300s, right?"

"Ah, 1320, to be exact, but I am impressed, Father Fitzpatrick. And Mr. Salvato, anything else stand out to you?" asked DuBois.

Angelo responded, "Timing seemed to be key and knowing exactly what they wanted and how to get it out. They were smart to come when the museum was most vulnerable—during operating hours when your other security measures aren't turned on due to the customers. You said this particular painting was on a wood panel, much more awkward to take than a canvas—so, they must have wanted this particular painting."

DuBois closed his eyes. "It is not just a painting, but an irreplaceable masterpiece."

"Hopefully, this theft isn't also a masterpiece. I haven't touched the hammer, but it appears some initials are engraved into the metal. Could be the owner's," said Angelo.

Billy watched as Brooks knelt down and carefully lifted the hammer with plastic gloves on. "RH. Anybody know any RHs?"

"Rembrandt Harmenszoon," replied Tom, playfully raising his brow.

"Harmen-what? I thought Rembrandt was his last name?"

"Rembrandt Harmenszoon van Rijn is his full name," DuBois replied with an apparent distaste for having to educate the uneducated. "Early on, he signed 'is paintings with *RH*, then *RHL*, then *RHL-van Rijn* or *Rembrant*, and then 'e added the *d* to *Rembrandt*."

Brooks stared closely at the engraving. "Huh."

All the photographs, fingerprints, forensics, and DNA evidence had been collected the night before. Brooks' eyes scanned the North Wall where the Rembrandt self-portrait had hung, noting the other impressive portraits, the eighteen-century Venetian chairs, and the opened arch balconies overlooking the courtyard below, which let the natural light enter the otherwise dark room.

Brooks glanced back down at the frame on the floor.

DuBois now held a purple handkerchief to his mouth. "This was ze work of art that convinced Madam Gardner to transform 'er 'ome into a private collection for everyone to see. You don't understand 'ow devastating this is."

Brooks pivoted and took a few steps across the irregular hand-made tiles toward the West Wall, where there were five arched windows with Corinthian marble columns in between. In front of them was an unusual setup of Venetian chairs and Italian tables facing each other with empty gold frames. "Are these normally set up like this?"

DuBois rolled his eyes again. "Detective, everything is as Madam arranged it—" DuBois turned and stared at the frame on the ground. "Except, of course, when brutes, who do not understand 'ow to live in a civilized world, do something like this!"

Tom pointed toward the wall. "The empty frames are from some of the paintings that were stolen in 1990. These two works of art were from a landscape by a pupil of Rembrandt named Flinck and Vermeer's *The Concert*, which was worth $200 million alone. That's correct, isn't it, Dr. DuBois?"

DuBois could not speak at the very mention of the lost works of art.

Tom continued. "Some paintings, due to their smaller size or detail, are meant to be appreciated with a level of intimacy as you sit and study them. I think that was the idea. You can see, on the back wall to your left, two other Rembrandts that were stolen in the 1990 heist."

Brooks turned to the South Wall and approached the large empty frame that once held Rembrandt's *The Storm on the Sea of Galilee*. The frame hung on a three-hundred-and-fifty-year-old green silk fabric drape-like wall covering embroidered with flowers, fruit, and birds. As he searched for clues, he peered down at the fabric-covered Venetian chairs that lined the wall under the painting and noticed one chair that was slightly out of alignment. Brooks turned and asked, "Would you expect these chairs to be straight?"

Touhey tilted his head and responded, "Normally, yes, but the guards said the first thief ran through this room, lifting the paintings along this wall to set off the alarms. I'm pretty sure he wasn't worried about the chairs."

"Huh." Brooks ambled further down the South Wall to inspect the other empty frame that had held Rembrandt's *A Lady and Gentleman in Black*. The only thing to see was the same green fabric that hung from high above to behind the chairs below. "Sean, where did you say you found the guard?"

Billy noticed Sean making his way to the darkest corner of the room and pointed to the floor. "She was here, and she might have been dragged a bit. You can see that the doorway into the room is narrow, so we got bunched up as he ran through it. By the time I got through the door, the first suspect was already out the other door. I think I was the only one to notice the guard on the floor, and I stopped to make sure she was alive. That's when I noticed the frame and tools on the floor."

Brooks glanced toward the corner of the room where the guard's body would have been and then turned to see that the opposite corner behind him would be just as dark. "Do you think the other suspect could have been in this other corner?"

"I don't know. Like I said, I never noticed him until I got that whack that knocked me over. I was pretty pissed and shook it off to tail after him," snapped Sean.

Brooks moved to the spot where Sean was pointing and then out into the hallway toward the marble staircase. "You didn't touch anything in this room?"

Sean paused for a moment. "Except for the guard, no."

They all followed Brooks as he hurried to the grand staircase. "When you reached this point, what could you see?"

Sean peered down the long, wide set of old marble stairs, then stood and bit his lip. "Let's see. I was running down the stairs and saw the commotion." Sean descended the stairs with everyone and then pointed. "Billy was against the wall, holding something, and Butchy was on the ground beside the door. There was no time to waste, so I grabbed Sully and took off after them." Sean stepped out of the front entrance and onto the sidewalk. "They had to cross Fenway, and car headlights created a glare on the painting one of them was carrying."

Billy held his hand out to stop the traffic as they all briskly walked across the busy street.

Sean pointed ahead. "We could hear them running down this path."

Brooks asked, "No one else was around?"

"It was pretty dark, but I didn't see anyone else. We were focused on not losing them," responded Sean as he glanced back and forth.

"There was that kid on the bike," said Sully.

Sean nodded. "Yep, yep. That was just down the path a bit. The bike was coming right at us in the dark at the narrow section, and we jumped out of the way."

With a sense of urgency, they trod too quickly for DuBois to keep up and reached the fork in the path.

"Here's where we split up. We couldn't tell if they took a left here and headed over that small bridge or continued straight. Sully stayed straight but said he heard no sign of them, so he doubled back to follow me."

The stone bridge arched over the gently flowing river as a light wind made the remaining fall leaves dance. Everything seemed peaceful compared to the panicked chase of the night before. They followed the path that ended at the soccer field and basketball courts, where no one was playing this early in the morning.

Sean stopped short in his tracks. "This is where we lost them."

Brooks smirked. "This is where you think you lost them. I understand there were backup patrol cars on both sides of the Fens Park and no sign of anyone leaving the park, especially with a large painting in tow. They didn't jump onto the street, and the river runs along the other side of the path, so you would have heard them if they tried to cross the water."

Sully nodded. "Yep. There were lights on the courts and a game going on."

Brooks turned to Sully. "And?"

"And, nothing. We questioned each one of them, but they said they saw no one running through, and nobody jumped into their game. They were all pretty sweaty, and none of them was wearing the black sweats or hoodies like the suspects were wearing."

Brooks peered over at Tom and then Angelo. "I wouldn't trust those players to tell you the truth any more than I trust this guy. I hope you got some real names we can follow up on."

Sean said, "I know a lot of the guys. Trevon's pretty straight."

Tom smiled. "Trev's a good baller, but I'm not sure he is going to give up one of his buds for the police. Did they just ditch the sweats?"

Sean frowned. "We only found one pair near the park entrance. Sully and I searched the area and couldn't find the hoodies, sunglasses, goatees, or—"

"Or the painting." DuBois, who had finally caught up, sighed. "Or the painting."

Brooks waved his hand. "We scoured this park last night with floodlights and then again in the morning. The bushes, the river, up and down every path. We found nothing and made sure no one came in or out of the park. Those guys were still playing when we arrived—so it doesn't look like they were in a hurry to escape, even if two of them were the suspects."

DuBois put his hands over his face. "Zis is 'opeless. We are ruined, and Rembrandt is in the 'ands of scoundrels!"

Billy put his hand on his back, and DuBois jumped. He said, "We'll find them, Doctor. Don't worry. We have a good crew here, and we know the city."

DuBois reached into his suit pocket for his purple handkerchief and wiped the corners of his eyes.

Brooks gave him a firm pat on the shoulder. "Think of the publicity, Doc."

Chapter 5

By the time they had canvassed the park, searched for evidence, and then retraced the steps of the robbery at the Gardner Museum, it was close to noon. Tom and Angelo stood with Brooks, Billy, and Sean back in the courtyard where the morning had begun.

Tom said, "I think a lunch break at Dempsey's Pub may be in order. What do you boys say? I'll buy!"

Billy smiled. "You drive a hard bargain, Father. I'm sure Sean's appetite alone will make you regret your offer, though."

Sean laughed as everyone else glanced toward Brooks for his response.

"I don't know if I want to be seen with this crew—*and* this is the end of the detective work on this case for the two of you!" said Brooks as he pointed his finger at Tom and Angelo. "The FBI will probably get involved, and I can't have Laurel and Hardy stumbling around on this case."

Tom turned to Angelo. "Well, here's another nice mess you've gotten me into, Stanley."

Without hesitation, Angelo scratched the top of his head and responded, "I'm sorry, Ollie."

Brooks quipped, "All right, just what I need. A couple of comedians."

Billy exchanged smiles with Dempsey as Tom led the crew down the street and into the pub for lunch. Dempsey pointed to an open booth and came over with a bar towel draped over his shoulder. "Tom, Angelo, Billy, Sean—oh, and Detective Brooks. The last time you visited my establishment, you were working on that Comghan case. Good thing you had these two to figure the case out for you."

Billy smiled to himself when he caught Brooks' uncomfortable glance toward Tom as he tried to ignore Dempsey's attempt at humor.

"What'll you have, boys?"

They ordered, and Dempsey returned with a tray of ice-cold beers and some chicken wings. "While you wait for your gourmet burgers, the wings are on the house."

As each of them grabbed their beer, they raised it in honor of the host.

Dempsey shook as he chuckled. "Hey, Billy, how's your bride faring these days?"

Billy straightened. "She never complains, but—" He could not find the words to finish the response.

Tom jumped in. "Let's make our toast to Mary."

They all clinked their mugs. "To Mary."

"Thanks," said Billy.

Sean tapped the table with his knuckles. "Let's focus on the case. Angelo, I hope you don't take any offense, but why would someone want to rob a painting?"

"Don't worry about offending me. Few have succeeded. That's a good question. Money is often the first reason. There's a lot of money in stolen art, and these jobs are usually pulled off by international organized crime syndicates. The money helps to fund drugs and even arms trades with terrorists. Or they may want bargaining leverage. The FBI may be willing to get mob members off from sentencing in exchange for stolen art being returned."

Sean asked, "You think those guys, last night, were part of the local mob or something bigger?"

"Probably not the latter. The crime bosses plan the heist and handle the quick disposal, but they usually use people not connected to pull it off. That way, they don't know anything or anyone, so they can't lead the police to any of the wise guys if they get caught. I think the FBI knows the guys who committed the 1990 heist, but it hasn't helped them locate the paintings because they probably aren't the real crooks behind it."

"Yeah, that makes sense. Do you think this was a local mob job?"

Angelo glanced at Brooks. "I don't know, but I can try to find out. It could also be the thrill of pulling it off more than the money. Stealing art is an art in itself."

Brooks asked, "Maybe you got the itch again for its challenge? I'll have to see if Father Tom here has any new paintings on his rectory walls."

Tom chuckled. "If it was for the challenge, Angelo, then it's not likely to be a syndicate job, right?"

Angelo sipped his beer. "Nope, and that might be tougher to crack—unless there was someone with a score to settle with the museum. In any case, they seemed to know when to hit at the right time. Most museums are secured like fortresses after hours, but the Achilles heel is when they are open to the public, and they do it in a blitz rather than working around elaborate security systems."

Tom shifted his sitting position. "Are those the only reasons, Angelo?"

Angelo shrugged. "Desperation."

This seemed to catch Brooks' attention. "Desperate for what?"

"Could be someone who has no other option. He needs the money for something and thinks that outweighs the cost of stealing. Fat insurance companies pay, no one gets hurt, and someone gets helped."

Brooks set down his beer. "So, it could be an inside job?"

Angelo glanced at the wing in his fingers. "Could be. Could be for any of those scenarios."

Billy turned to Brooks. "Goin' to need to interview that museum staff to see if there's a likely candidate."

Sean laughed. "My money is on DuBois."

Everyone chuckled and then sipped their beers.

Brooks held out one of the teriyaki wings. "I don't understand how two men could enter that park and disappear with a large painting like that. They couldn't roll it up. There was a river on one side of the path and cruisers on the street surrounding the park. Even if they climbed a tree or rolled under a bush, they'd have to come out eventually, or we would have found them during our search."

Tom asked, "What if they rolled down the bank and then slid into the river after Sean and Sully passed?"

Brooks shook his head. "I don't know. That painting is on a wood panel. They would have destroyed it in the water. And officers were checking the river on both ends of the park with floodlights last night to make sure no one escaped."

"Yeah," Tom said, "it seems like a longshot, but they may have floated along with it. What about a hiding spot under one of the bridges?"

"Already checked that last night," Brooks answered. "Nothing under the bridges, in the bushes, the gardens, or up in the trees. They must've slipped into that basketball game last night."

Sean said, "But we saw no sign of the disguises or the painting—anywhere."

Brooks nodded. "I know, but it looks like the only way they could have disappeared like that." He turned to Tom. "Why did DuBois think you'd be interested or helpful in this case?"

"Well, Angelo has a good eye."

"Yeah, but he asked you over as well."

"He did. I don't know. Maybe it was because of my interest in the 1990 robbery?"

"Are you one of those amateur experts?"

"Amateur, yes. Expert, not quite. It's just one of those stories I've been interested in."

Sean pulled himself forward. "I don't know much about it. What happened?"

Tom considered the men in the booth. "I don't want to bore anyone."

Brooks motioned with his open palm to proceed, and everyone else nodded.

"Well, this was the single largest unsolved art heist in history; thirteen paintings valued at $500 million and still missing."

Sean asked, "What has it been? Twenty years?"

"Almost. In the wee hours of March 18, 1990, two men sat in a red Dodge Daytona by the side entrance of the Gardner Museum and waited for an hour as people passed, leaving various St. Patrick's Day parties. Some witnesses even came forward, saying they saw two policemen sitting in a red car as they walked by that night. At 1:24 a.m., they pushed the outside buzzer and told the security guard at the desk that they were responding to a disturbance call. The front door guard was a 23-year-old Berklee music student, kind of a hippie-rocker type, who was told to never let anyone in, but he wasn't told what to do if the police showed up. He could see them dressed in uniforms, stepped out from the desk where the only police alarm button was, and let them in. Once in, the men in police uniforms announced to the two guards, 'Gentlemen, this is a robbery,' and then duct-taped them to pipes in the basement and went to work."

Sean stared at him, open-mouthed. "No one came in during the entire robbery?"

"They were in the museum for eighty-one minutes. That's a long time for a robbery. Motion detectors tracked their movements as they went first to the Dutch Room."

Billy nodded. "Huh. Same room as the Rembrandt was in this time."

"Actually, the first painting they tried to take was the Rembrandt self-portrait that we're now searching for. They took down the heavy frame, setting off only an internal alarm that they smashed. It was too hard removing the wooden paneled painting from the frame so they gave up on it. Next, they turned to the Rembrandts on the wall behind them and cut those canvas paintings out of their frame, then the Vermeer and Flinck in front of those desks. They took some Degas drawings, a Manet, and a few other items but oddly left two Raphael masterpieces, a Botticelli, and a Titian—all very expensive pieces."

Sean asked, "Why would they leave those?"

Tom sighed. "That's a great question. Some say it was the dumbest robbery in history because the items they took were too hot to ever sell to anyone. Some think they might've been amateurs, or maybe some collector wanted specific pieces. So many questions but few answers."

Brooks pushed his beer aside as Dempsey came forward with five juicy-looking burgers. "The FBI has been on a worldwide hunt for those works of art for a long time, and there's a five-million-dollar reward for any information that leads directly to the recovery of all the items in good condition."

His brow raised, Sean said, "Five million! Just for information? Sounds like that much dough should have smoked out someone who knew something!"

Tom bit into his burger and chewed. "There've been several dead-end leads. Before they left, the thieves even took the time to say to the guards, 'You'll be hearing from us in about a year.' At one time, they thought this Boston mob gangster, Bobby Donati, was a possible collaborator because he was seen with a bag of police uniforms shortly before the robbery. Still, he was murdered a year after the robbery—found beaten and stabbed with his throat slit in the trunk of his car." Tom stopped from taking a second bite of his burger and continued, "The FBI has followed leads in Boston, Philly, and Hartford. At one point, they thought Whitey Bulger may have masterminded it, but a lot of people still put their money on Myles Connor, the country's most notorious art thief, even though he was in jail when it happened. They've also been to Scotland Yard, the French police, and Ireland many times, thinking the IRA did it to fund the release of prisoners. Seventeen years of investigation, a long list of suspects who are all dead, and no paintings."

Brooks interrupted. "That's why we need to move hard and fast on this one. As with any art theft, time is the enemy."

Angelo nodded. "I think he's right. If these were professionals, those paintings will be long gone as soon as the heat is off. If they were amateurs, we might have a shot at finding some careless clues left behind."

Billy asked, "Such as?"

"Such as nothing yet," Angelo said. "They seemed to have had a plan that they'd practiced and stuck to. They knew how much time they needed to create a distraction, but they took a big chance thinking they could get out that door with a large painting on wood and the police blocking it. It's really odd they didn't take the smaller painting too."

Tom mused, "The Giotto. Billy, you said the first suspect handed it to you?"

Billy hesitated as he thought about the chaotic scene. "You know, he was swingin' that thing like a weapon to prevent the guards from convergin' on him, but then he stopped and approached me with his hands up; I reached out for it, and it was almost as if he was presentin' it to me. I think it was a distraction tactic, because I was surprised by it. Before I could react, I was knocked aside by the second suspect sprintin' with full force down the staircase."

Angelo said, "It seems like he could've whacked you with it and escaped without giving it up?"

"Huh. Maybe he wanted to—I don't know. It's odd, to be sure."

Brooks frowned. "What's odd is me discussing another case with a priest and his ex-con sidekick."

Tom finished his beer. "We are only here as a favor and to help."

Brooks stood up. "Well, do me a favor and help by staying clear on this one, okay?"

"We'll do our best."

"That's what I'm afraid of," quipped Brooks.

Tom started to reply and then hesitated.

"What is it?" asked Brooks.

"I was just thinking about Myles Connor."

Billy sneered in disgust. "Junior. Myles Connor, Jr. He's nothing like Myles Senior. He was as fine a cop as there has ever been in this state, but his son was a heartache—nothin' but a two-bit thief."

Tom shrugged. "I understand, but he may be someone we want to talk to. He's possibly been involved in hundreds of art heists, including strolling out of the Museum of Fine Arts with a priceless Rembrandt in 1975."

Brooks scoffed. "You're right that he would likely know potential players in an art heist, but he's unlikely to talk to us, never mind give us any valuable info."

Angelo rubbed his hand across the table. "I might be able to help set up a meeting with him."

Brooks stood up, followed by everyone else. "Hmm. Thick as thieves, huh?" He turned to Billy and Sean. "Quinn. O'Donnell. I'll probably need your help at the station tonight. We need to talk with each player in that game last night."

They both nodded as Dempsey came to the table with the check and placed it in front of Tom.

Tom raised his brow as he studied the bill. "I did say something about this being on me, didn't I?"

Everyone chuckled.

Outside the pub, Billy stood with Sean.

Sean asked, "See you at four?"

"Sure. Hey, have you heard how Kenny Green's doin'?" asked Billy.

Sean stopped and hesitated before responding, "Oh, the guy who was shot last night. No. Why?"

Billy scratched his cheek. "I don't know. I might drop by to see if he's okay."

"I'm sure he's fine. Do you think he's part of your family now that he has some of your blood?"

Billy laughed. "Yeah. I wanted to invite him over for Thanksgiving."

"Do you want some company?"

Before they knew it, they were at the Boston Medical Center, standing outside of Room 316, Kenny Green's room, according to the nurse at the desk. Billy leaned his head into the room to see if Kenny was awake and ready for visitors. The head of the bed was elevated, and the man's eyes were closed. They stepped in quietly and stood at the side of the bed. Kenny's eyes slowly opened, and his body pulled back as he spotted the gun in Billy's holster before making eye contact. "Sorry, just an instinctive reaction. I'm not too partial to guns at the moment."

"How're you doin', Mr. Green?" asked Billy.

"You can call me Kenny. I think I'm doing all right. Thanks to your donation, I hear. I didn't think I'd get a chance to thank you for that."

"Do you need any more?"

"I think I'm good. Who's your friend?"

Sean said, "O'Donnell, Sean. I was the one that showed up when you were shot and called the ambulance."

"Oh. I guess I owe you a thanks too. I wasn't paying much attention to faces last night." He turned gingerly toward Billy. "Why did you do it?"

"It's my job."

"No. Why did you offer your blood to me?"

Billy shrugged his shoulders. "I don't know. You lost a lot, and we have something in common."

Kenny seemed confused.

"We're in an exclusive club—O negative. We can give to everyone but only take from each other. It narrows down the available donors since only seven percent of people are O negative."

"How did you know?" Kenny squinted.

Sean grinned. "I asked you."

"So," Billy asked, "how did they say you're doin'?"

"Luckily, the bullet didn't hit anything vital. It looks like the world is stuck with me for a little while longer. You saved my life. I want to repay you for that."

"I don't know about that, but I understand you're on parole," Billy said. "Do you have a job yet?"

Kenny shook his head. "Not yet, but I ain't goin' back there. No way."

"You can repay me by keepin' that promise. I'm glad to hear things are goin' okay. Do you know who'd want to shoot you?"

Kenny pursed his lips, glanced away.

"Okay. If you think of any possibility, let us know."

Kenny nodded and began to close his eyes again.

As Sean and Billy reached the door, they heard Kenny say, "I didn't expect visitors. I appreciate it."

"Take care of yourself," said Billy.

Chapter 6

Back at home, Billy only had a few hours before his evening shift.

Mary greeted him with a smile and a hug. "Good to see you back, Mr. Quinn. You up for a cup of tea?"

"I'll never turn down a date with my girl."

Billy took a seat at the kitchen table, and Mary carried two cups of piping hot tea over and joined him. "Any clues uncovered this morning?"

Billy held up his cup and let the steam warm his face. "This's goin' to be a tough one. The two guys we chased vanished into thin air."

"In the museum?"

"No. Sean and Sully chased them into the Back Bay Fens Park, and we had cars on both sides of that narrow strip to make sure they didn't escape."

"They've done such a nice job fixing up that greenway. I love that rose garden."

Billy sipped his tea. "Well, you know that path we walked to the garden?"

"Sure, we had a picnic there for our anniversary. That was a nice day. The river runs along that path. What if they jumped into it?"

Billy rubbed the back of his neck. "Sean or Sully would have heard some sort of splash."

Mary held her cup with both hands next to her chin. "Hmmm."

Billy could tell that the wheels were turning in her head. He gazed at her face while she thought. Even with the addition of wrinkles that came with time, smiles, worries, and tragedies, she was still beautiful. Those lines and wrinkles were hardly noticeable in his loving eyes. Magazine models may have had greater technical beauty, but they often lacked the beauty that shined from deep in their souls.

"What if they put the painting into something floating on the river, under the bridge, and out of the park?"

"You missed your calling as an art thief."

Mary squinted. "And I don't have an alibi for last night."

Billy laughed and spluttered his tea. "Well, you had an accomplice, and you've learned to run a lot faster than you could when you were younger."

Mary raised one eyebrow. "You might be surprised. As they say, we need to focus and think outside the box. What about using a balloon to float the painting out of the park? Wait! A wire would be even better!"

"A wire?"

"Sure. A loose wire could have been hooked high to a tree. They could have loaded the painting into a bag hooked to the wire, and then someone across the street could have lifted it high and let it travel down the wire and out of the park."

"Mrs. Quinn, you're trying too hard." Billy made a mental note to check the park for any sign of a wire.

"We'll figure this one out. I'd miss that portrait, and it's just wrong to steal it from everyone."

"We will, indeed, Mrs. Quinn."

Mary's smile disappeared. "Billy, is the young man okay? The one who was shot last night."

After sipping his tea, Billy sighed. "I visited him just before I came home today. It looks like the bullet missed any vital organs, and he'll be okay. I hope it inspires him to stay straight."

"Maybe you can help him find a job?"

Billy stared down into his empty teacup. "Huh. That's a nice idea. I just need to make sure he's serious about living up to any recommendation I give."

"We all deserve a second chance."

Billy's thoughts quickly drifted off to his daily wish for Mary to get a second chance.

"I know that look. Please don't worry so much."

Billy's eyes filled with tears as he made eye contact with her. "I'd have no life worth living without you."

Mary reached across the Formica table and clasped his hands. "We don't know what'll happen."

Billy gazed into her eyes. "All those doctors have said the same thing—you need that operation. They all think you'd be as healthy as ever with a new kidney and maybe a new liver. I've watched you struggle, and I know how much pain you're in."

Mary gave him a half-smile. "But we both know how unrealistic it is for us."

Billy's face flushed as he clenched his fists. "Money! I'm sick of it. You're worth everythin' we have and more. There's no way we're not gonna take care of you—no matter what. I can't believe the insurance won't cover most of this!"

Despite his clenched fists, Mary continued to hold onto them, and she squeezed tighter. "We can't change what is. Five hundred thousand was the low estimate for something that isn't even guaranteed to work."

"I told you I can cash in my pension to pay for it. There's nothin' more to discuss. I'm not gonna let you down. I'm not. I love you too much to let you go."

"We've gone over this. Taking that much out wouldn't leave you enough to live, and you can't keep working with that back of yours. You've been struggling with that since you came home from the war. Don't put this all on yourself. We've got to trust God's plan."

"Well, His plan isn't workin' too well so far, and He hasta expect us to do our part."

Mary's shoulders dropped. "Billy, I know how much you care, and I don't want you to be alone—I just—I just—"

"What is it?"

"I'm just trying to focus on Paddie today."

Billy gazed into his bride's water-filled eyes. "Ah, Mar, I'm sorry. I should've thought about this bein' All Soul's Day. And I know how much you pray for Paddie." He paused. "You went to Mass this mornin' for him, didn't ya?"

Mary nodded. "I'm sorry."

"You have nothin' to be sorry for. I didn't mean to upset you—and thank you for never givin' up on Paddie. He's, ahhh—he's—"

Tears rolled down Billy's cheeks, and his throat tightened.

Mary lifted his hand and kissed it.

Even after fifteen years, this was a pain deep in his heart that would not go away. The pain was all he had left now of his only son. The emotional onslaught tore through him. He stood up and kissed her on the cheek. "Okay if I close my eyes for a bit before my shift?"

Mary nodded before he retired to the bedroom.

Friday night shifts were often unpredictable in this section of Boston, but tonight was fairly quiet as Sean and Billy patrolled their usual route. Sean turned down the street where Kenny Green had been shot the previous night. "You seem quiet. Everything okay?"

Billy was in a daze as he stared down the darkened street lined by old parked cars.

"Billy, are you okay?"

"What? Sorry. What'd you say?" Billy replied, shaking himself from his memories.

"I asked if you were okay."

"Sure. No different than any other day. I was just thinkin' about—"

He didn't have to finish because Sean already knew. Billy only worried about two things—Mary or Patrick.

"It's okay. You don't have to talk if you don't want to."

He turned his head toward Sean. "I don't want you to ever feel afraid to ask me anything. You've always been there for us, always."

"You two are everything to me, so why wouldn't I be there?"

Sean pulled in front of the Harrison Street Police Station. They entered the station to submit their reports from the prior evening.

Desk Sergeant Doherty's eyes widened. "The two Rembrandts of detective work are here!"

Sean smirked. "Give us a chance. It's only been twenty-four hours."

Billy peered past the desk and down the hall to see Tom and Angelo exiting the detective's room. He waved to them. "Did Brooks actually hire you two for the case?"

Tom laughed. "Billy. Sean. It's been a long time. We just dropped by to bring in some possible evidence."

"Evidence?" Billy asked. "From the Gardner?"

"Maybe. Angelo checked out the Back Bay Fens on foot and found nothing. Then he widened his—Angelo, you did all the work; tell them."

Angelo took a step forward. His fit, muscular body belied his seventy-plus years. "Well, since the thieves couldn't still be in the park, they had to get out or at least get the evidence out, so I started searching in circles around the park and the museum. I kept widening my circle until I noticed something caught on the bushes lining the Ruggles Street sidewalk."

Sean quirked an eyebrow at him. "Ruggles? That's going the other way from where they were running."

"What did you find?" Billy asked.

"A black knit ski mask. It might not be from the robbery, but I don't believe in coincidences."

"Hmm," Sean said. "There's no way they could've been heading down that road. We saw both of them run into the Fens, and there was no route past the cruisers for anyone carrying a painting and ski masks. Why would they take a chance on a road that close to the museum?"

Tom said, "Maybe someone else picked it up and dumped it off?"

"I had to untangle it a bit from the bush," Angelo responded. "I have a feeling it got caught and was pulled from someone's grip or something since it was low on the bush. Definitely not tossed."

Billy patted Angelo on the back. "That's good work. I hope it leads to somethin'."

Sean pulled Angelo aside. "Thanks for helping out on this. Billy promised we would solve this case, so anything that might help is appreciated."

Angelo grinned. "He means a lot to you, doesn't he?"

Sean cocked his head. "You know Billy means the world to me. I don't know where I'd be if they hadn't taken me in as a boy. I think of them as my parents."

Angelo's smile grew wider. "I believe you. *Il sangue ti rende imparentato ma la lealtà ti rende famiglia.*"

"*Ill sanga*—what? What does that mean?"

"It's an old Sicilian saying. 'Blood makes you related, but loyalty makes you family.' As long as I have known you and the Quinns, you have been as loyal as anyone I know."

Sean's brow furrowed. "Loyalty. Do you really think you can be family without being a blood relation?"

"What do couples say when they get married?"

Sean scratched his head. "I do?"

"Exactly, and that's my answer to your question. *I do* believe you can."

****

Billy waved Tom to the side. "Father Tom, do you mind if I talk with you for a second?"

"Sure. What is it?"

Billy sighed as he ran his hand across his mouth. "Look. I'm, ahh, I'm humbled that you are giving the speech for me tomorrow, but—" He stopped and squeezed his chin. "I just don't feel comfortable about the whole thing."

"I think the reason you are so uncomfortable is the same reason so many people want to be there to honor you. You are humble about a life and career to be proud of."

Billy stared at the floor.

Tom continued, "I'm proud of you. I know Mary admires her man, and a very long list of officers do as well. I know how you feel, though, and I'll try not to overdo it—okay?"

Billy raised his head with a sincere sigh of relief. "I'd appreciate that."

<h1 style="text-align:center">Chapter 7</h1>

After an unusually quiet breakfast, Mary stood at the ironing board, pressing Billy's dress uniform. Billy appreciated his bride's efforts as he paced from one room to another.

"You're going to wear yourself or that rug out before the dinner tonight."

"I don't know why they bother with these silly things."

"Because the man I admire most in the world deserves some recognition after almost forty years of impeccable service to this city—that's why."

"I don't know about that. It's still silly."

Mary picked up the water bottle and squeezed the spray handle toward Billy. "You're the only one being silly here. Everyone coming tonight thinks the world of you. Think of it as a fun night at a nice restaurant with a few hundred friends. You love that Italian restaurant, don't you? Plus, you'll have the prettiest gal in town on your arm tonight."

He gazed into her eyes. "You've got that right, Mrs. Quinn."

A little before four o'clock, Sean pulled up to Billy's house to pick them up.

As they got into his car, Mary said, "Where's *your* date, Sean?"

Sean laughed. "You two are my date."

Billy shut the passenger-side door. "He's too picky."

"He should be picky." She leaned forward from the back seat and patted Sean's shoulder. "I'm sure there's a nice girl out there for you, Sean. Don't waste your time on the others. Don't you want to get married someday?"

"It always seems like there's too much going on. Working the night shift doesn't help, but I love it," replied Sean as he entered the Expressway and headed to the Venezia Restaurant, which was tucked away on a small waterfront peninsula of Dorchester.

Across the inlet, Billy could see the sandy but empty Tenean Beach, sometimes called "Tin Can Beach" by the locals. Seven years earlier, he was on that same beach when the body of Paul McGonagle was being dug up. McGonagle was the South Boston's Mullins Gang leader who had disappeared in 1974. His wallet was found floating next to a stolen car in the water near the docks of Charlestown. Billy remembered staring down at the shallow grave as they frantically worked to retrieve the skeletal remains, faded shoes, fragments of clothing, and a gold claddagh ring before the high tide washed them out to sea.

At that time, Whitey Bulger was still on the run as second only to Osama bin Laden on the FBI's most-wanted list, but one of Whitey's soldiers,

Kevin Weeks, had implicated Bulger and Stephen "Rifleman" Flemmi in the murders of three people, including McGonagle. The bullet holes in his skull were clearly visible. Billy tried to shake off the still vivid memory as they pulled into the parking lot on the pier overlooking the Boston skyline across the water.

Sean raced around to open the doors for Billy and Mary, the honored guests for this evening's festivities.

"Do we really have to do this?" asked Billy as his glance shot back over toward the small beach.

"The night will be over before you know it. Try to enjoy yourself, Billy," responded Mary as she took Sean's extended hand. Sean helped her out of the car. She stepped back and studied Billy and Sean in their dress uniforms. "Don't you two boys look handsome tonight?"

To that, Billy took Sean's arm and started strolling toward the restaurant's front door as if Sean were his date, leaving Mary behind.

"Hey, I'm sure there are a few other handsome men in uniform here tonight," called out Mary.

Without hesitation, they both returned and let her take each of their arms. They then escorted her into the bright dining room with a grand view of the harbor and the boats on the pier. The voices were loud as a sea of blue-uniformed officers gathered at the bar. They turned to see Billy enter the room.

A broad grin came to his face, and he was sure his cheeks turned red. They turned and raised their glasses with a loud, "Hooyah! Hooyah!" He approached the men gathering around him, patting him on the back and shaking his hand. Over his long career, he had gotten to know so many other officers who had risked their lives together to protect the city they loved. The bond was strong and not always something he could fully describe to Mary—but she always knew it was there.

Many of these men had only known a life of service, often coming from the military, and each day on duty carried a heightened sense of knowing that the next minute of life was never guaranteed. Over the years, they had lost many fellow officers and always came out in full force to support the surviving families and each other. Retirement was certainly not the same as death, but the visible support was the same, and there was a sense of losing someone in a different way. The room became much louder as jokes and laughter filled the air. Billy blushed as he noticed Mary smiling and watching her man being admired by so many friends.

"You're stuck with him now," said one officer.

"Not for another six months, Brian O'Leary! He's still yours till then!" answered Mary. Loud laughter of the men and women met her comment in this now festive atmosphere.

Billy beamed at Mary, knowing she was undoubtedly forcing herself to appear fine despite her unceasing fatigue.

"I heard he has to stay until he finds that painting from the Gardner!" yelled out one man.

"I heard something about that promise too. We may never get rid of him!" added another.

"Yeah, I heard Billy brought in a priest to solve it—the power of prayer can't be underestimated!" The third man laughed.

A fourth man asked, "Any clues yet, Billy?"

Billy glanced at Sean and started to respond as the police chief entered the room with Tom.

Chief Danny Duggan was as tall as he was broad and created a presence in any room he entered. "So, what are all these Micks doing in an Italian restaurant in Dorchester? No good cooking at home?"

Matt Connolly handed Duggan and Tom each a glass of bourbon on the rocks. "Hey, if no one else is going to brown-nose the Chief, I will!"

The room exploded again in laughter as people started to move into smaller group conversations.

Billy and Sean stood with Duggan and Tom as the chief said, "I spoke to Detective Brooks about the Gardner case. He may be asking for some more of your time to help with leads that come up. You both okay with that?"

Sean smirked. "Brooks? He's got Father Tom here and Angelo hot on this case. What does he need us for?"

Duggan faced Tom. "Ah, I see. Seeking to break into a new career, huh, Father? One case solved wasn't enough for you? Now you've got the bug?"

Tom sipped his drink. "I don't know what you're talking about, and I have a speech to focus on."

"A *short* speech!" interjected Billy. "You promised, and I know priests don't lie now."

Ignoring the interruption, Duggan peered at Sean and then Billy. "So, are there any leads?"

Billy responded, "Not yet. No one could ID the suspects, and they vanished into thin air that night. They couldn't have gotten out of the park, so we have to interview the guys that were playin' ball that night. The suspects could have slipped into that game, but—"

"But that doesn't explain how their clothes and the painting could have disappeared," added Sean. "We scoured that park all night and the next day. Nothing but one pair of sweatpants."

"Well, try to step back and think on it. Some details aren't so obvious at the time."

Tom said, "They seemed to have done their homework, so it's odd that they chose such a hard painting to steal and hide. A rolled-up canvas is a heck of a lot easier than a three-foot wooden panel."

Sean, Billy, and Duggan all smiled, seemingly amused by the earnest expression on Tom's face. He blushed. "Right, let me go practice my *short* speech."

Tom's speech was not short. He had talked with a large number of officers and people who had known Billy over the years and pulled together their stories of a humble but great man who had served faithfully: from his modest beginnings living in a three-decker home of a largely Irish neighborhood to his heroic and decorated service in Vietnam, his thirty-seven years on the police force, and the many volunteering efforts in the Boston community. Tom talked about Mary putting up with Billy for all these decades, about his active commitment to his faith and his family. There was a long moment of silence in recognition of their son, Patrick. The stories were both funny and often moving as Tom painted a portrait of a great man, a man of courage and conviction, and a man who was loved and admired.

When Tom finished, Billy strode to the podium, his body tense. The buzz in the room became very quiet as Billy struggled to find his first words. He exhaled as the people watched in anticipation. "I really don't know what to say. I love everyone in this room. I love my wife more, but I still love all of you." Muffled laughter rippled through the room. "I really don't know who Father Tom's speech was for. Obviously, he grabbed the wrong one because I don't deserve all the kind words he spoke. I would like to meet that guy, though." The laughter grew louder, and he noticed Mary grinning widely. "I do want to tell you how blessed I feel to have each of you in our lives and the support you gave us when P—" Billy tipped his head upward to keep the tears from spilling down his cheeks, but it was to no avail. He could not continue as a painful lump rose in his throat. He held his right hand up as a sign of gratitude and sat down as everyone clanked their spoons against their water glasses. He knew he was among friends, but only his wife really understood his grief.

Billy regained his composure during dinner, which allowed for a long line of speakers to make the evening fun and to help Billy to relax.

Once home, Mary was in bed and asleep fairly quickly, but Billy stayed up for several hours into early Sunday morning. As they dressed for Mass in the morning, he remained quiet.

Mary broke the silence. "That was really nice last night, wasn't it?"

"Sure. I'm just glad it's over."

"Come on, you enjoyed most of it, didn't you?"

"I guess. We should probably get moving if we want to make Mass."

"All right, Mr. Quinn."

After Mass and breakfast, Billy was still restless. He went for a walk and ended up at the church again, taking a seat in the back pew as the third and last Mass of the day ended.

He saw Father Tom approach him after everyone else was gone. "Billy, I thought I saw you at Mass this morning. Did you forget something?"

"No, I just wanted to sit for a bit. It's peaceful here when everyone's gone."

Billy slid over in his pew as Tom sat next him.

"I hope it wasn't too bad for you last night?"

"You did lie to me," replied Billy, turning to catch Tom's grin.

"I may have lied about you, but how did I lie to you?"

Billy shook his head. "You were supposed to keep it short."

"I guess I got a little carried away, but it's hard to fit all that good stuff in a short speech."

"Yeah. Yeah. Excuses will get you nowhere." Billy glanced around the church. "Remember where you are, Father."

"Good point. Patrick is still weighing heavily on you. I can imagine how much you must miss him, but you do know he is in the best of hands, don't you?"

Billy's brow tightened. "How do we actually *know* where anyone is?"

He caught Tom staring at the tabernacle. "You're worried that Patrick isn't with God right now—because of the circumstances?"

Billy didn't respond as he struggled to even broach the subject for the first time. "Yeah—the circumstances. Can you go to heaven with a mortal sin on your soul?"

"I can see why you'd worry. Here's what I can tell you. First, we have to trust in God's unconditional love, mercy, and plan. He had one for Patrick. Yes, the Church teaches that taking the life of anyone, including ourselves, is against God's plan."

Feeling a pang in his chest, Billy replied, "I get that—but he was so young."

"Billy, we are responsible for our lives. God gifts us with this life, and we are obliged to honor it for our salvation. Our life is not ours to dispose of. It contradicts nature, hope, and love itself, and it impacts the people we leave behind. But—pay close attention to what else the Church teaches us."

Billy shifted uncomfortably. "You mean that anyone who commits suicide goes straight to Hell? That teaching?"

"No. The Church teaches that the person is not one-hundred-percent morally culpable if they weren't fully aware or in their right mind at the time." Tom paused. "People can suffer greatly from anguish, depression, or fear that can diminish their responsibility. Christ will always judge us fairly and justly—and with love. This is why I pray for Patrick, and you, and Mary, every single day."

Sighing loudly, Billy said, "I still don't know why he did it." His throat tightened."I miss him so."

"It pains me to see you suffering. I don't believe he rejected God, and I can't imagine the pain he must have been experiencing. Depression and mental illness are not sins. Second-guessing yourselves would be a natural inclination for loving parents, but I'm sure you and Mary did everything you could."

"I think I'm going to sit for a while if you don't mind?"

Tom put his hand on Billy's shoulder. "Stay as long as you like. The church is always open. I'll be in the rectory if you need anything." Then he patted Billy's shoulder as he stood, genuflected toward the tabernacle, and left Billy sitting with his thoughts.

Well over an hour later, Billy tapped at the kitchen door to the rectory.

"Come in. Come in," Tom welcomed him.

"Sure I'm not interrupting anything?" Two empty bowls with spoons were scattered on the table, and the chess pieces were mostly gone from the board.

"Never. Are you okay?"

Billy shrugged.

Tom waved him down the hall. "I have a really good book on what we were talking about. It might help a little."

Billy left his coat at the table and followed him to his office.

As Tom searched through the bookshelves in his office, Billy noticed a print on the wall and stepped toward it. He remembered seeing it before but never took the time to study it. Tom pulled a book off of the shelf and approached Billy. He held out the book. "What do you think?"

"What's it about?"

"Tell me what you see."

Billy leaned in and squinted. "I'm not a connoisseur of paintin's. It looks like a rich man bein' compassionate to a poor beggar and three people watchin'—wait, four people watching. I couldn't see the woman in the shadows. There's a lot of dark in the paintin'."

"That's really good. Would you believe me if I told you that this one was painted by Rembrandt too?"

"You steal it?" responded Billy with a smirk. "Is this really a Rembrandt?"

"Yup. It was the last painting he did, just before he died, and it's called

The Return of the Prodigal Son. It's my favorite painting and parable by Jesus."

"I think I know it. Father has two sons, and one wants his inheritance now and squanders it on sinful living until he's broke and comes home to ask his father if he can be a servant. So the man on the ground is poor, and the father is comforting him. I never got why the father doesn't hold him accountable to earn his way back. It's like he's spoiling an ungrateful son when his other son has always been loyal." Billy caught Tom's nod.

"Think of the painting as Rembrandt's deep understanding of what Jesus is trying to tell us in the story. The son has lost his way, his dignity, and his identity as the son of the father. Despite turning his back on his father and shaming him and his family every day, the father looks out for his son's return. Jesus is telling us about what kind of father His Father is—an unconditionally loving, merciful, and compassionate Father ready to embrace us without question. Rembrandt uses light and dark to communicate the radiance of God's love and mercy that can only be found in Him, while sin only leads to emptiness and a loss of our identity as a son of the Father."

"Huh. All that in one paintin'?" Billy reached out to almost touch the father's loving hands in the painting.

"You can touch it. There's a lot more in this painting than that, but the main thing is that it was never a question about God forgiving the son, but if the son would accept the forgiveness—coming back to the home that was always his. We are called to be like the Father in our love, mercy, and forgiveness of others—and ourselves."

Shoulders tightening, Billy asked, "Forgive ourselves? How can we do that?"

Tom put his hand on Billy's back. "By trusting that God is always ready to forgive us completely first. Hey, guess what I found at the used bookshop on Tremont?" Tom picked up a rolled-up poster and unrolled it. "Hold this. I want to tack it to the wall. It was a photo of the painting of a young man in seventeenth-century clothes."

As Billy stepped back to look at the picture now tacked to the wall, he asked, "Why are you so excited about this paintin'?"

Tom pointed to the poster. "This is the one we're looking for—Rembrandt's self-portrait at age twenty-three. I forgot how magnificent it was."

Billy peered at the portrait of the young man again. He now recalled seeing the same portrait with Mary in her Isabella Stewart Gardner book. He remembered the plumed beret and the fancy dress on the young man. "What's so magnificent about it?"

"Well, it's an outstanding painting for a twenty-three-year-old, but his use of light and dark again and the story he is conveying seems to be beyond his years. Rembrandt did fifty self-portraits, and they form an intimate biography of an artist that was self-reflective and, over time, willing to look at himself without vanity and with total sincerity."

Billy scratched the top of his scalp. "Did he grow up rich? He seems to have a sense of self-importance and is dressed in rich clothes—and look at that feathered hat."

"I believe he grew up in a large family with modest means. See here, the light strikes his hat, his shoulders, and the side of his face, leaving his eyes and much of his face in the dark. The dress was how an ideal painter with a noble patron would dress and not how he actually appeared as a young painter at the beginning of his career. As a young man, Rembrandt may have just been starting to find himself. Over the next forty years, he painted forty-nine more self-portraits, each giving more insights into his perception of himself. He painted his last and probably most honest self-portrait the year he died, showing his full humanity, not hiding his strengths or weaknesses, his confidence or his uncertainty, his hope or his sorrows."

Billy stared more closely at the young Rembrandt. In the shadows of this face, it was hard to look deeply into his eyes. He recalled Mary asking if you can really know someone from the outside. Maybe Tom was asking a deeper question: Do most of us have the courage to see ourselves honestly and humbly, to look at our own true selves? Billy didn't want to think about that at the moment. "Hey, I've got to get going. Thanks for the art class, though."

"You know you can drop by anytime. You do know that, right?"

"I do," answered Billy as he grabbed his jacket from the table and headed out the door.

Billy left without taking the book. He assumed it might be on coping with a child's suicide and was glad that he got out of range before Tom remembered, although he thought he could faintly hear his name being called from the rectory.

Chapter 8

Billy reached his white two-family home feeling less comfortable than when he left it. Instead of going in, he continued, slowing down as he reached the local bakery that was closed on Sundays. The gold letters painted on the window read *Boccaccio's Bakery*. Billy stepped up to the window to see past his reflection to the bakery shelves full of different loaves of bread, colorful cookies, cakes, and desserts. Even from the outside, the comforting smell of the bakery was almost as good as the imagined taste. When he finally moved backward a few steps, he could see his reflection in the window. It was as if he could see right through himself, something he often feared that others could do.

He stared uncomfortably into his own eyes, trying to see himself as the young Rembrandt had painted himself—trying to portray what he wanted the world to see. Billy wondered if he was hiding his real self the same way Rembrandt had. He thought of what Fr. Tom had said about Rembrandt's last painting, how he had exposed himself humbly and sincerely, something that few people had the courage to. *Did he really show everything in his portraits? Would our subconscious even allow anyone to do that? Maybe the paintings would be as translucent as my image in this bakery window. And how honest have I ever been in reflecting on myself?*

Billy started to feel more uncomfortable with his thoughts as he suddenly saw another figure behind him in the window's reflection. The figure stood right behind him but was taller, so Billy could instantly tell who it was. "Haven't you had enough of me today?"

Tom responded, "I was going to ask you the same question. Smells good, though, doesn't it?"

Billy turned.

Tom held a book in his left hand as he stepped to the window, putting his right hand up over his eyes to allow him to see the treats inside. "What is it about a bakery? We can't live by bread alone, but it does seem pretty tempting to try."

Billy nodded. "Sorry I left the rectory so abruptly. I just needed some air and time to think."

"No need to apologize to me. I didn't mean to interrupt your bakery inspection. I just wanted to offer you this book I mentioned. I thought it was well done and might help with what we were talking about in the church." He held it out, almost like the art robber who had handed him the

Giotto painting the other night.

"Thanks, Father Tom. I'll see what I can do. I appreciate it. All these years, I've never learned to say Giovanni's last name—B-o-kah-kio?"

"Most of the time, Italians pronounce each letter the way it sounds—bo-ka-che-o. *Ch* for the second *cc*. I never asked Giovanni if he's related."

"I don't think he's from the old Sod, do you, Fitzpatrick?"

Tom laughed. "No, I don't t'ink so, Mr. Quinn. I was actually thinking about the poet from the 1300s from Florence. Giovanni Boccaccio. Same spelling."

"I don't think our Giovanni would be much of a poet. What did this guy write?"

"One was a series of a hundred short stories during the Black Plague called *Decameron*."

"Sounds uplifting."

Tom shook his head. "Certainly not at times, but he might have been inspired by Dante to consider what was important in life and looking honestly at himself."

Billy stared at the letters of Giovanni's last name again painted on the window. "Kinda like Rembrandt doin' so many self-portraits?"

"Kind of. He wrote about a man with a fortune who was learning to overcome it."

Billy tilted his head. "He can give it to me because I could certainly use it. Why was he tryin' to overcome it?"

"I think it was a bit of honest reflection and asking about what it was to be truly noble. He thought a man must accept his life as it is, accepting the consequences of his own actions without bitterness—even if those events were tragic or contrary to his expectations. Burying yourself in regret and not accepting your limitations makes it impossible to be happy in this life."

Billy glanced back at his reflection in the window. "I thought you always said that you needed God to be truly happy?"

"I do. I think Boccaccio focused on the human aspect of this life and how we can be the source of our unhappiness by not accepting our failings as human beings. It hurts us, and it hurts our relationships too. Interesting way to look at it, don't you think?"

While heading home, Billy thought about Tom's question. How much had he shortchanged his own son, Patrick, growing up and, now, Mary, even more so? When he entered their second-floor apartment, Sean was already there helping to prepare the weekly Sunday afternoon family dinner: pot roast, mashed potatoes, greens, and some bread from Boccaccio's Mary had purchased the day before.

Mary glanced up. "Ah, 'tis himself, home just in time."

Sean gazed at Billy as if to get a read on the man's feelings. Billy was normally there to carve the roast. "How's my partner and main man doing?"

"He doin' just fine. Thanks for takin' over carvin' duty. Save Mary an end piece."

"I'd never forget that," replied Sean as he brought over the roast. Everyone sat, bowed their heads for the blessing, and then finally dug into the delicious meal.

Mary turned to Sean. "So? What's the update on this case you're working on? Billy said you chased the suspects through the Fens, but they disappeared into thin air."

Sean blew a long breath. "That's what it felt like. One second we could hear them running, and then they were gone. No suspects, no painting, no nothing—oh, except for one pair of sweats, so we know they went that way, but then Angelo, from the church, found a black ski mask at a totally different location. I really don't know what to make of it."

Mary grimaced. "I hate this. If they wanted money, why not steal money? People can always get more money, but you can't paint another Rembrandt—and I love that painting."

Billy chewed his beef. "Mary, don't get yourself worked up. We'll do our best to find these guys and get that paintin' back for you."

Mary glanced around the room, from wall to wall.

"What are you lookin' at?" asked Billy.

Mary raised her brow. "I was figuring out where we are going to hang it."

Sean burst out laughing. "I like that. Any other paintings you're interested in?"

"I think the Rembrandt will do."

Sean turned to Billy. "Do you want me to pick you up in the morning? They're rounding up the players from the park to go through another round of interviews. Well, Brooksie will probably interrogate them himself."

"Sean, do you think the robbers got into the game just before you got there?" asked Mary.

"We don't know, but we're going to find out. That's why we're bringing them in."

Mary sighed. "How many players were there?"

"Five on each team."

"Is that the normal number?" asked Mary as she took some mashed potatoes and passed the serving bowl to Sean.

"You can play with less, but that's the normal number."

"Huh. What're the odds there just happened to be eight players, and they would have had room for exactly two more? Hey, I know. Ask them each what the score was when you got there. I bet the last two won't know."

With his mouth full, Sean turned to Billy and wagged his fork. "She's very good." He turned back to Mary. "You're very good. You still watching *Mrs. Marple* these days?"

Billy chuckled. "Mrs. Marple has nothin' on this sleuth."

Mary blushed. "It's *Miss Marple*, and I know you two are making fun of me. Sean, when are you going to bring some nice girl for dinner some Sunday? You spend too many evenings with this guy. You didn't answer when I asked you last night, but do you want to get married someday?"

Sean put another two slices of roast beef on his plate. "I have my family right here."

Chapter 9

As Billy strolled into the police station with Sean, the desk sergeant tilted his head, motioning their attention to the long benches in the waiting area. The ten black men in their twenties and thirties looked unhappy about the imposition on their Monday morning. The shortest and most animated stood up and approached them. "Didn't we tell you what's what the other night? I need to get my rest, or I don't got game for tonight's balling—you know what I'm sayin'?"

Sean lifted a hand in appeasement. "Trev, we just have a few more questions for everyone. Cooperate, and your head will be back on that pillow in no time."

"Why do we got to cooperate? Can't play ball now without being harassed?" quipped Trevon.

Billy added, "We just need to know what everyone saw and if anyone just happened to join your game that night. The help would be appreciated."

"I help my friends. For others—that help is worth somethin'. There's gotta be somethin' in it to jog the memory a bit," answered Trevon as he ran his hand across his lips and then adjusted the brim of his cap that he wore backward.

Billy glanced down the row of players. They were all wearing black hoodies with black sweatpants, as did Trevon. He turned back to Trevon with a smile. "Nice touch. Does that mean you're all confessing?"

Trevon scowled. "No one's fessin' up to something we didn't do."

"Did you see anyone that night?" asked Sean.

Trevon didn't respond.

"We'll be talking to everyone individually to check stories."

Trevon shrugged. "This is four days later. You don't think everyone's story is goin' to check?"

Billy knew he was right. None of these guys were going to help the police, and if two of them were the thieves, they were smart enough to know how to cover their tracks. *If two of them were the thieves, how the heck did they ditch their disguises and that painting?*

One by one, they brought each player into the interrogation room, where Detectives Brooks and Mullen questioned them as Billy and Sean sat, listening to see if anything they said didn't line up with what they saw. The answers were surprisingly consistent.

"What did you do that day?" Brooks asked.

Most said sleeping in, hanging out, and then going to the park and playing a bunch of games under the lights.

"Do you have anyone that can vouch for where you were during the day?"

All named one or two of the other guys that were playing.

"When did the game begin?"

There were different answers based on when they showed up at the park.

"How many players were in each game?"

Three on three. Four on four. And then finally, five-on-five games.

"When was the first five-on-five game?"

Everyone said it was pretty early. No one remembered two players jumping in the game at the last minute.

Sean leaned over and said to Billy, maybe Miss Marple's suggestion could come in handy. Sean asked, "Do you remember when *we* showed up?"

Everyone responded, "Yes."

"What was the score of the game, and who won?"

Billy knew that Trevon would have known exactly what the score was and known for sure who won. Sean had played at these courts many times, and he had mentioned to Billy that Trevon always played each game as if his reputation and very life were on the line. Not everyone had the same exact score, but most were in the same ballpark, except for Dougie Jones and Reggie Hope. Dougie couldn't remember to even guess, and Reggie wasn't close with the score but got the winner of the game right. When each player was done answering their questions about the game and their whereabouts before and after the robbery, they were moved into another room to avoid giving any heads-up to the players who were still waiting to go in.

Once the questioning was finished and they let everyone go home, Brooks sat at his desk perusing his notes. Detective Mullen, Billy, and Sean stood in front of his desk, waiting for him to comment. "That was interesting. Let's corroborate their alibis and whereabouts as soon as possible. I think we need to focus on Jones and Hope." Brooks tipped his glasses and peered up at Sean. "That was a great question to see if they knew the score and who won that game you interrupted."

Billy smirked.

Brooks asked, "What's so amusing? O'Donnell asked a great question. Sign of a good detective if you ask me."

Billy glimpsed Sean. "Oh, I'm sure it is."

Billy and Sean were tasked with keeping tabs on Dougie Jones and Reggie Hope. The records showed that they had recently spent some time together in prison for a large package store robbery. The store owner said that Jones had pulled a gun on him when he walked over to help him in one of the liquor aisles, out of sight of the surveillance cameras. Without finding a gun on them, there was no conviction for armed robbery, which meant a shorter sentence.

Billy checked over their files as they sat in the patrol car down the street from the apartment building where Jones and Hope lived. He asked Sean, "What do you think? From these files, it seems like they're a team, and I'm not talkin' about basketball."

Sean reached over and rotated the sheet with photos from the liquor store robbery. "I saw the video of this robbery. From the camera footage, it's obvious they worked well together, followed a plan, and knew where the camera angles were—but that's a liquor store robbery. It'll take some more convincing to believe they could plan and pull off an art museum heist—successfully!"

"Successful, so far. It sounds like they were the shakiest on their answers to Mary's—sorry, *your* great detective question." Billy laughed.

"Yeah, yeah. You can call me *Mr.* Marple."

Billy stared out the cruiser window at the darkened street. Two of the streetlamps had been broken for some time and never replaced by the city, adding to the sense of vigilance one had to take to avoid an unwanted surprise.

Up ahead, the silhouettes of a gang gathered on the stoop of the project entrance. Some were sitting, while others stood, watching two of the guys engaging in an animated story.

"We've got to figure a way to know where these two were before and after the robbery," said Billy.

Sean took a sip of his coffee. "And maybe even during. If they weren't in that game like they said, it might change the conversation a bit."

"That's a tough one. All the other players are vouchin' for them. I don't know if any other witnesses could tell us if there were only eight players on that court just before you showed up. You didn't see anyone else watchin', did you?"

"Nope. I would've mentioned it."

Billy peered down the street again, noticing things getting a little physical between two guys in the gang, but nothing worthy of intervening and blowing their cover. "Just trying to jog your memory. Hey, wait a minute—you said a biker also hit you on the path."

"Yeah."

"Maybe the kid was coming from the court?" Billy asked him.

"Maybe, but we've got to find that kid."

"Or the bike. Anythin' unusual about it?"

Sean shrugged. "To tell you the truth, we were moving so fast, and it was so dark, I can't picture it."

"Maybe Sully will know?"

"Maybe. He was behind me, though, but we can ask him. Hey, I wanted to ask you something."

Billy turned in his passenger seat. "Ask what? You want to know what I want for Christmas this year?"

Sean laughed. "I know. Same as every year—nothing, but I never get you what you want, so get used to it. That's not it, though. You seem kind of quiet lately, especially at dinner yesterday. Everything all right?"

Agitation filled Billy. "I'm fine. Next question."

Sean lifted his hands in surrender. "I didn't mean to pry. I just care how you're doing, that's all. Is it Mary? Or is it Paddie?"

"He doesn't mean to pry." Billy sighed. "I always think of them, especially these days with Mary's health. She's fightin' me takin' out that retirement money to pay for the transplant." Raising his voice, he said, "Money! Nothin' is worth more than her life. What the hell good is the money if she's gone?"

"Heck, you can have all of my pension. I have time to save up, but you're done, and you need to be with her. We can figure something out, okay? So, if you're always thinking about them, what's been different lately? Is there something else gnawing at you?"

Billy looked aside, saw his reflection in the window, and changed the topic. "It is time for a break yet?" A buzz on Billy's cell phone broke the silence. "Quinn."

Tom's voice spoke loud and clear. "Billy, Angelo got us a few minutes with Myles Connor. Are you interested in driving down to Blackstone?"

Chapter 10

The next morning, Billy was standing in front of the Harrison Street station with Brooks when Tom pulled alongside the curb in his old, broken-down blue Honda hatchback with Angelo riding shotgun. They stepped out of the car to let Billy and Brooks squeeze into the backseat.

"Why are we taking our lives in our own hands in this bucket?" sneered Brooks.

Angelo slid back into his seat. "It doesn't help to show up to a criminal's house in a police car."

"I guess you would know better than me. Why, again, did this Connor guy agree to talk to us?"

Angelo replied, "As a favor to a friend, and I think he is interested in setting the record straight with all the stories going on about him."

"That rap sheet and his prison time wasn't just a story," said Billy.

During the one-hour drive, Brooks shifted his body around, trying to get comfortable. "This better be worth the trip."

"Myles is an interesting character," Tom shouted over the vibrating of the muffler. "I think he likes it that way. He had a rock band called The Wild Ones, robbed banks, dealt in drugs, was involved in shootouts, spent a good deal of time in prison, including Walpole during those riots, but his claim to fame is all the art heists he's successfully pulled off—including that Rembrandt from the MFA in '75. Don't underestimate him. He's got a very high IQ and seems to be fearless about taking risks."

Billy leaned forward. "I thought you said he was still a suspect in the first Gardner robbery."

"Though he may not have been the mastermind behind it, a lot people believe that he knows exactly what happened. He's the first person the FBI thought of, but Myles was in federal custody in Illinois on a murder charge on March 18, 1990. Funny thing was that they still called the prison and asked them to check to make sure he was in his cell. He was," said Tom with a laugh.

"Likely, that's where he should be now," mumbled Brooks.

Angelo rapped on the front door of Connor's modest home in Blackstone, a small town southwest of Boston on the Rhode Island border. No one answered.

Standing back, Billy observed the house. "I always wonder why these thieves never seem to be living the life of Riley with all that money they steal."

Just then, the door opened, and there stood Myles Connor, Jr. He was no taller than five foot six, with thinning, unkempt white hair. He wore a leather jacket, tee-shirt, and old khaki pants. Instead of inviting them in, he stepped out onto the front stoop. "You must be Angelo."

Angelo nodded. "Thanks for being willing to see us. Johnny appreciates it. This is Tony Brooks, Father Tom Fitzpatrick, and Billy Quinn."

Myles chuckled. "Two cops, a priest, and a reformed thief. Is this an intervention to save my soul, or are you trying to put me behind bars again?" He waved them to the back yard, where cackling chickens and barking dogs welcomed them. He grabbed the chicken feed. "What can I help you with?"

Brooks responded, "I think you know that a Rembrandt from the Isabella Stewart Gardner was stolen."

Myles laughed as he scattered some of the feed, and the chickens scrambled and gobbled it up. "It's always the Gardner. That's all anyone wants to talk about. Yes, I heard about that. A very nice painting, to be sure. Do you want to know if I stole it?"

Father Tom said, "That's not why we are here, but since you asked—"

"I could probably give the same answer I did for the 1990 heist. If I were going to go to all the trouble of robbing the Gardner, you would have known it was me because I would have taken Titian's *Europa*. That's the real masterpiece at the museum, but the Rembrandt is no slouch and certainly more of a challenge since it's painted on that large wood panel," said Myles as he set the feed aside and stroked the two dogs at his feet. "I always wanted a large family. Now, I have four dogs, two cats, a brood of chickens, and my horses."

Billy couldn't make eye contact with Myles as he chided, "All earned by good honest work, right?"

Myles grinned as if the offense was more of an interesting challenge. He stepped closer to Billy. "You're a uniform, right?"

Billy nodded.

"So was my dad."

Billy lifted his head. "Didn't you ever want him to be proud of you instead of being a dishonest thief?"

Brooks grabbed Billy's arm to stop him from going further.

Myles raised his hand. There was an unusual presence about him, almost as if life entertained him, and he had no fear or sense of shame. "Officer Quinn, only a fool has no regrets in life. I've pulled over thirty heists and spent too much of my life behind bars for it, but my biggest regret is for my family. My father was decent, compassionate, and had incredible integrity—never bending to compromise his character." Myles peered deep into Billy's eyes. "Can you say you have always had that level of integrity and no regrets?"

Defensive rage filled Billy. "I didn't kill two teenage girls if that's what you're askin'."

Myles narrowed his eyes. "I was acquitted of that charge. Now, what is it you want?"

Tom stepped forward. "Myles, we are simply interested to know if you have any idea who might have been involved with this latest Gardner heist. Why would they steal something they can't sell?"

Myles took a deep breath and regained his playful grin. "Ahh. Motive. That is a great place to start when trying to solve any puzzling crime. Well, there are certainly black market opportunities to sell a great piece. There are very rich men in places like Saudi Arabia who would pay handsomely to own a masterpiece. The other two reasons are probably more likely here."

Brooks lit a cigarette and took a long drag. "What would those be?"

Myles smirked. "People want their masterpieces back, so they are always a great bargaining chip if someone wants a reduced sentence. Fine art for freedom is a very effective strategy. It was for me and would be for someone else."

"Like you did with the Rembrandt from the M.F.A., right?" asked Tom.

Myles nodded. "Yeah. It's a lot of negotiating, but it works very well."

Billy furrowed his brow. "Wait. You steal something valuable and then you get to use it to negotiate less time in jail?"

An impish grin came to Myles' face.

Brooks sighed. "And, what's the other reason?"

"Reward. Just wait a bit, and when the museum doesn't think they will get back their precious works of art, they will pay. They will pay millions. You don't have to sell the art; you can just collect the reward to make it worth the risk. There's nothing like the rush of being in a museum all by yourself and knowing you can take any priceless work of art you want, but the reward money can also be the reason you take the chance."

Exhaling cigarette smoke, Brooks stole a glance at Myles. "It's still possible you masterminded the 1990 heist. Why should we believe you weren't behind this one?"

Myles ambled over to one of his horses and stroked its nose. "You can believe whatever you want, but I wish I had thought of it. What a great challenge—to rob a museum embarrassed by the largest art heist in history. Pulling that off would have been like a hit of cocaine." He let out a deep breath. "Okay. So, who might it be this time? I don't know, but I do know who robbed the Gardner in 1990."

Tom squinted. "You do?"

"I do. I cased the museum several years prior with Bobby Donati. He asked me if I ever thought of knocking off the Gardner, and we checked it out. Years later, he and his accomplice dressed up as cops and pulled off the heist. There was little worry since the security was so bad; they knew there would be time. David Houghton worked with Bobby and confirmed it, saying they robbed it as a bargaining chip to help get me off my life sentence. I had worked with both of them many times."

Tom shook his head. "Unfortunately, both of them died a year later. Bobby Donati was found hog-tied, stabbed, and his throat slit in the back of his Cadillac in Revere, and Houghton died of a heart attack. There seems to be a long list of dead bodies for most of the possible suspects and a cold trail to the loot."

Myles grinned. "I have my guesses, but I don't know where those pieces are, and I don't know anything about this latest heist, swear to God."

"You may be taking a big chance mentioning God to an Irish priest," said Tom with a laugh. "You're Irish Catholic, aren't you?"

"Was. I got hauled to Mass every weekend by my folks, and the ritual made me skeptical of organized religions."

Tom raised his eyebrows slightly. "I always wondered about the appeal of disorganized religions. Remember the thief on the cross next to Jesus was saved in his final hours, so I won't give up on you, Myles." Tom patted his shoulder.

"Hey, I've often felt cheated by my own lack of faith. I'm not blind to the peace and purpose of religion, and God can bring hope to some people. I've just never experienced it." Myles led them back around to the front of the house.

Angelo shook Myles's hand. "Thanks for being willing to talk to us."

Myles nodded. He glanced up at Billy. "No hard feelings? I actually appreciate good cops—when they don't catch me."

Brooks said, "I wish you could have told us more, but thanks."

"Look. I'd like to say, 'Good luck' but I'm not really in the business of helping the police. I heard two guys pulled the theft off. They probably aren't the ones who planned and sponsored this thing, but they'd want to get paid somehow from the reward money," replied Myles.

Tom shook Myles' hand and gazed into his eyes. "God bless you, Myles. We can give up on Him, but He never gives up on us."

Myles Connor stood at the end of his driveway as Tom, Angelo, Brooks, and Billy squeezed into the old Honda.

As Tom nodded to him, Myles said, "Peter Buck."

"What?" asked Tom.

Myles grinned and turned down the driveway.

As Tom started the noisy car, he said, "He's certainly an interesting character."

"He certainly thinks so," replied Brooks.

"Who's Peter Buck?" asked Angelo.

Chapter 11

Few would notice, but Billy always felt uneasy. There was an exhausting tension created by the gulf between the person everyone saw and the person Billy knew lay under his skin. Today, however, feeling particularly uncomfortable and fidgety, he took a morning walk with no direction in mind. Within minutes, he entered the north side of the Back Bay Fens, where the community gardens were being put to sleep for the upcoming winter by neighborhood gardeners. The suspects couldn't have reached this far before the streets were blocked off, and those gardens were scoured multiple times to see if either of the culprits had buried themselves or the painting—no such luck.

The river that ran through the elongated park became wider in spots as it curled through it like a serpent. He crossed over to the rose garden that still dazzled with the colorful rose bushes that would not surrender until the end of the season.

Billy had taken Mary to this garden on their first date. Her eyes had sparkled as if she were a princess entering her castle. That enchanted look caught his attention when passing her in the halls in junior high school. Mary Elizabeth Quigley's entire face had shone with goodness and a love for life. Billy had become as infatuated with her. Thoughts of her had consumed every waking moment, so much so, he had wondered how he ever did any homework or was able to focus as captain of the basketball team. He had also been shy with girls and afraid she would end his fantasy if he asked her out—something he had waited to do until he was twenty-two, back from the war, and starting his career in the police force.

A couple strolling the circular garden stared when Billy chuckled out loud. It was in this spot that Mary had given his arm a good whack on that first date.

He had leaned his head backward. "This is how you treat someone that tells you how much they like you?"

Mary had glared at him. "You just said you've liked me since junior year in high school!"

He had taken her hands in his. "I was head over heels for you. Isn't that good news?"

"I sat home for two proms because of you. Why didn't you ask me out?"

He had stared down at the gravelly path. "I was afraid you'd say no and I'd lose you."

She had smiled and had gazed fondly into his eyes, reaching her hand up to stroke his cheek, but he had pulled back. "Why are *you* the one pulling away now?"

"You pack a good punch. I just wanted to make sure you didn't put me down for the count before we finish our first date." Then he had laughed out loud.

"What? Making fun of *me*, now?"

At this moment, Billy had stared deeply into her eyes. *What will she do if I ever tell her I love her?* She was the best thing to ever happen to William Patrick Quinn. She admired everything about him, but he alone was aware that he deserved none of that admiration.

This haunting thought was what brought him back into the discomforting present he lived in. He wandered out of the rose garden and approached the section of the park that held the basketball courts and soccer field. He was back to being Officer Quinn and slowly scanned the area for any missed clues. There were plenty of trees, a pond, and paths on both sides. If Jones or Hope did pull off the robbery and then jumped into the game that night, how did they get rid of their sweatsuits and the painting? Billy's mind was blank, and he felt uncomfortable, as he did most of the time.

He ambled down the remaining path until he stood in front of the Gardner Museum. While he was in street clothes, he always carried his badge in his pocket. He entered through the main doors.

The desk security guard recognized him. "Officer Quinn, right?"

Billy half-smiled. "Last time I checked. You're Dudley, aren't you?"

"Last time I checked," he responded as his shoulders straightened, probably proud that Billy remembered his name. "Are you here to investigate?"

Billy hadn't thought about why he had entered the museum. "Oh, ahh—yeah. Do you mind if I look around?"

Dudley motioned forward. "Not at all. Let me know if you need help with anything."

Billy stepped into the courtyard garden as the morning sunlight streamed through the high arched windows. He thought that Mary was right; one never got tired of the beautiful sight. It was early, and few patrons were in the garden as he ascended the large marble staircase and entered the Dutch Room. On the wall hung the slightly damaged large gold frame that had held the portrait of young Rembrandt. Behind it was only the green silk wall covering. He stopped and looked squarely at the frame, and an image of himself as an eighteen-year-old in his Marine uniform came to mind. He was young and just beginning his life, but knowing he was heading to Vietnam made him realize that he might possibly be closer to death than he was ready for. He remembered feeling nervous but proud, ready to defend his country and find out what kind of man he really was. He imagined more details, almost as if he were painting his own portrait as he stood there—and then he jumped.

The solitary quiet of the moment was broken as heard a voice say, "This is my favorite painting too."

Billy turned to see Father Tom standing next to him. "Do you want to give an old cop a heart attack? What are you doin' here?"

"I guess I could ask you the same. What are *you* doing here, anyway?"

Billy ran his fingers across his forehead. "I wish I knew." He glanced up at the frame and chuckled. "Maybe they could put your poster into the frame so people would know what was there."

Tom pointed down at the small table placed underneath the frame. An art photo book was opened up to a page with the portrait of the young Rembrandt. "A poor substitute, but at least people will know what's missing—hopefully, not for long."

"I'm definitely stumped," Billy replied as he took a closer inspection of the portrait photo. "Is there somethin' different about the eyes in this paintin'?"

"Well, he painted his eyes in the dark, and they don't reflect light. That's what strikes me most. I think I read that this revealed a secretness of heart and mind and an absence of spiritual life, but then the eyes are directed toward the light."

"Huh, what does that mean?"

"Kind of like what we talked about with the *Prodigal Son* painting and how he used dark and light. Remember, we talked about self-portraits being a form of analyzing oneself and becoming self-aware. Rembrandt wanted to know himself deep inside, in the dark places, and become enlightened about his potential and his limitations as well. We are all more complex people than we often show the world—pushing the ugly or uncomfortable parts we fear most into the dark corners to avoid them from being seen and rejected."

"All that with a few strokes of the brush, but the painter can create any image he wants." Billy leaned closer.

"Sure, unless he wants to know and understand himself. The light can be scary, but it becomes the place we have the real freedom to be ourselves—to forgive, accept, and love ourselves."

Billy glanced back up at the empty frame, visualizing his own image again. "I don't know. Maybe some people don't deserve to be loved?"

Tom put his hand on Billy's back. "That's probably how the prodigal son felt, but God always has a better plan for his unconditional love and mercy."

"Yeah, maybe—but maybe some people don't deserve mercy."

Tom squeezed Billy's shoulder. "If we deserved it, it wouldn't be called mercy, would it?"

Billy merely nodded as they left the Dutch Room.

Tom motioned to the staircase heading upstairs to the Gothic Room. A tall painting of Isabella Stewart Gardner herself was at one end of this room, ensuring everything remained as she had arranged it. In front of where they stood was Giotto's *The Presentation of the Christ Child in the Temple.*

Billy studied the painting, which even he could recognize as special. "Someone gave this to me once." Billy chuckled.

"You should have kept it." Tom laughed. "It's quite a painting—expressive. I love how the baby Jesus is struggling to get back into his mother's arms as he is presented publicly in the Temple, as their child and as our Savior—the Son of God."

Billy scratched the top of his head. "I never thought about there being so much thinkin' goin' into paintin's."

"It captures the dramatic moment from Luke when Simeon and Anna recognize who Christ really is. As I said, you should have kept it when he *presented* it to you."

"It's kinda funny. It felt like he was presentin' it to me. It stunned me for a second."

"Not to change the subject, but any leads yet?"

Billy raised his hands. "It's a dry well so far. We have two guys from the basketball game that we are watchin', but nothin' solid to tie them to the robbery."

"I heard that from Angelo—Jones and Hope, is it?"

Billy rolled his eyes, peering up at the arched ceilings. "He isn't supposed to know any names like that. Who told him?"

Tom shrugged. "He seems to have a lot of informative connections. I never ask him about it because I don't think I want to know. He brought it up to me because of the Hope guy—it's Reggie, right?"

"Maybe. What if it was?"

"Reggie Hope. RH."

"I never heard of him being referred to as RH before."

Tom replied, "No. RH were the initials on the hammer that was left on the floor. Maybe he left in such a rush he didn't remember it was there?"

"Well, how about that? I thought you said it was for Rembrandt Harm-something?"

"Rembrandt Harmenszoon van Rijn. I was joking a bit there."

Suddenly they heard an unexpected-but-not-unfamiliar voice. "'ow can zis be a time for the joking?" Standing behind them was Dr. DuBois, looking severely agitated. "I see you 'ave not yet caught these two 'oodlums! When will we 'ave our Rembrandt back where 'e rightfully belongs? Is there no justice in this country of yours? Should France take back the Statue of Liberty?"

Billy shot a glance at Tom and replied, "We'll find it, Doc. You're just goin' to need to be a little patient with the process."

DuBois scoffed and responded. "Ah. *Les mots sont bon marché!*" He squinted as he scanned the room and left in a huff. "Results are all zat matter."

Billy turned to Tom. "What did he say to me?"

"I think it was something to the effect of 'Words are cheap.' Don't pay any attention to him. He's just frustrated."

"And French."

Tom chuckled as they started down the flights of stairs. "Hey, Angelo also asked about the bike."

Billy tilted his head. "Bike?"

"Angelo and I were playing chess the other night and brainstorming about how the painting could have disappeared from the park. The only thing Sean and the other officer—"

"Sully?"

"Yeah, Sean and Sully were chasing the suspects into the park. They said there was a kid on a bike that almost ran into them. Did we hear that right?"

As they reached the last step, Billy responded, "Yeah, he said a boy on a bike. I pressed him on that, but he said it was too dark, and they were goin' too fast to tell. He assumed it was a boy because the bike was lower than an adult bike."

"Anything else he could remember about it?"

Billy squeezed his chin and shook his head. "No. Wait! He said he had to arch his body because the bike had those large baskets on each side of the back tire."

"Interesting. Remember what Detective Brooks keeps saying? It's—"

"All in the details. I've heard that from him often enough. Well, I'm goin' to get home to Mary. She'll wonder where I disappeared to."

"Good seeing you, Billy. Just let me know if you ever want to follow up on that talk we never finished."

"Thanks, I appreciate that," he replied as he started home.

Billy struggled to clear his head of the discomforting thoughts that were becoming permanent guests. He had spent decades avoiding his true identity and whether he was worthy of the admiration he received from Mary and this Boston community. Still, the protective walls of distraction and busyness seemed to be cracking open. For what must have been an hour, he strode through the streets with the intent of pushing the invading thoughts from his conscious mind, but memories started to pour through those cracks as he reached the familiar streets of his youth. He stopped at the end of Hallam Street, a short narrow street lined with old three-deckers, common in Dorchester. Little had changed since the summer nights he remembered—hanging out on these porch steps, playing catch in the street before listening to the Red Sox on the radio and coming to understand the meaning of the broader family that existed in this neighborhood.

Billy's mother, Betty, depended on that extended sense of family most after his dad was killed in action in the Korean War when Billy was five and his younger brother, Jimmy, was four. Betty went to work at a local factory and needed Billy to take on responsibilities beyond his years. She needed to depend on him as he grew, but he let her down on many occasions, drinking too much with friends, getting in trouble at school, and even with the police on occasion.

One of those occasions involved breaking into a house two streets over. He had been hanging around with several other boys who were bored and wanted some excitement—the rush of taking a big chance when Billy hoisted himself up to a window to pry it open. If his father had been alive, Billy knew he probably wouldn't have done it, but at the time, he didn't care about right or wrong. He just wanted to belong. It didn't take long for the neighbor, whose apartment house was less than five feet away, to call the police, and Billy was soon sitting at the station. An officer at the station who had been an old friend of Billy's father pulled him aside for a long talk and a warning before letting him go home. His mom never knew—not about that.

His mother couldn't provide the mentoring and guidance he had missed from his dad, and Billy knew it as well. Anxiously, Betty permitted him to join the Marines at age seventeen. Jimmy joined him a year later. Billy grew up fast in the Marines, even being decorated with the Navy Cross for extraordinary heroism in combat in Vietnam, while Jimmy gave his life. Billy's mother had died of cancer shortly after Billy returned from his tour of duty, and her funeral was the last time he had stood on this street.

Almost forty years hadn't erased his sense of guilt and shame for letting her down, and he didn't want anyone to recognize him as he quickly turned and strode back home, feeling no sense of valor or heroism. *I can't change the past. I can't fix the past. I need to focus on today. Marines take care of those in their care right now, and I can't let Mary down. She has to have that operation, come hell or high water—no matter what!*

His stride continued to pick up as he thought. Tom always said that faith was God's work in us that we respond to. Billy had to respond to those most in need, and that was clearly Mary right now.

Chapter 12

As Billy approached his home, he noticed that Sean's squad car—number 316—was parked in front. Sean was sitting at the kitchen table talking with Mary when he walked in. "A little early, aren't you, Officer O'Donnell?"

Sean jumped to his feet. "Where've you been? The judge approved a search warrant to check out the apartments of Jones and Hope. Brooks wants us at their place within a half-hour."

"Well, what are you waitin' for? Let me change, and let's go!"

Their positive energy drew a smile from Mary. On their way out the door, she shouted, "Make sure you check the ceiling tiles to see if they hid the painting in the ceiling!"

Though they laughed loud enough for the whole first floor to hear, they admitted to each other that it wasn't a bad idea.

"How did they get the warrant?" asked Billy as he got into the passenger side and adjusted the gun in his holster.

"Both gave shaky answers; they've stolen together before and shared prison time in the past, and because of the RH initials on the hammer left at the scene," responded Sean as he pulled away from the curb and drove to the project apartments where Dougie Jones and Reggie Hope lived.

Detectives Brooks and Mullen were already there, along with Sully and Butchy. Instead of working one apartment at a time, they split up into teams of three and planned to search both apartments at the same time. The building was old, the dark hallways in need of painting, and the doors worn and broken. Break-ins and gunshots were common.

Dougie and Reggie had been friends ever since childhood, and their apartments were on the same floor and only a few doors apart. Billy took a deep breath as he knocked on the door. His heart pounded, aware of the unpredictability of the situation. Anyone not from these apartments was considered an enemy. Frequently they were: police doing an investigation, competing gangs, loan sharks wanting to get paid, and collection agencies.

They were met with silence. The door cracked open. A large woman wearing a floral apron appeared behind the mostly closed door. She was wary but still friendly as she asked how she could help them.

"Ma'am, sorry to intrude, but we have a warrant to search your apartment," responded Sean.

The door didn't budge. Her brow furrowed and her eyes squinted with a look of confusion as sweat glistened on her forehead. "What? You must have the wrong apartment."

Brooks asked, "Does Reggie Hope reside here?"

Her shoulders drooped as she opened the door to let them in. "I'm his mother, Rozzy. What's he done now? I've told him and told him to keep himself clean and stay out of that place."

Old pictures of young boys dotted the walls, along with a framed portrait of Jesus. Billy could now see the heartache in her eyes as she stepped aside to let them search the living room and kitchen.

"Where do you keep your tools?"

She frowned. "Tools? Who do you think is using tools here? There's a lot that could use fixin' around here, but that ain't happenin' with my boys."

Reggie stepped out of one of the bedrooms barefoot and wearing a tee-shirt and black sweatpants. "What's going on? I answered all your questions at the station. I told you I had nothing to do with that robbery."

Rozzy moved toward him. "What robbery? You didn't say anythin' about a robbery?"

"Ma, don't worry. We were playing ball. I think they think black boys can't do anything except steal things. What would I do with a painting, anyway?"

Her eyes narrowed. "Painting? Why would you steal a painting?"

His voice rose in volume and tone. "I didn't steal anything! Once guilty, always guilty. We told them everything we know, and they still want to harass us. It doesn't matter who actually did it, as long as they find someone." Reggie shook his head as he reached for a cigarette.

Brooks said, "Mr. Hope, we aren't here to harass you. We have a warrant. If you're innocent, then you should have nothing to worry about."

Reggie lit his cigarette and took a long drag. "Nothin' to worry about? That's what they said the last time, and I spent a chunk of my life in the pen avoiding J-cats, prison wolves, and getting shanked for the fun of it."

Sean raised his hands. "It's hard to argue with video evidence. Mind if I search your room?"

"Does it matter what I mind?" He followed them, stood tensely, and watched them check every drawer, wall panel, floor rug, the undersides of chairs, tables, and beds.

Billy wondered why he appeared so nervous if he had nothing to hide. He reminded Sean of Mary's suggestion, so they peered up at the ceiling. They didn't have the ceiling tiles Mary had envisioned, but there was one panel for access above. Sean took a long flashlight and pushed open the panel. It moved easily. Reggie shifted from one foot to another and glanced at the doorway. Sean stepped on a chair as Billy and Brooks watched and ensured that everyone stayed where they were. Sean lifted out a plastic bag and lowered down what appeared to be a stash of pot that he handed to Billy.

Brooks took the bag and held it up to Reggie. "Easy violation of parole, isn't it?"

"I don't know where that came from."

"Well, we can ignore it, or we can turn it in. I'm going to let you think about it for a bit to see if you can help us out on this Gardner heist. Maybe a little incentive might help jog your memory to keep you away from all the fun in the pen?"

Reggie took a long drag from his cigarette and exhaled it. "I don't need no favors, and I swear on my mother's grave, I didn't rob that museum."

Rozzy interrupted, "Your mama ain't dead yet, so don't swear on me for anythin' yet. You tell these officers what they need to know. Did you steal that paintin' they're lookin' for?"

Reggie made eye contact. "Nope."

Rozzy turned to Brooks. "My boy ain't perfect, but I know when he's tellin' me a lie, and he ain't tellin' me a lie. Are you done with your searchin'?"

Brooks nodded to Rozzy and then glanced over to Reggie. "For now. Let me know if that little plastic baggie helps you improve your memory."

They met Detective Mullen and the rest of the crew, who had searched Dougie Jones' apartment, in the hallway. They found no painting, no clothing, no tools, and no other evidence that would help tie them to the robbery—just an eerie feeling that something didn't fit. Brooks asked Billy and Sean to continue to keep an eye on them.

At their eight o'clock break that night, the desk sergeant held up a piece of notepaper as Billy and Sean entered the station.

Billy asked, "What are you smilin' about, Doherty? Did you win the numbers today?"

"I wish. You've been summoned."

Billy pulled the note from his hand. "Summoned to what?"

"Your favorite priest wants to see you. It's bad enough when you decide it's time to go to confession, but when your priest has to call you in, it can't be good." Doherty smirked.

Billy glanced at the note. *Please drop by the rectory as soon as you can.*

Billy showed Sean the note, and they turned around to head to St. Francis.

The street was quiet as they pulled into the driveway. They could see the kitchen light on in the rectory. After climbing the steps, Billy tapped on the door, which Tom answered with his usual warm, welcoming smile.

"What's up, Father?"

"Come in. I hope I didn't interrupt anything, but Angelo may have a lead you'd be interested in."

Sean stepped inside. "What kind of lead?"

"I was talking to Angelo about how the painting and disguises could have gotten out of the park. Sean, you said the only person you saw leaving that park during your pursuit was a bike heading the other way."

Sean exhaled through his closed lips. "That's right, but that was some kid."

Tom motioned to the fridge. "Do you want a drink or anything?" He pulled out glasses and fixed them a cold tonic. "Are you sure it was a kid?"

Sean took a long swig from his tall glass. "I think so. It was pitch-black out, and the bike was short—so Sully thought it must have been just a kid. Why are you asking?"

"Like I said, Angelo and I were discussing the evidence. When I mentioned the bike, he thought you should focus on it, especially considering that's where the black ski mask was dropped in the bushes. It was heading in the same direction, and it would have been the right height. Billy mentioned that Sully thought the bike had large wire baskets over the back tire."

"Yeah, something like that. I had to jump to the side to avoid them."

"Angelo thought the biker might be part of the escape plan. They could quickly stuff the evidence into the baskets and head in the opposite direction."

Billy rubbed his cheek. "I don't know. That paintin' would have been too large to fit into any basket."

Tom nodded. "That's definitely a problem to solve. Angelo spent the day scouring the neighborhoods in the biker's direction. It took him pretty much all day before he found a potential candidate."

Sean asked, "He found the bike? Where?"

"It was at the other end of Ruggles, near the Madison Park High School field. A guy was riding it, and the baskets were full of returnable cans and bottles, but the bike fit the description."

"Are you talkin' about Bubblegum Bob?" Billy asked. "He supplements his income by collectin' returnables and helpin' out at the high school. He's been kind of like the mascot and cheerleader for the sports teams over the last thirty years. Bob might be limited in a few ways, but he's practically a neighborhood institution. He's a good guy. I don't think he'd get mixed up with anythin' like this."

Tom said, "Angelo didn't think so either. When he approached him, Bob handed Angelo a stick of gum. Angelo struck up a conversation, and it turned out that his bike had been stolen last week. Angelo was able to help him narrow it down to Halloween night, and it showed back up in front of his apartment the morning after the robbery. It seems like too much of a coincidence, doesn't it?"

"Way too much," Billy said. "That is some great detective work on Angelo's part."

Tom nodded. "The other thing that seems like too much of a coincidence is that Bubblegum Bob's apartment is just around the corner from Dougie Jones and Reggie Hope. If they end up being the two robbers, we're still going to need to find out who was riding the bike. Maybe it was a kid just doing his small part is—but he might be the link to everything else."

Chapter 13

Bubblegum Bob was easy to spot. He always wore a bright red Madison High Cardinals team jacket with his name sewn on the front. He wore a matching red baseball hat in the summer and a bright red wool cap in the winter, both with a proud flying cardinal embroidered in front. Billy hadn't mentioned to Sean that he was going to drop by Ruggles Street the next morning.

He arrived in street clothes to avoid attention, but Bob recognized him. Bob, always friendly, had talked with Billy many times over the years at sporting events in the neighborhoods. "Hey, Bob. How's it goin' today?"

Earnest and excited as usual, Bob grinned. "Doin' real good, Billy Quinn. How about you?"

"Always better when I see you, Bob. How many sticks of bubblegum have you given out so far? What are you up to?"

Bob placed his hand on top of his cap and looked up to the sky, trying to calculate how many sticks of gum he had given out over the past thirty years. "Um, I want to beat the Guinness Book record. Let's see—"

"Well, how many is the record?"

"A lot."

"And how many do you think you've given out so far?"

"Um, a lot. Really a lot. I give out sticks of gum every day."

Billy's eyes widened. "So, it sounds like you are tied for the record and can beat it real soon!"

Bob's wide smile reached his eyes. "I hope so. Do you know the record for the most sticks of bubble gum chewed at the same time? Ninety-eight by Randy G!"

"That's very cool." Billy circled Bob's bike. The handlebar had streamers and an old bell, and the large baskets were full of the cans and bottles he had collected that morning. "You've had this same bike for a long time, haven't ya, Bob?"

"Oh, yeah. Long time. It's a good bike. Someone wanted to talk about it yesterday too. At first, I thought he wanted to take it, but he just wanted to talk about it."

Billy asked, "Has anyone ever taken your bike before?"

Bob's head bounced up and down. "I lost it last week for a few days, but someone brought it back."

"Did you see who it was?"

Bob paused before he replied, "Nope. Nope. It was just here when I got up in the morning. I was happy, but they took all my bottles out. I wasn't happy about that. Collecting takes a lot of work."

Billy put his hand on the bell. "It sure does. Can I see how this sounds?"

Bob nodded, and Billy pulled the metal lever to hear the bell make a ring-ring sound. "Bob, when do you use this bell?"

Bob grinned. "I use the bell every time I reach a sidewalk or intersection—especially in the dark. That way, I won't hit anyone."

"Do you usually ride your bike in the dark?"

"Nope. I have my TV shows on at night."

"What did you watch last Thursday night? Do you remember?"

"Oh, yeah. Thursday's my favorite—*Survivor* at eight and *CSI* at 9. They're good shows. Do you watch them?"

"I have to work at night, so I miss all the good shows."

An elderly man crossed the street and called out. "Glad you got your bike back, Bob."

"Me too, Mervin. I've had this bike for a long time."

Mervin stopped next to Billy. "It was nice of the boy to bring it back."

Billy quickly interjected, "You saw someone bring Bob's bike back?"

Mervin nodded. "Yeah. I forgot to take the trash out Thursday night, so I got up early on Friday, and I saw him riding it back."

"Do you remember what he looked like and which direction he came from?"

Mervin's hand clenched his chin as he peered up at the sky to think. "He dressed like all those boys from down the street there, except he had this orange streak in his hair. I'd say he was maybe thirteen."

Billy thanked him, and Mervin ambled on. Billy turned back to Bob. "Football game comin' up for Friday?"

"Oh, yeah. Friday football for the Cardinals. They need me there. We've won all our home games. You should come."

Billy patted Bob on the back. "Maybe I will. It was good seein' you, Bob. Really good." As he made his way down the sidewalk, he could hear the faint sound of the bell on Bob's bike as he passed people. Billy spent several hours making his way up and down each street in the area until he reached a vacant lot and made a call from his cell phone. "Brooks, this is Quinn. Do you think you and Mullen can come to the parkin' lot in the back of St. Katharine Drexel's Church on Ruggles?"

The two officers arrived within a few minutes. "What do you have, Billy?" asked Brooks.

Billy led them to a spot behind the parking lot of the magnificent church building, one of the few open areas with grass and large trees instead of a building or a parking lot. At Billy's feet were the charcoaled remnants of a small fire.

"What are we staring at?" asked Brooks.

Billy stood with his hands in his pockets. "On the night of the robbery, the only person anyone saw leave the park was possibly a kid or someone riding a bike—a bike with large wire baskets on each side of the back tire. It looks like that bike was stolen around the corner from here. Remember Angelo found the ski mask snagged low to a bush on the part of Ruggles near the Museum? We found a bike that was stolen before the robbery and was returned the day after."

"Okay, so why are we here?"

"Take a close look at the items that weren't fully burned in this little campfire."

Brooks and Mullen squatted down and carefully sifted through the small pieces of material, some sticks, and a piece of metal. "What's all this?"

Brooks stood up. "Hopefully, there's no Rembrandt in there. I'll get forensics down here. How did you know about the bike?"

Billy hesitated.

Brooks frowned. "Never mind. I don't think I want to know. Where's the bike now?"

Billy told him about Bubblegum Bob, and later that day, forensics was able to take samples from the tires without taking the bike from Bob. They confirmed that the ashes from the fire showed fibers from black cotton sweatpants and hoodies. They found wool fibers that the masks could have been made of, synthetic material from the gloves, thin wood sticks, some vinyl material, and a metal clip that rotated. There wasn't any evidence of a painting.

After Billy updated Sean, they stopped by Brooks' office. During their evening shift, they sat around Brooks' desk analyzing the pieces of evidence and photos of the potential suspects. Silence loomed for a moment.

Brooks stood up and approached the large whiteboard. "What do we know so far? Forensics confirmed that the bike with the wire baskets had been in the Back Bay Fens Park within the past week based on the gravel in the tires. That same bike suddenly disappeared just before the robbery and magically reappeared afterward. There was a fire to destroy what clearly could be the evidence from the robbery, and this all happened right around the corner from our two friends, Jones and Hope, who can't keep score at a basketball game they claimed to have been in from the beginning. They both fit the build and agility of the suspects, but we have no witnesses to their involvement, no evidence to tie them directly to the robbery, and no painting. Aren't we doing just great for a week's work?"

"Hey," Mullen said, "we've got another day before it's a week. I can canvas the neighborhood to see if Dougie or Reggie used any kids or anyone to run for them. We know they are still involved with dealing. Maybe they used the same kid to steal the bike, wait in the park, and stuff the mask and things into his baskets before taking off and burning the evidence."

Brooks pointed to the photo of the two suspects. "Why do I doubt that they masterminded this? They look more like thieves than planners of an art heist."

Sean said, "It's hard to believe they'd want to take on a job this risky just after getting out of the pen."

Brooks shrugged. "The reward alone will probably be pretty high, so think of what that painting would fetch. That would make the holiest angel at least think about it."

Chapter 14

Sean dropped Billy off in front of his apartment a little after midnight. The quiet side street was dark and empty at this time of night. "Get some sleep, Billy. You look exhausted."

"I'm fine. Be careful going home."

"I will. I know something's bothering you, but I know not to ask until you're ready to talk—so let me know."

As Billy closed the car door, Sean rolled down the window.

Billy said, "I told you I'm fine."

Sean quietly drove away.

Upstairs, Billy tried to slip into bed without waking Mary, but she turned over and kissed him on the cheek. "Good to have my hero home safe and sound."

"No place I'd rather be, Mrs. Quinn," said Billy as he leaned over to kiss her cheek. He was very tired but still unsettled. As he prayed for Mary and Patrick, he wondered which would win—sleep or restlessness? Finally, sleep took over, and he drifted into a dream.

He could see himself walking in a field of tall grass bending in a gentle breeze under a bright sunshiny sky. He smiled with contentment until the meadow became covered with large trees that blocked the sun, and everything grew darker. At his feet were the remnants of a fire with embers feeding off of whatever was remaining in a shallow pit. Suddenly a flame burst from the embers, and the fire roared; he backed off and ran into the church, where a wooden casket sat in the center aisle in front of the altar.

He was alone in the large church with its high arching ceilings and rows of wooden pews. A powerful urge pushed him forward to open the casket's lid to see who was inside. His legs felt like lead as he approached, then paused as needle pricks of nervousness swept over him. Reaching out, he was suddenly overwhelmed by the fire that shot several feet into the air. The casket would be quickly consumed. He panicked. His son, Patrick, lay helplessly inside, crying out for him.

Billy jolted from the dream, sat up, sweat rolling down his back, his heart pounding, and his body trembling and weak. As he slipped out of bed, he sighed with relief that he hadn't also woken Mary. The earlier restlessness became worse. He couldn't sit still, and he didn't want to pace the apartment, so he got dressed and eased his way out the door to walk off his unmanageable anxiety. He marched the streets for miles but found no sense of relief.

Eventually, he found himself standing in front of St. Francis Church. He thought the last thing he should do after such a nightmare was to go back into a church, but he felt tugged inside, where he instantly felt he was no longer alone.

His footsteps echoed as he strode down the center aisle of the darkened church, lit only by the gentle light of a handful of prayer candles. He slid into a front pew, his whole body still trembling. He tried to talk to God. He tried to yell at him for letting his son suffer instead of him, but his mind couldn't focus on any coherent prayer. His impulse was to get up and leave immediately, but he felt too exhausted to stand. As he sat in the silence, working to calm his emotions, he heard the sound of the entrance door being gently closed. He didn't turn to see if anyone was there and heard no footsteps, but he was startled by the sudden feeling that someone was standing beside him. He closed his eyes in hopes of the feeling going away, and a sudden voice let him know that wasn't going to happen.

"You're a little early for morning Mass. If you're afraid there won't be any seats; I can tell you that won't be a problem."

Billy resisted glancing up, praying that his trembling wasn't as noticeable as it felt.

Tom took a step into the pew and sat quietly next to him for several minutes before Billy noticed that Tom's feet were bare, his legs covered by pajama bottoms and his top with a jacket over a tee-shirt. "Is this the new attire for Catholic priests these days?"

"Only at three in the morning."

"I didn't mean for you to get up. You said the church was open any time."

"Indeed, it is. I hope I'm not interrupting anything. Angelo is a light sleeper, so he let me know you were here. I figured I'd offer an ear if you needed one."

"Is that what the temple guard said to Peter when they came to take Jesus away?"

"Very good." Tom smiled. "So, am I a friend tonight or an unwelcomed intruder?"

Billy responded. "You can stay. I just may not say anything."

"Whatever you need, Billy. Whatever you need."

Billy sat for a while, started to talk several times, and then pulled back.

"Sometimes, just starting anywhere helps."

Billy took a deep breath and exhaled slowly. "Do you know what Mary says when I come home from work every night and slip into bed? She says, 'It's good to have my hero home.'"

"Well, you are her hero, as you are to a lot of people in your life."

Billy's eyes closed, and he felt his heart beginning to pound against his chest. He turned to Tom, his fury unleashed as he snapped, "I'm not anyone's hero! I'm not even a good man."

"Aren't you being too hard on yourself?" asked Tom with compassion in his eyes.

"You don't get it!" exclaimed Billy as he looked for an exit from the pew.

"I want to get it. Help me to get it."

Shakes racked Billy's body. "I keep trying to be honest with myself, but it just makes things worse."

"That's often the case at first, but it's the only way to real peace. We tend to avoid what is uncomfortable and escape into our coping mechanisms. Avoidance can feel like protection but never leads to anything good, only self-destruction and poisoned relationships."

Billy's tears began to fall. "You don't get it. Patrick is dead, so there is no relationship. Tonight, I dreamed of him calling out to me in a burning casket, and I couldn't save him. I feel like he is burning in Hell right now because of me. It's my fault! He doesn't deserve this—I do!"

Tom leaned forward. "Why do you feel like it was your fault?"

"I wasn't there. He needed a dad, and I wasn't there for him. The anxiety, depression, and sense of hopelessness he must have been feelin' are because of me. He killed himself because I wasn't there to save him, to love him, to stop him!" Billy's eyes swelled with tears, anguish overwhelming him.

He stood and tried to maneuver his way around Tom, but Tom got up and put both of his hands on Billy's shoulders. Just as Billy pushed past Tom, Tom said, "Billy, I don't believe his death was your fault. That is not the man that I know. The man that Mary knows."

Billy turned sharply, glaring at Tom. "You don't know me!" he shouted before he turned to hurry out of the church. The heavy doors banged shut behind him.

Billy didn't undress after returning from his late-night walk. He slept on the couch until Mary woke.

"Up early today, huh?" asked Mary. She kissed him. "Mr. Quinn, don't you know I can tell when you aren't in bed?"

"I know all about your supernatural powers, Mrs. Quinn."

"I don't need extra powers to see there's been something heavy weighing on you. You can talk to me, you know—or talk to someone you can trust."

Billy laughed and mumbled, "A lot of good that does."

"What are you murmuring about? Since you're up, do you want to come to Mass with me this morning?"

Billy was quiet for several moments. "I don't think so today. I might drop by Sean's for a bit."

"Can't wait for your evening date with him." Mary laughed.

Billy strode over to Sean's apartment. He lived in a two-family home, similar to Billy's. The woman who owned the house let Sean use the garage to work on his car and do projects, which is where Billy found him. The large garage door was open, and Sean was using a wood plane to fix a door for his landlady. Sean jumped as Billy said, "Are you sure you wouldn't be a better carpenter than a cop?"

"Hey, don't do that."

Billy took the old planer from Sean. "Is this new?"

Sean laughed. "Only new to me. This guy had some very nice tools at his yard sale. I think he figured out he was too old to be using them anymore."

Billy handled the tool, appreciating the quality. "How old was he?"

"I don't know, maybe your age," responded Sean as he took back the planer and returned to making his passes as the thin shavings curled and landed on the cement floor.

"Wiseguy. I was going to take a walk over to Orchard Park and didn't know if you wanted to come along."

Sean glanced up with curiosity as he leaned into a pass with the planer. "Sure. What are we looking for?"

"I heard exercise is a good thing for old guys, and I could use some fresh air," responded Billy.

They headed out, zig-zagging their way through the South End until they reached the street to the Orchard Park affordable housing apartments.

Sean glanced around. "Well? What's here?"

"Let's just stay here, out of sight, for a bit." Billy pulled Sean back. "So, our only suspects are from here; the bike that may have been used was from around the corner, and, just over there, a fire was used to destroy the evidence. It seems like a lot of things pointing to this area."

They patiently stood out of sight and watched the street in front of the Orchard Park apartments for several hours, but neither Reggie nor Dougie made an appearance.

"What do you think, Sean? Do you think these two are the ones?"

Sean leaned back against the chain-link fence. "I don't know. We haven't found anything to tie them to the robbery other than a lousy answer on the basketball score and the coincidence of living near other circumstantial evidence. Maybe two of the other guys in the game did it? Maybe they were more attentive to the score or did their homework before coming in to be prepared? You know what I mean?"

Billy leaned in to see if he was missing anything. "You know, I thought that same exact thing. I don't think Trevon would get involved, and Big Russ was too big. Some of the other guys were too short or too fat. I could only see three of the players who had the build and agility of the thieves, and only two of them had worked together before. Three years in the pen is plenty of time to plan out something like this."

"Good point, but I'm starting to wonder if it's any of the guys in that game," responded Sean.

"Maybe you're right. Maybe we aren't even on square one yet in solving this. I don't think anythin's goin' to happen here today. Thanks for takin' a chance with me."

Sean put his arm around Billy's shoulder. "Anytime."

When Billy got back home, he could hear voices in the apartment. His shoulders sank as he realized Mary had invited Tom back to the house for lunch.

"I'm like a bad penny, Billy," said Tom.

"I won't argue with you today—at least, not again."

Mary poured some tea into Tom's cup as he nudged a cup closer to Billy. "What are you talking about—again?"

"Never mind, Mrs. Quinn," responded Billy. After lunch was over, Billy nodded to Mary. "Father Tom and I are going for a walk."

Outside, Tom said to Billy, "I'm sorry for barging in. Mary insisted I come over. She's really worried about you."

"Huh. She's the one who's sick, and she's worried about me. Look, I want to apologize for bargin' in on *you* last night and for my abrupt departure. Even if my point was accurate, you deserve more respect, and I know you were just tryin' to help. I've just had a lot on my mind lately."

"To be honest, you were barging in on God, which I don't think He minds, and then I barged in on you. I was intruding on your time and pushed my way into places I wasn't invited to go." He looked at Billy. "I do care a lot about you."

Billy sighed as they strolled down several streets in silence. As they passed by Ramsay Park, Tom mentioned his old friend Gus Busbi and the young man he had befriended and mentored named Jamiel Russell, who loved to play on this court. Then he said, "I just want to be there for you, Billy, but I don't want to make things worse."

Billy stopped in his tracks. "You can't know. You can't know what it's like to lose someone who was everything to you to suicide and know it was your fault. You just can't know." Billy felt empty inside. He finally looked up to find tears streaming down Tom's cheeks and and his face twisted in grief. He'd never seen Tom like this. It was so sudden; did he feel the same kind of agony?

Billy started to apologize, but he just started crying—not just for himself, but for both of them. "I'm sorry. I'm so sorry, Father Tom."

Tom put his hand in his chest pocket and pulled out a picture of a young woman. Billy could tell that Tom wanted to say something, clearing his throat but remaining speechless, appearing as tormented as Billy himself. He could only put his hand on Billy's shoulder as they walked in a different type of silence, their pain shared.

Billy took Tom down the street to where Bubblegum Bob lived. He showed him where the bike had been stolen and then to the small tree-covered park behind the church where the remnants of the burned evidence remained. Thinking about the case would take their minds off things. "Both of these pieces of evidence are right around the corner from our only two suspects who live in Orchard Park."

"And you don't believe in coincidences."

"And I don't believe in coincidences, but we have nothin' solid yet to tie them to the robbery, and we don't know what they did with the painting," said Billy as they stopped at the end of the street. This was where he had stood with Sean that morning. He moved Tom out of sight of the entrance doors to the project apartment buildings.

"What are you looking for?"

Billy shrugged. "I don't know. Just a hunch."

A voice from behind startled them. "What're you two crackers doin' slummin' in my neighborhood?"

They turned to see Trevon tossing a basketball back and forth between his hands.

Tom sighed. "Oh, it's you, Trev. Don't do that."

"Hey, you the ones that're spying on my boys."

Billy stepped forward. "Why do you think we're spyin'?"

Trevon tilted his head forward and peered up at Billy. "Cause I know what's what. Who you lookin' for anyway?"

"If you know what's what, then tell us."

"What's in it for me?"

Tom playfully tipped the ball from him. "Reggie Jones told us if they hadn't joined that game at the end, you would never have won it. We just wanted to find out if that was true."

Trevon grabbed the ball back. "He's full of you know what. I already had that game under control before he sh—hey, I don't know what you're sellin'."

Billy jumped in. "So he did jump into that game?"

Trevon bounced the ball and turned. "I never said nothin' like that. You boys should be movin' on to safer streets. You know what I mean?" He walked away.

Tom and Billy raised their eyebrows as they glanced at each other and then back down the street to watch people coming in and out of the apartments. Finally, Billy grabbed Tom's jacket as he saw Dougie Jones standing on the sidewalk. Reggie Hope joined him a few minutes later. The two stood and talked as if they were waiting for someone. Within a few minutes, Billy spotted a teen crossing the street heading toward them, panning around to see if anyone was watching. As the teen reached them on the sidewalk, Reggie put his arm around the boy and handed him something that Billy thought was a yellow envelope.

"What is it?" asked Tom.

"See that kid? He has an orange streak in his hair."

With a look of confusion on his face, Tom asked, "What does that mean?"

"Bubblegum Bob's neighbor said he saw a kid droppin' the bike off early in the mornin'. That kid had a bright orange streak in his hair. Coincidence?"

Tom patted Billy on the back. "I know you don't believe in coincidences."

Billy nodded.

"How old do you think that kid is?"

Billy thought for a second. "Twelve, maybe thirteen. Why?"

"I wondered if he was young enough to go to Orchard Park school?"

"Maybe, but it's obvious he ain't goin' to school every day."

"I've had a chance to work with the principal at the school. He's young but very good. They designated it a pilot school and gave him the flexibility to bring in the teachers he wanted, have school uniforms, and exchange the security guards for art and music programs. They've seen a remarkable turnaround in the kids that go there now. I've wanted to see what programs we could use at St. Francis. Maybe he knows that kid."

As they entered the school's administration office, the principal approached and recognized Tom immediately. "Good to see you again, Father Tom. What're you doing in the neighborhood?"

Tom shook hands with him. "Hi, Andy. Good to see you too. We've been trying out some of your ideas at St. Francis, and they've been working really well. Oh, this is Billy Quinn. He's an officer for the Boston Police."

Andy's expression darkened. "Officer Quinn. Hopefully, you don't have bad news?"

"Hopefully not."

"Andy," Tom said, "we just wanted to ask about a boy who may be a student here. We don't know his name, but he has an orange streak in his hair."

Andy nodded. "You must mean Tobin. He goes by Tobey. He's in the eighth grade, but he has been showing up less and less these days. I've talked to his mom, but she insists he's coming every day. She won't believe otherwise, so it's been tough to address. Have you seen him lately? Is he in some kind of trouble?"

Billy shrugged. "We don't know. It's possible he was involved in something, and also possible he doesn't actually know what was really happening."

Andy sat on the edge of the desk. "I hate to lose him. Tobey's a smart kid, but I think he's mixed up with some men in the neighborhood that may be pulling him in the wrong direction. I caught him dealing some drugs several months back—small stuff, but that's how it starts, and that's when he started missing school. I hope I'm wrong and this is a temporary thing."

Tom shook Andy's hand. "Thanks, Andy. What's Tobey's last name?"

"Oddly, his last name is Hope. If you see him, please tell him that I'm missing him and his talents."

Tom nodded. "Will do."

After Tom and Billy left the school building and turned a corner, the young man himself was coming right toward them. As they neared each other, Tom dropped his keys on the ground in front of him. The boy bent down, retrieved them, and handed them to Tom. Tom smiled and said, "Thanks, Tobey."

The boy stepped back, frowning, with suspicion in his eyes. "Do I know you?"

Tom hesitated. "I'm Father Tom. I visited your school last year. Principal Russet pointed you out in an art class and remarked on your talent. I don't think you had the new style then, though."

Tobey appeared relieved. "All those kids, and you remembered me?"

"I guess you come across as someone with the potential to lead and do great things with your life. I think Principal Russet thought so as well. He seemed to care a lot about you."

"Yeah, he's always checking in on me. He's a good guy, I guess."

Tom peered into Tobey's eyes. "I think so too. I think I remembered because of your last name—Hope. It's a great name. I play basketball over at the Fens, and I think I remember playing with someone with that name—um, let's see—I think it's Reggie. Yeah, that's it. Good player."

"He's my uncle. He's all right, but I can take him."

Tom patted Tobey on the shoulder. "I bet you could. You're a good height for the eighth grade. Work on your game and stay in school, and I bet you could be a good player. I coach at St. Francis if you ever want some pointers. You can come by any time."

Tobey seemed taken by the positive attention. *Maybe he didn't experience much of that growing up.*

"Maybe I'll surprise you sometime," responded Tobey as he started to leave.

"Anytime," called out Tom, waving goodbye as the boy took off down the street.

"That was something," said Billy with a laugh. "I underestimated your talents. I would have tipped him off with my question, but you just slid in there smooth, and he never knew what hit him. Now we know there's a connection between Reggie and the Tobey kid."

Father Tom sighed. "I hope I accomplished more than that."

Chapter 16

Billy asked Sean to pick him up a little early for their shift so that they could talk to Detective Brooks about the case. As they entered the detective's room, Brooks said, "Okay, what has Angelo found for us today?"

Chuckling, Billy said, "Actually, we've been doing a bit of our own recon work in the Orchard Park neighborhood."

Brooks sat up and leaned forward. "What've you got?"

"Two suspects, a lead on the bike that may have been used, and the remnants of a fire to burn the evidence all within a few streets of each other."

Brooks sat back, disappointed. "We know all this."

"Well, a neighbor said that he saw a boy bringin' back Bubblegum Bob's bike in the early mornin' the day after the robbery. He mentioned that the boy had a distinctive orange streak in his hair. Sean and I spent a good chunk of the morning watching the street Jones and Hope live on, but no luck."

"Is that it?" asked the growingly impatient Brooks.

"No. I went back later with Father Tom."

Brooks rolled his eyes.

"And we spotted Jones and Hope this time. We also saw a boy, maybe twelve or thirteen, cross the street and take an envelope from Hope. That boy had an orange streak in his hair—his distinctive mark."

Brooks sat back up again. "Now you've got my interest."

"That's not all. We went to the local school and talked to the principal. The boy is in the eighth grade and seems to be a good and talented kid but has recently been skipping a lot of school and getting hooked up with drug dealing. Get this; his name is Tobin Hope."

"Hope?" asked Brooks as he stood up.

"Yeah. Well, Father Tom and I walked the neighborhood and ended up meeting with Tobey. Father Tom is one slick operator. Without ever looking at Tobey, he dropped his keys on the sidewalk in front of him. Tobey stopped to pick them up. Father Tom acted as if he recognized him from a visit to his school, paid him a few compliments, and before he knew it, got him to tell us that Reggie Hope was his uncle."

"So, we have a strong connection."

"We do. We didn't let on that he told us anything, and Father Tom offered to work with him on his basketball game if he was ever interested in playing in high school. I think you've got to hire Father Tom and Angelo."

"Yeah. Yeah. Somehow, I feel as if they're already on the payroll whether I hire them or not. We need to find a way to talk to this Tobin or Tobey Hope kid. I don't want to signal anything to Jones or Hope. The kid doesn't know you're a cop, does he?"

Billy shook his head.

"Maybe we can pick him up on a drug-dealing thing, and he'll be scared enough to let us know where he was last Thursday night. You may very well have found our breakthrough."

"I wish I could take the credit."

"Okay, we'll give Father Tom and Salvato a box of donuts if this pans out."

Sean said, "Maybe they should get more than donuts," as he held up the Boston newspaper showing the front-page headline that read 'Gardner Offers $1.5 M for Return of Rembrandt.'"

Brooks stepped to the whiteboard and added Tobey's name in code to the possible evidence. "The reward isn't for finding the perpetrators; it's for finding the painting, so we've got to make this connection stick and let it lead us to the actual painting, intact, to make Father Tom the richest priest in town."

Billy nodded. "Even if Jones and Hope were the thieves in the museum, they might not be the masterminds or even know where the paintin' disappeared to."

Brooks sighed. "That's, unfortunately, a very likely scenario."

* * * *

On Friday, Brooks had squads patrolling the Orchard Park area as discreetly as possible until they spotted Tobey taking money from someone at a vacant lot. They picked him up with small bags of pot in his oversized sweats and a roll of bills in his pants pockets. When he was brought into the station, he was shaking like the lone leaf of a tree on a windy fall day as he sat in the interrogation room. Things had probably been easy, doing small runs for his uncle up until now, but now was probably the first time he had faced the police.

Brooks entered the interrogation room with Detective Mullen and an assigned youth advocate. They hadn't arrested Tobey and were, at the moment, more interested in getting information than taking any action on a drug-dealing charge.

Mullen spoke first. "Tobey, you know that dealing drugs is a serious crime at any age, right?"

Tobey continued shaking as he stared at the cleared desk in front of him.

"Being honest with us today can go a long way to avoiding serious consequences and getting back on the right path."

He hesitated several seconds and then nodded.

"It would be helpful if you tell us everything you did, starting with today and going back at least a week."

Tobey glanced up.

The advocate said, "If you feel uncomfortable or have a question, just ask me."

Tobey started describing his daily routine, when he got up, where he went, and what he did. Brooks could tell when he was leaving compromising stuff out, but Tobey seemed smart enough to be plausible and not to make himself look like an angel either. When he finally got to the previous Thursday, Brooks moved up in his chair with interest. As Tobey got closer to the time of the robbery and hadn't mentioned the bike or the Back Bay Fens, Brooks asked if he could check on a few things.

"Tobey. Do you like to play basketball?"

"Yeah. Sure."

"Do you ever watch some of the older guys play, to pick up techniques and learn the game?"

"Yeah. I love doing that, and then I practice those moves the next day."

Brooks nodded. "I like that attitude. Sign of a good player. Have you ever watched games at the Fens courts?"

Tobey hesitated. "A few times. They have some good games, and the courts are in good shape. Sometimes, they let me play a little if they don't have enough players."

"They had some really good games on Thursday night. Did you catch any of them?" asked Brooks.

"Oh, yeah, they were really goo—wait a minute. I don't think I was there on Thursday," responded Tobey with a cracked voice.

"I'm pretty sure someone saw you on a bike in the park that night."

"Thursday night? I guess I'm not sure then." Tobey squirmed.

Mullen gazed steadily at him. "Tobey, you were on a bike but can't remember the night?"

"Um, yeah. I don't remember the night."

"Do you remember where you got the bike?"

Tobey ran his hands down his face. "Um, I borrowed it."

Brooks nodded. "Okay. You're doing good. Who did you borrow it from?"

"I don't remember."

"Okay, that's fine. I think the person said it was a bike with wire baskets in the back?"

Tobey put his head down on the table. "Yeah, I think so."

"But you did take it back. It's not like you stole it. Could it have been Bubblegum Bob's bike you borrowed and then took back on Friday?" asked Mullen softly.

"Yeah, that guy Bob. I didn't damage his bike, and I didn't steal it."

Brooks stood up and paced the floor a few times. "Tobey, take a few deep breaths. We don't want you to be nervous or afraid. Do you want some water?"

Tobey nodded. When Mullen gave him a glass of water, Tobey drank it in a few gulps.

"You okay?"

Tobey nodded.

"So, Tobey, did you ride back on Ruggles Street? I think that would be the straightest route from the park."

Tobey nodded again.

"Did you have matches to light the fire in the park behind St. Katharine's Church?"

Tobey glanced up with a look that said, *How does he know this?* He didn't respond.

Brooks didn't want him to start clamming up. "Any good ballplayers in your family?"

Tobey seemed relieved in the shift in the conversation. "Yeah, a few."

"Who's good?"

Tobey blew air out of his tightened lips. "I heard my dad was good when he was around. My uncle and a cousin of mine."

"Sounds like talent runs in the family. How did your Uncle Reggie play at the Fens on Thursday night?"

"What? He didn't play there that night."

"So, you do remember being there and that your uncle wasn't there?"

Tobey asked for more water, seemingly trying to stall to think of the right answer. "Yeah, maybe that was the night I was there, but Uncle Reggie wasn't there. He didn't play that night."

Brooks picked up the pitcher of water and filled Tobey's glass again. "So you watched some of the games, and then you left, and you didn't see your uncle play any games that night."

"Right. He wasn't there."

"When you were there. Maybe he showed up after you left?"

Tobey took another drink of water. "I guess he could have, but I don't think so."

Brooks leaned forward and stared Tobey in the eye. "I think you're telling the truth to us, and we appreciate the honesty. You said you borrowed

Bubblegum Bob's bike and rode to the Fens Park to watch some games, and up until the time you left, your uncle didn't play in any of those games."

Tobey nodded.

"At some point, you rode down the path and out of the park and rode home on Ruggles Street. Is it possible that someone stuffed something into your large bike baskets before you left the park?"

Tobey closed his eyes and began to sweat. He remained silent, and the advocate said, "You don't have to answer any questions you are uncomfortable with. Please don't say anything false to the detectives. That will never help you."

"I'm, I'm uncomfortable with all of this, but I don't want to go to jail either. My mother is going to kill me just for being here, so I can imagine what she'll do if she finds out about the other stuff."

Brooks put his hand on Tobey's shoulders. "You are a very young man right now. We can help you stay out of trouble, and we can help you with your mom."

Tobey straightened. "What are you asking me to do?"

"We need you to be completely honest about last Thursday night. We don't think you knowingly did anything wrong, so you can avoid getting caught up in anything serious if you can help us by telling us the truth."

Tobey took several deep breaths. "What can you do when my mom comes? She's going to want to know why I'm here and what I did. She will kill me, and my uncle will literally kill me. I can't win."

Brooks could hear anguish in Tobey's voice. "I think I can solve all your problems before your mom arrives. If you promise to give up that crap with the drug dealing and commit to going to school again, I can solve your mom issue. As far as your Uncle Reggie goes, I won't make you tell me anything, but I will ask you to shake your head if I get anything wrong."

Tobey looked confused but listened intently to Brooks' description of Thursday night.

"So, you borrowed Bob's bike and stayed to watch the game, and at 8:30, you started down the path and waited in the dark just before the entrance. Two men, Reggie Hope and Dougie Jones came running into the park and stuffed their sweats, ski masks, and a painting into the baskets of the bike. You immediately started riding the bike out of the park, almost hitting two police officers. You rode across the street, down the full length of Ruggles Street until you reached St. Katharine Drexel's Church, where you rode to the parking lot behind. It was dark and protected in the grassy area under the trees, and you lit a fire to burn the items in the baskets—except for the painting. Early in the morning hours, you returned the bike to Bubblegum Bob's house, and several days later, your uncle gave you a yellow envelope with cash for doing what you were asked to do."

Tobey didn't shake his head at any part of Brooks' depiction of the events of that evening.

Brooks looked at him closely to see if there were any signs, but Tobey gave none. Brooks said, "Last thing. Do you or do you not know what happened to the painting on a large wood panel?"

Tobey stood up and glanced at Brooks and then Jan. "If I answer this last question, will you keep your promise when my mother comes?"

Brooks responded, "Only if you answer it honestly. If you don't, your mom will be the least of your worries."

Tobey stared Brooks straight in the eye. "I never saw it and don't know what happened to it. I swear that is true."

Brooks continued to stare into Tobey's eyes. "I believe you. Thank you for being an honest man. Don't worry about your mom. Police make mistakes all the time when they bring people in."

Tobey heaved a deep sigh of relief.

Brooks could now bring in Reggie Hope and Dougie Jones for another round of questioning and hopefully solve the case.

Chapter 17

At the beginning of Billy's Friday night shift, Brooks asked him and Sean to bring Dougie Jones and Reggie Hope back in for further questioning based on what he had confidentially learned from Tobey. They weren't hard to find, and Reggie became agitated with having to go into the station again.

"Why are you guys always harassing the brothers? Why don't you spend some time in your own neighborhoods? They ain't exactly angels over there, ya know."

Sean opened the squad car door to let Reggie and Dougie into the back. "It's just some questions. We appreciate you helping out."

When they got to the station, Reggie asked for a state-appointed lawyer who instructed them only to answer questions they were comfortable with answering. Billy and Sean let them know that they were not under arrest and were needed to clear up some details on their last interview. Reggie and Dougie sat down next to their lawyer, while Brooks and Mullen sat across from them with Billy and Sean sitting behind.

Brooks started, "We appreciate you coming back in, Mr. Hope and Mr. Jones."

"Did we have a choice? I still call this harassment. That's what it is."

Mullen placed a folder on the table and said, "We'll try to make this as short and painless as possible."

"Too late for that." Reggie huffed.

"You both said you were playing at the Fens courts most of the evening last Thursday. Is that statement still accurate?" asked Brooks.

"Yeah. Probably around six-something to after nine."

"What if I told you that we have a witness that claims you entered the park much later than six-something, and neither of you was playing in most of the games that night?"

Reggie scratched his head and glanced over at the lawyer. "Who are you going to believe, the person who was actually playing or some lying guy passin' by?"

Brooks answered, "I didn't say it was someone passing by, and I didn't say it was a guy. What if I told you they saw you running into the Fens around the time of the robbery from the direction of the museum?"

Reggie shrugged, and Dougie remained uncomfortably quiet.

"What if I told you that evidence from the robbery was found just around the corner from your apartment?"

Reggie glanced at the lawyer again. "I don't gut to say nothin', right?"

The lawyer nodded.

Looking stubborn, Reggie didn't respond.

Brooks sat forward in his chair. "Little plastic bags and breaking parole isn't a good thing for either of you. How about if we cut to the chase—I mean literally. You ran out of the Gardner with a large painting on wood—right?"

"No," responded Reggie.

"You're going to tell me that you didn't steal that painting?" asked Brooks as his fingers tapped against the top of the table.

Reggie stared right into Brooks' eyes, "I never took that painting. I didn't steal no painting from the Gardner or from anywhere! I am telling you the truth—I didn't take it!"

Brooks' stare shifted to Dougie. "Dougie, you've been super quiet. Let me ask you the same question—"

Dougie glanced up, a furious light in his eyes. "He didn't take that painting, and I didn't take that painting. We didn't steal it, so stop assuming we did just because you haven't found out who did."

Mullen said, "You know that lying to enforcement officers about a crime is a crime. It's serious stuff."

Dougie seemed to grow more upset when the lawyer patted the side of his arm. "It's not us. We both told you the truth—we didn't take it."

Mullen closed her note folder.

Brooks slid back on his chair and threw his hands up in the air. "Okay, you can go for now. Don't disappear on me."

Reggie and Dougie could be heard grumbling as they left the interrogation room.

Billy and Sean remained and sat with Brooks and Mullen. Sean asked, "So, what are the next steps, Chief?"

Brooks wiped his brow and played with the cigarettes in his top pocket. "Just when you think you are that close, it suddenly seems like we are a million miles away. Somehow we're going to have to hit them up separately. I've never seen that much conviction in someone's denial before. It was kinda eerie."

Sean asked, "How are we going to isolate them?"

Brooks rose and got himself a glass of cold water, taking a sip before responding, "I don't know. Talk to their friends and family on their whereabouts, any slips in talking about the robbery, places they could have purchased the sweats, ski mask, spray paint, and such."

Billy said, "So, what you are really sayin' is that we have a lot of work in front of us?"

"Ah-yup," responded Brooks as he poured another glass of water.

* * * *

As Billy made his normal patrol rounds with his partner, Sean commented, "You seem a little better today."

"Maybe. I think I'm just focused on other things. Like I said, I'm fine. It's Mary that's most important right now—not me."

"I gotcha. Hey, how did you find that kid with the orange thing going on in his hair," asked Sean as he turned the corner toward the Fens and passed in front of the Gardner Museum.

"A little old-fashioned footwork."

"Oh, and what else have you found out?" asked Sean as he headed down Ruggles and he passed by the Orchard Park apartments. On the cement steps in front of the apartment building was a gang just hanging out. As they passed by, Reggie spotted the officers, and they just stared at each other until the car had passed the entrance.

"Hey, I haven't lost it yet. Give me a few more months before you put me out to pasture."

Sean laughed. "Okay. You deserve a final favor—old man."

The radio dispatcher said, "We have a 246 — shots fired at 90 Lenox Street. Repeat, active shooting at 90 Lenox. Return fire has been reported."

Billy grabbed the radio mic. "316 will respond. Will need more than one backup. 316 within 1."

As Sean made the turn onto Lenox, they could hear multiple gunshots. Billy pointed to a red car on the side of the street. Shots were being fired from the apartment building at the red car, and gunfire was being returned from inside the vehicle, where it appeared that rival gang members might have been pinned down. Some wondered why he would risk his life for people trying to knock each other off, but Billy never felt that way.

"Sean, let me out here and then turn your sirens on when our backup arrives." Billy made his way up the dark sidewalk to get a better view of where the shots were coming from.

When the backup unit arrived from the other end of the street, Billy signaled to Sean to turn on his siren and blue flashing lights. The shooting stopped, and Billy got closer to the red vehicle, ready to apprehend anyone who got out of the bullet-filled car. As he edged closer in the dark silence, he heard another shot and the ping of metal being struck, and then a sudden burning sensation in his left arm. He had been hit and instantly dropped to the ground to avoid any other shots.

Sean pulled up closer as Butchy and Sully approached from the other end. Billy watched Sean get out of the car with his gun drawn. Sean spotted Billy down with one knee on the sidewalk and clutching his arm as he continued to watch the red car. "Billy, you okay?"

"I think I got hit by a ricochet. It's just my arm. Watch that car."

Sean held his gun straight out in front of him as he scanned the apartment building doors and windows and then back to the car. The driver was bloodied and hunched over the steering wheel. Another man appeared to be dead, and the third was hit but clutching his gun with fear in his eyes.

"Put the gun down, and we can get you some help. An ambulance is on the way."

The frightened boy appeared to be maybe fifteen years old and was clearly injured. He put the gun down and raised the one hand that he could.

Sean took the gun and checked the others to see if there was any sign of life to these gang members who, more likely than not, had never expected to live past their mid-twenties.

Butchy and Sully were covering the apartment building with its blown-out windows.

Other backup units and two ambulances arrived. Flashing blue and red lights lit the entire street as neighbors slowly started appearing at their windows and on the street to watch. The surviving boy received attention first as they carried him to the ambulance, and then the other EMT team began working on Billy's arm as Sean watched.

Billy asked, "What are we lookin' at?"

Sean responded, "Looks like two dead in the car. I recognize the driver as one of the Columbia Point Dawgs. Hopefully, the boy will be okay, but he was hit more than once."

Sully relayed that there was at least one dead outside of the apartment entrance, a member of the Lenox Street Cardinals. "It was probably a drive-by hit that went bad."

Billy rubbed his forehead. "It seems endless—and senseless."

"Let's make sure you're okay," said Sean.

"I'm fine."

Sean picked up Billy's cap. "We'll let the doctors decide how fine you are, Pops."

****

Later that evening, Billy lay on a hospital bed as Sean and Mary entered the room where he would stay overnight.

No matter how many times Billy said, "Don't worry, I'll be fine," he knew a night like this didn't make her feel so sure.

While Billy may have been the one wounded in a hospital bed, Mary seemed frailer and more tired tonight. She was noticeably uncomfortable, and Billy knew it wasn't because she was worried about him—her compromised organs were taking their toll.

He felt restless all night and, at times, more afraid than he could ever remember feeling in his life. Now in tears, he started to plead with God: *Please, God, heal Mary. Don't worry about me, but please don't let her suffer from this condition. I know I don't deserve your favors for me; I've let you down too many times, but she is so good, so faithful to you, and doesn't deserve this! Please. Please. Help give her the time until we get her what she needs. I don't want to lose her. I can't lose her! I'll do anything to save her.* He tossed and turned the entire night, sensing no answer to his pleas.

In the morning, a restless Billy gave a half-smile when Sean returned with donuts and coffee which he proceeded to finish by himself.

"I don't know why they have me in here wearin' this backless dress when I am fine."

Sean grinned while chewing the last half of his donut. "Sure. 'I'm fine. I just have a bullet hole in me, and I have no reason to be in the hospital.' Sounds logical to me."

Billy glanced up to see Brooks standing in the doorway. "I can't believe you came to visit. I should be getting out any minute now."

Brooks entered. "I'm glad it wasn't serious."

"Not too, but I can't be sittin' here when we need to be workin' Jones and Hope to solve this case."

"Yeah. Jones and Hope."

Billy felt confused. "Who else?"

"A few minutes ago, I had a call from the famous Dr. DuBois."

Billy sat up, and Sean stepped closer to Brooks.

"It looks like he was contacted early this morning by someone who says they can lead us to the painting. He wants confirmation of the conditions of the reward money that was offered."

Billy's jaw dropped. "Did he identify himself?"

Sean added, "Did he tell DuBois where the painting was?"

"Nope and nope. DuBois told him that the only condition was that the person had to have information that led to finding the undamaged painting. The caller said he could do that and would check back mid-afternoon to confirm."

Sean gaped at him. "What? Doesn't he have to lead us to the thieves that took it? What if the person who called was Hope or Jones? Do they get to collect the reward?"

Brooks raised his hand. "No, they can't. You are disqualified if you had anything to do with stealing it in the first place."

"Huh. What if we can't prove they were the thieves?" Sean asked. "Can they argue they have a legitimate claim?"

"I don't know, but let's get the painting back first before we worry about these technicality games. I'm going to be at the Gardner at two this afternoon if you want to see where this thing goes. My hunch is that this is one of many hoaxes we will get on this." Brooks was obviously hesitating to say what was on his mind.

Billy tilted his head. "Was there something else you found?"

Shaking his head, Brooks replied, "Not me. Angelo located a man named Peter Buck."

"Peter Buck. That sounds familiar," said Billy.

"Yeah. It's the name Myles Connor said as we left his place. Buck operates down at the Seaport area. He imports and exports goods for a particular set of customers willing to pay premium dollar for rare items. Somewhat shady dealings, I suspect. He's had issues with taxes, export compliance, and possession of stolen goods. Angelo believes he's running a major fencing operation for the black market and New England crime families as well."

Sean sat down on the end of Billy's bed. "Huh. Did he find any reason to think he's connected to the Gardner heist?"

Brooks lifted his head. "He collected a reward for a stolen artifact from the Museum of Fine Art a few years back and—"

Billy raised a brow. "And?"

"And Angelo got some info that Buck was seen talking to our favorite duo in Orchard Park."

"Hope and Jones? Do you think he's the one who will show up to claim the reward this afternoon?"

"I don't know, but I'm not waiting until then to find out. We are heading to talk to Mr. Buck right now. Maybe he orchestrated this heist and was going to sell the Rembrandt overseas unless the reward money was a better return on his investment. Or maybe he approached Hope and Jones after the heist and made an offer to them, knowing the reward money would be coming."

Chapter 18

Saturday morning was a busy day at the Seaport in Boston. Rebandaged and dressed, Billy climbed out of the car with Brooks and Sean and peered up at that sign over the warehouse that read, 'Peter Buck Global Enterprises.' Billy turned to Brooks, who was shaking his head. "What's wrong, Brooks?"

"Why am I ever surprised?" responded Brooks.

Billy turned to see Tom and Angelo talking with a man who seemed larger than life, tall and heavy set, snow-white hair and mustache, wearing a broad-brimmed coffee planter's hat, which matched his off-white suit. Forklift trucks were moving cargo in the warehouse as they approached, and, even in the midst of his conversation, Buck pointed them in different directions with his ivory-handled cane.

They approached, and Brooks said, "Peter Buck, I assume?" Glancing aside to Tom, he added, "And I see you've already met our advance team?"

Buck focused on Billy. His eyes were soft and blue, and he had more the look of a confident salesman than an underworld gangster. "Yes, Father Tom and Angelo were just introducing themselves. Is there something, in particular, I can do for you, gentlemen? Are you looking for a donation for the church raffle or the policemen's ball?"

Brooks quipped, "Not quite. I'm Detective Brooks from the Boston Police. Is there any quieter place we can talk?"

"I know who you are, and I apologize, but I have lots to accomplish this morning, and I'm hoping we can keep this short. Can we?"

"All right, Mr. Buck."

"Call me Peter."

"Okay, Pete. We know you help connect buyers and sellers of very expensive items around the world. We know that not all of those items have always been legally obtained." Brooks held up his hand when Buck motioned to balk at the last accusation. "We know you were seen talking with two suspects of a recent art heist, and we know you've collected rewards for stolen artworks in the past. Did I get anything wrong?"

Buck leaned on his cane and replied, "Pretty much everything, but I'm not surprised."

"So you've never spoken to Reggie Hope or Dougie Jones in Orchard Park?"

"Not that I'm aware of, but I go for walks through the neighborhoods all the time. It helps to keep moving with my arthritis. There's no crime against being friendly, is there? Now, is there anything else I can help you, gentlemen, with?"

"If we search your warehouse, would we find any Rembrandts hanging around?"

"Listen, Detective. I don't want to waste either of our time. If I had anything to do with the Gardner heist, you wouldn't find the painting here, and if I didn't have anything to do with the heist, you—"

"Wouldn't find the painting here. I get it," said Brooks with a sigh.

Tom cleared his throat. "$1.5 million in reward money is a lot of incentive for any shrewd businessman to get their hands on a hot commodity. What do you think an interested party might be willing to pay for it in today's market? Just wondering."

A broad smile reached Buck's face. "Quite a bit more—I would imagine. I would love to spend more time with you, but I have an important appointment this afternoon, so I do need to get back to business." He took a few steps away from them and turned, "I'm sure it will turn up soon." He left Brooks and the team scratching their heads, knowing they had nothing on him yet.

Brooks said, "If he walks into the Gardner at two o'clock with a painting, there will be plenty of questions he's not going to weasel out on."

"I hope we didn't scare him into selling it, instead," said Angelo.

Brooks' glare indicated that it was a real possibility.

* * * *

Two o'clock on a Saturday afternoon was a busy time at the Gardner Museum. Billy, bandaged arm and all, didn't want to miss anything as he made his way with Sean and Security Chief Bob Touhey to Dr. DuBois' office door where Tony Brooks and Jan Mullen waited. After speaking on the phone, DuBois hung up, stood, waving them in and looking very anxious. "That was the man who claims to know the whereabouts of our Rembrandt. 'e wanted to know the exact conditions of the reward money before 'e would be willing to lead us to the painting. Gentlemen, I feel breathless but very nervous at the same time."

Sean crossed his arms and frowned. "How do we know this isn't the thief who planned on collecting the reward all along? You can't be giving money to the people who stole the painting."

DuBois rolled his eyes with an impatient sigh. "I was very clear that no one involved in any way with the robbery would be eligible for the reward money. The recovery of Mrs. Gardner's painting is all I care about, and then we can solve your silly mystery."

Bill watched Brooks step forward. "Okay, so this guy got his answer to the conditions of the reward. What's next, Doc? Did he tell you who he was or when he would come forward?"

"He knows ze conditions, and he said that 'e qualified for the reward," responded DuBois.

Brooks interrupted, "And?"

"I wish you were not so impolite, but I understand that you can't 'elp it. Ze man did not give me his name, but 'e said 'e is coming to the museum in a few minutes. He was finishing up some business."

They all stood in nervous anticipation as they waited for DuBois' phone to ring, telling them that the man had arrived. DuBois jumped when it finally rang and picked it up before the second ring. "'ello. Yes. Please bring him to my office. Merci beaucoup, Mr. Dudley."

Finally, the door opened, and Dudley let in the mystery man, the man Brooks would have to assess with suspicion and doubt until he proved himself differently.

As he entered, Billy exclaimed, "Kenny?"

DuBois's mouth turned downward as if he had just bit on a sour lemon. "You know each other? Is this a club you belong to with your matching arm slings?"

Cautiously, Kenny Green entered the room. He held his bandaged arm close to his body and winced with each step. "Officer Quinn. O'Donnell. I didn't expect to see you here."

Sean responded, "The feeling is likewise. We didn't expect you to be walking through that door. You're not here about the reward, are you?"

DuBois waved Kenny toward a seat. "Can you tell us who you are and, more importantly, where our Rembrandt is?"

Kenny paled as he shrank into his seat, anxiously scanning each of the faces in the room. "My name is Kenneth Green. I'm here to help you recover your painting—the one with a reward."

Brooks moved in front of Kenny's seat and tilted his head to the side. "Where is the painting, and how did you come by this information?"

As he waited for Kenny's response, Billy heard Brooks whisper to Mullen to call into the station and do a search on Kenny Green.

"I know where the painting is, but I don't know who the information came from. There was a note left at my door with the information. I have had it for several days, trying to decide what to do. I didn't know if it was a joke or a setup, but my gut feeling said it was for real."

"Where's the note?"

"The note ended with *You deserve a second chance if you do good with this reward. The only condition is that you destroy this note before claiming that reward.* I couldn't figure out what it meant, but somehow I believed it was real, so I'm here to help you get your painting back and do some good."

DuBois closed his eyes and clasped his hands in front of his face. "Please, say this is true! Where is ze painting? And tell me it is in good condition."

Kenny stared at him a moment, then glanced at the others. "It should be in very good condition. Does anyone have a glass of water? It's pretty hot in here."

DuBois waved his hands motioning to Bob to bring Kenny some water. Suddenly everyone glanced up as two more faces appeared in the doorway. "No," grumbled Brooks. "Why are you two here?"

There stood Father Tom and Angelo. "We heard you might have some good news," answered Tom.

"Don't you have churchy things to be attending to? Never mind," said Brooks as he turned his attention back to Kenny. "Can you tell us where the painting is now? Wait, first, do you know a Myles Connor or a Peter Buck?"

Kenny's brow furrowed, and his eyes narrowed with confusion. "Who?"

"Never mind. Go on. Tell us where the painting is."

"That's why I am here, but are there any papers to sign for the reward? I don't want to get stuck here with empty pockets after you've gut what you want."

DuBois narrowed his eyes. "I made it very clear to you what the conditions were, and I am a man of honor. If you can lead us to the painting, and it is not damaged in any way, and you were not part of the shameless scheme to steal the painting, then the reward is yours in full."

Kenny sat in silence as he mulled over what DuBois had promised.

Tom glanced over toward DuBois and said, "I think he would feel a little better if you put what you said in writing and signed it. Is that right, Mr. Green?"

Kenny nodded, and DuBois snorted. Once DuBois had signed a copy of the reward agreement, he handed it to Kenny, who stared at it for several minutes, adding to the tension in the room. Then Kenny stood up and exited the office. A worried DuBois exclaimed, "Where are you going? I have given you my word and signed it!"

Kenny held the signed statement closely. "I'm ready to bring you to the painting."

DuBois exclaimed, "Wait, let me get my coat and scarf. There is a chill in the air today."

Kenny smiled for the first time. "No need. We won't be going outside."

Tom appeared intrigued as he moved aside to let everyone out of the office to follow Kenny.

"I've never been to your museum, so you'll need to direct me," said Kenny, peering around.

DuBois's eyes widened, seemingly stunned. "What are you saying? Do we not 'ave to go to the painting?"

"We are," responded Kenny. "I think we need to go to the second floor if I've got it right."

Suddenly, the anxious energy was evident in DuBois's stride as he walked briskly down the hall and out to the courtyard full of patrons admiring the unique and beautiful space. Everyone turned to see what was happening as this train of professional and amateur detectives followed DuBois and Kenny up the marble staircase until they reached the top floor.

"Okay, um, we need to go to the Holland Room."

DuBois closed his eyes as panic set into his body. "What is this? Mrs. Gardner does not have a Holland Room! Is this a joke?"

Kenny shook his head. "No. It's no joke. I don't understand."

Tom asked, "Kenny, did you, by chance, mean the Dutch Room?"

Kenny glanced up with a large sigh of relief. "Yes, yes. That's it. I was thinking of those flowers to help me remember all the details before burning the note. Dutch Room, right."

Before the group entered the Dutch Room, DuBois asked the security guard to clear the room and not allow anyone to enter while they were there. After the room was cleared, DuBois entered with Kenny, Bob, Brooks, Billy, Sean, Tom, and Angelo. Kenny gazed around the room, wide-eyed. The dark wood paneling, open arched windows overlooking the courtyard, the large fireplace, and the empty frames caught most patrons' attention at first.

DuBois remained impatient. "I do not understand. We know ze painting was stolen from this room. You can see ze empty frame. Why are we here in the Holl—ze Dutch Room?"

Tom asked, "Kenny, are you saying the painting never really left this room?"

Shaking his head, DuBois said, "The police and my security team saw those uncivilized thieves carrying the painting out of this room and into the park."

Kenny didn't respond but circled around the perimeter of the room, stopping to inspect each painting, until he reached the empty frame on the wall opposite the missing Rembrandt self-portrait. Kenny read the small label on the large empty gold frame: *Rembrandt's* The Storm on the Sea of Galilee *was stolen from the Isabella Stewart Gardner Museum.* "This is it," said Kenny. "This is the one."

Brooks approached to inspect the label. "What? This was a Rembrandt, but not the one we are looking for. Do you know what you are talking about, Green?"

Angelo nodded. "Remember when we inspected the room after the robbery? The chairs under this frame were out of place." He looked up and down at the silk-green fabric that draped and covered the wall behind the painting.

Kenny said, "Your painting is behind the shining green cloth under this frame."

DuBois stepped back and asked Bob to disable the alarm for this section of the Dutch Room. Then they lifted each of the old cloth-covered Italian chairs before carefully removing the large gold frame from the draped wallcovering. DuBois and Bob held each end of the bottom of the draped wallcovering and gently lifted it away from the wall and saw nothing on the wall behind except for the original wallpaper itself.

Kenny straightened and furrowed his brow. "I don't understand. The note said this is where we would find the painting."

DuBois and Bob slowly let the cloth drape back down against the wall.

Patrons were at each of the two doors to the Dutch Room, peering in to see what was happening. Most visitors knew of the recent theft.

DuBois wiped his hands on a handkerchief. "We need to make sure they dust these drapes. This charade was a complete waste of time." He began to walk out of the doorway with the others following closely behind.

They stopped as Brooks turned and saw Tom and Angelo still standing by the wall. "Are you two thinking of stealing the wallcovering for the rectory?"

Angelo said, "If you did want to hide the painting, what would be the fastest and best way to do it?"

Everyone came back into the room, circled that section of the wall, and started to peer around the room for possible places to hide a large painting.

"Dr. DuBois, could we lift the draped wallcovering again?" inquired Angelo.

DuBois squinted and pursed his lips as he and Bob lifted the heavy silk cloth again. Angelo positioned himself against the wall to inspect the backside of the wall covering. "Very clever."

Brooks moved over to Angelo's vantage point. "What are you going on about?"

Angelo pointed to the back. And Brooks moved behind the cloth to see what caught Angelo's eye.

"I don't suppose this is part of Mrs. Gardner's plan," said Angelo.

DuBois leaned over. "What is this cloth pouch hooked to the back of the wallcovering?"

Tom and Sean reached the hooks and lifted the pouch from the back of the drape, opening the top to reveal a painting inside.

DuBois and Bob carefully lifted the *Self-Portrait* out of the pouch, and a tear rolled down DuBois's cheek as the missing masterpiece came into view.

Tom gazed at the painting and grinned. "Great news, Henri! This is the first time I've ever seen you speechless."

DuBois didn't respond but continued to stare at the young man in the painting.

Billy moved to see the actual painting that he had only seen pictured in books and on a poster. The real thing was striking, the actual painting of the man who painted a series of portraits of himself. This young version of Rembrandt appeared as someone presenting himself as something more than he was, a reality that was all too personal to Billy himself.

DuBois finally recovered from his delighted shock. "Let's carefully put everything back in place and take ze painting to ze restoration room to ensure that it's authentic—although I can tell it is. I can tell. Mr. Green, you will need to come to my office to sign some papers, and as soon as we validate zat ze painting is original and ze inspectors can validate zat you had no connection to ze robbery, I believe you will receive your reward."

Mullen had come back, and Billy spotted her whispering something in Brooks's ear, and Brooks said, "Doc, do you mind if we use one of your rooms to talk to Mr. Green?"

"If you promise to leave everything alone, you can use my office. I will be with our beautiful Rembrandt," responded DuBois as he followed the painting up the stairs.

Kenny Green sat at the table with Brooks, Jan, Billy, and Sean. Kenny asked, "What's this about?"

Brooks scratched the side of his head. "That reward is a lot of money."

Kenny's eyes widened. "You're tellin' me. I want to do some good with it, though."

Brooks cocked his head. "A lot of money can get us to do strange things, say almost anything."

"Hey, are you sayin' I'm lying about somethin'?" Kenny squirmed in his seat as he took off his worn baseball hat.

"I don't know what you're doing. I just know that's a lot of money."

"You keep sayin' that. I didn't lie about anythin'."

Brooks placed his palms down on the table. "Where were you on the night of November first?"

"I don't know."

Sean said, "Yeah, you do. You were in the hospital with a bullet hole in your side."

Kenny glanced up at Brooks. "That's right. Day after Halloween. I can show you my wounds."

"Do you know a Reggie Hope or a Dougie Jones?"

Kenny slumped in his chair. "I don't know. Maybe a little."

Brooks leaned forward. "Maybe? A little? You grew up in the same neighborhood and spent time in the same prison as these two. A little?"

Kenny shrugged. "They're younger than me and a little more hardcore if you know what I mean. I know who they are, but it's not like I hung out with them. They were in a different section of the prison than me."

Brooks said, "The three of you live practically in the same building and just happen to be connected to the same painting that is now paying you over a million dollars. Coincidence, huh?"

"Coincidence, yeah. I don't have a connection with them. How are they connected to this painting? Did they put in for a reward, too?"

Brooks laughed. "Their only reward might be another visit to the pen, and I hope to hell you aren't involved."

"Why would they go back to jail for this?"

"Stealing multi-million dollar pieces of art is still a crime, in case you didn't know."

Kenny glanced around the room and responded, "Was something stolen?"

Brooks hesitated to respond as it must have finally hit him that nothing had been stolen. All the paintings were still in the museum. "Well, insurance fraud is also a crime. If they see a penny of this reward, I guess we'll know the answer—if there is any reward money."

Chapter 19

When Sean arrived for the usual Sunday afternoon dinner, Billy could tell he was in a good mood. The roast and sliced potatoes were in the oven, sending an irresistible aroma throughout the apartment.

Mary was tired and sat with Sean in the sitting room while Billy took out the roast and began carving. Mary asked, "Sean, when are you going to bring a girl over for dinner? You should be dating some nice girl at your age."

Sean blushed. "Okay. Okay. I have been seeing someone for a while now. I think you'll like her too."

"Why don't you bring her over?"

"I don't know. It seems like something you do when you are really serious or engaged, you know?"

Billy laughed. "And we know Sean isn't the serious type. He probably takes her to the park to let her watch him play football or basketball. That's his idea of a romantic date."

Sean's face turned red again. "Hey, I know how to treat a girl right. You guys taught me how to respect her and be a gentleman."

Mary grinned. "Don't listen to that old man. I'm sure you treat her right. What's her name?"

"Jennifer."

"I like that. I think it goes with you. What's she like?"

"Hopefully, she likes me. She's twenty-six. She's from Salem and just finished her master's in education at Boston University."

"That's really nice. What does she want to teach?"

"She got her undergraduate in art history and went back for her education to teach art in high school. She has a nice family, two brothers and a younger sister."

Mary sat up. "Oh, so you've met her family, have you?"

"Well, yeah. But that's a little different."

As Billy carried the carved roast to the table, Sean and Mary got up and joined him. They took their seats.

Mary patted Sean's arm. "Well, let's make it *not* so different. You should have her over. Okay?"

Sean nodded. "Okay."

Billy had caught Mary up on the status of the "robbery" on Saturday. After saying grace, Mary glanced at Sean. "Can you believe that precious painting was in the museum all along?"

Before Sean could respond, Billy said, "I don't believe in coincidences. If they went through all that trouble of stealing it, how could they bring it back and why?"

Sean said, "Maybe they realized it was harder to sell than they thought and decided to return it so they couldn't get prosecuted for grand theft?"

"Yeah, then how does Kenny get caught up in this?"

"That's a good question," responded Sean as he took his first bite of the tender roast beef. "What I do know is that this is really good beef."

When they finished and returned to the sitting room to talk while the game was on the television, the phone in the kitchen rang. Billy answered it. When he came back, he appeared as white as a ghost.

Mary said, "Billy, what's wrong? Who was that?"

"Oh, it was nothing. I tried to swallow too large a bite, and it just took a few seconds to go down the right pipe. It just scared me a bit."

Mary glanced at Sean. "I keep telling him to chew more." And then back at Billy. "Are you okay?"

"Yeah, I'm good. Let's have some of the dessert Sean brought from Boccaccio's."

Later that afternoon, Billy took a walk to Sean's house.

Sean was busy repairing the leg on a dresser for his landlady and jumped when he finally noticed Billy standing in the large open doorway. "Billy, don't scare me like that. Did I leave something at your house?"

"I don't think so. Patriots aren't playin' until tomorrow night, so I was just walkin' and thought I would drop by."

"Nine and 0, so far. They're playing great. It feels like a Super Bowl year with how they're clicking."

"Yeah, maybe a perfect season, nineteen and 0?"

"What's on your mind, Billy? I can tell when something's up."

Billy picked up one of Sean's tools and toyed with it for a moment. "You know I think the world of you, don't you, Sean?"

"I hope so."

"You would probably do anythin' for Mary and me—wouldn't ya?"

Sean nodded. "I would. I'd do anything and more. I didn't go to war like you did, willing to give your life for us, but the least I can do is sacrifice a little for you two. You gave me a home, love, and mentoring. I don't know where I'd be if you two didn't sacrifice for me."

"How far would you go?"

"I don't know. Like I said, I would do anything for you two. You're everything to me. Why are you asking?"

Billy put down the tool. "Ah, no reason. I knew the answer, so I don't know why I asked. You're a good man, Sean. Stay a good man."

"I try to. I try to be like you in every way I can."

Billy laughed as he ambled out. "You don't want to be me. Trust me and be yourself, your best true self. At this point, you have a better chance than I do."

Sean stared at him, but Billy could only return a sad glance before he disappeared into the early evening darkness.

Billy walked for some time, thinking about the conflicting forces now pulling at him. He had never been faced with a dilemma like this one in his entire life, and he truly didn't know what to do. It was several hours before he stood at the end of the St. Francis driveway and stared at the warm orangy yellow light from the rectory. *Why am I here? Of all places, why am I here?*

He took a deep breath, stepped slowly down the driveway, and found no answer to his question as he rapped on the door.

Tom opened it with a grin. "Hey, we were just talking about you, Billy. Come in."

Billy entered the warm kitchen and sighed at the smell of beef stew.

Angelo sat at the kitchen table, mulling over his next move in a chess match with Tom. "To what do we owe the pleasure?"

"I don't know. I was just passin' by."

Tom nodded. "That's the best reason for a visit. You can sit down and watch me crush Angelo. I feel it's time to stop letting him beat me every time."

Angelo laughed. "You've got one possible move."

Tom sat to try to find it, most likely having fallen into one of Angelo's traps. "What do you think, Billy? Can I save my queen?"

Billy peered down onto the board, which now held more of Angelo's black pieces than Tom's white ones. The queen seemed surrounded, and it looked like the only piece that could save her would be the king, but then the game would be lost. "I'm not seein' a way out," said Billy as Tom moved his hand from one piece to another in search of the move Angelo had spotted.

Tom scratched his head and finally moved his king to protect his queen. "I can't *not* protect her."

Angelo moved his rook across the board and knocked down the king. "Checkmate."

Tom tilted his head. "Have I ever beaten you? What move did I miss?"

Angelo began placing the pieces back into the box and held up a white piece. "You could have used the bishop to cover for the queen and then moved your queen back toward the king." Angelo focused on Billy. "He has too much chivalry to play this game."

Tom laughed. "I just recognize the inevitable when trying to play against you, Mr. Salvato. You think too many steps ahead." He turned to Billy and pointed to the kettle. "Would you like a warm cup?"

"Sure. It's gotten a bit nippy out there lately."

In a few minutes, Tom brought over three cups of hot tea. "So, just passing by, were you?"

Billy tried to take a sip, but it was too hot, so he set his cup aside. "Just wrestlin' with things lately."

"What do you think about that Kenny guy and knowing where the painting was? Information like that doesn't just drop from heaven no matter what this one will tell you," quipped Angelo, thumbing toward Tom.

Billy nodded. "Who knows? The insurance company will be investigating, but the reward conditions are pretty straightforward."

Angelo set down his mug. "I heard he was in the hospital with a gunshot wound the night of the robbery?"

"He was, and I was with him. We're like blood brothers now, I guess."

Tom asked, "You gave him some blood?"

"I did. Rare blood type—O negative."

"Ah, the most precious blood."

Billy took a long sip of tea, warming his hands on the cup as he looked Tom in the eye. "I have a question for you if we're done sleuthing."

"Sure. We're good with questions, not always great with answers, but we try."

Billy clasped his hands together and pressed them against his lips as he struggled to figure out what he wanted to ask. "Okay, what if there was somethin' really important and good you could do for someone who absolutely needed it, but you had to compromise on honesty to do it?"

Tom sat forward. "Like what kind of good and what kind of compromise?"

Billy's face tightened as he replied, "Like, life and death good, and you're not sure you are doin' anything wrong kind of compromise."

Tom blew out a breath. "Generally, it isn't right to do something wrong to achieve something right."

Billy continued, "You know the other day we were at Orchard Park, and we were talkin' to that boy, Tobey? You knew there was a larger good if he felt comfortable enough to trust us and be honest. Maybe you told a small white lie there to make him trust you?"

Angelo looked up as Tom blushed. "Well, yeah. I've been to the school and could've met him. All right, it wasn't the right thing to do."

"But it helped us out a lot. We were able to make a connection on the robbery, and you were able to make him promise to get back in school and off the streets. If you add it all up, that was a good thing, right?"

Tom wiped his chin. "Well, it was good, but I should have been honest with him. It was an instinctive reaction, but that doesn't make it right."

Billy stared down, pressing his palm on the kitchen table. "What you did was a tiny thing, and the good that came of it was huge. If your child was starvin', could you pinch a piece of bread to feed them—if someone was about to be hit, could you run a red light to save them?"

"Sure. Sure. I'm sorry, Billy. I'm not trying to be so black-and-white here. You have to look at the options available to save someone. I wouldn't judge anyone that did those things to save someone's life, literally or figurately. We should just see if it's the only way."

"Yeah, the only way. I gotcha. What if it is that dire, but you know it's somethin' not so small, somethin' that makes you personally feel uncomfortable? Should you put that person's welfare ahead of your discomfort? Even your own soul? You always talk about self-sacrificing love for others."

"I think you need to consider each situation honestly. I could rob a bank and give the money to starving children, but that wouldn't be right, and it wouldn't be the only way to help those children. So, I would have to think hard about those other options. I would always recommend praying on it for guidance."

"Yeah, doesn't seem like those prayers always work, though," replied Billy as he stood up and thanked Tom for the tea and the talk.

On his way to the door, Angelo asked, "What's happening to those suspects from the robbery?"

Billy stopped. "That's a good question. What robbery?"

Angelo raised his finger to his lips. "That's a good point. Nothing was stolen, but it seems as if they wouldn't go through all the trouble and risk for nothing. If one of them hid the painting, somehow it seems like they are involved with Kenny, or at least with Kenny finding out where to find it. There's got to be a connection."

"I don't believe in coincidences, so I bet you're right on that," answered Billy as he headed out the door and back home to his worried spouse.

Chapter 20

Mary glanced up from the television when Billy opened the door. "Did you spend all that time with Sean?"

Billy sank into his favorite chair and closed his eyes a moment as he answered. "Some. I was just walkin'." After a moment, he turned and gazed into Mary's eyes as if it might be for the last time. "There's nothin' wrong. I was just thinkin' about things."

Mary sat on the arm of Billy's chair and put her arm around his shoulder. "Mr. Quinn, you do know you're talking to me, don't you? I can always tell when something's not right. I can definitely tell it isn't good news."

He put his hand on her knee. "Well, it may very well be good news, so maybe you don't know me as well as you think?"

She shifted and leaned closer. "I think I know you as well as anyone in the world, but—" She hesitated for several moments.

"But, what?"

She replied, "I've always felt like some part of you is a stranger to me—hidden and protected—I'd hope you could someday tell me and trust that I would love you through it, no matter what."

Unexpected tears fell down his cheeks, and fear filled him.

"Billy, are you okay? Did I say something?"

He couldn't respond. He wiggled out of the seat and stood back up, figuring out what to do and where to run. His coat was still on as he made his way to the entrance door.

"Billy!" Mary shouted, panic in her voice.

He opened the doors and went back out into the cold once again. He strode briskly, knowing where he was headed. Twenty minutes later, he stood in the dark of the street in front of a plain, low-budget apartment building next to Orchard Park and dialed a number on his small cell phone. "It's Quinn. I'm in front of your place. Are you here?"

"I'll be right down."

Within a few minutes, the entrance door to the five-story affordable apartment building opened, and a man in a gray hooded sweatshirt, dark jeans, and basketball shoes appeared. By the time he stood face-to-face with Billy, he was shivering in the evening chill. "It's damn cold tonight, isn't it?"

"Why are you doin' this?" asked Billy.

"I told you on the phone. You saved my life, and I want to start doing some good in the world. I'm not used to thinking that way, but I want to do it, and I know you need it. I heard she needs it pretty bad—right?"

Squinting, Billy said, "We're strangers to you. I don't get why you would give up that kind of money. A hundred bucks is probably a lot of money to you, and you just decided to offer half a million dollars to people you don't even know?"

He cocked his head. "Man, aren't you in a desperate situation? Doesn't your lady's life depend on that operation? You saved my life, and now I can repay you—and still have a lot left for me."

Billy let out a heavy sigh and ran his hand along the back of his scalp. He tried to look him in the eye to see if there was any sign of insincerity, but it was too dark to see clearly. "Yes, she needs this desperately, and I've been prayin' night and day for a miracle because that's what it would take to find the money for the bills, but—"

"Let me do this for you—for her."

"It's not goin' to look right for a police officer to be the beneficiary of reward money, especially for a crime he's investigatin'. I don't know. Somethin' doesn't feel right."

"Why does anyone need to know? When I get the money, I can just pay the bills. We don't need to be broadcasting this or anything."

Billy shuffled his feet back and forth to generate some body heat. "Kenny, how well do you know Reggie and Dougie?"

Kenny scratched his head. "I told you. I don't really know them. I'm thirty-four; they're in their twenties. They're guys in the neighborhood, that's all. What do you think—I'm part of some master scheme and shot myself for an alibi? Man, if that's what I'm all about, I wouldn't be offering anything to you, would I? Do you think those two would give up part of their share if they were in on it?"

"I don't know what to think. All I know is if this isn't on the up-and-up, nobody's getting any of that money."

Kenny started back to his apartment entrance. "You'd better hope that ain't the case—for Mrs. Quinn's sake."

Billy strode off without knowing if he should be feeling elated or troubled. This deal could provide the chance to fund the transplant operation Mary needed to live a long life—a life he couldn't imagine living without her. His throat choked up at the thought of losing her. Why was he worried about his wild suspicions when the life of the most important person in his life was on the line and this was the only hope in sight? If God was answering his prayer, why didn't he trust His way of providing that answer? What else could it have looked like?

When he returned home, he gave Mary a long hug. "I'm sorry for walkin' out like that. I've just been worried."

"Worried about what?"

Billy hesitated for a few seconds. "About you. I have nothin' else I worry about. I guess it is retirement comin' up, and I don't want to live my life without you—and I don't want you goin' through this stuff. You're too good to be facin' this."

"And look who's talking about being good. Don't worry so much, or we won't enjoy any of our time together," responded Mary with a hug.

It was Veteran's Day. Billy never enjoyed the day, despite his awards for bravery and service. Maybe it reminded him of losing his only brother.

The following week, Billy didn't see Mary much since he was out during the day.

Late Friday morning, Billy visited Sean, who was working on another project in his favorite place—the garage. The large door was open. As Billy approached, Sean glanced up from his workbench. "You've been over here more in the past two weeks than you have the whole year. Missing me more these days?"

Billy hummed to himself as he entered the garage and ran his hand across the top of the cabinet Sean was refurbishing. "You like saving old things, don't you?"

"Some people see junk, but I see something of quality that just needs some attention and a little loyalty."

"Loyalty?"

Sean ran his sanding block over the top of the piece. "Yeah, sticking with something, even if everyone thinks it's a piece of nothing. This will be a piece worth keeping in the family."

"Sounds like you'd do anything to save somethin' you thought was worth savin'? Kind of like redemption, huh?"

"Maybe."

Billy picked up the wood plane he had held in his hand the previous week and looked it over. "Are there people in your life you would do anything for?"

Sean ran his hand over the smooth wood as he answered. "You know the answer. I would do anything for you and Mo—Mary."

"Anything?"

Sean picked up a tack cloth and wiped the surface. "What are you getting at?"

"How did you come up with it?"

Sean squinted with confusion. "Come up with what?"

"I will have to say that I'm pretty impressed with your planning and pulling off something like this."

Sean froze in place. They stood there staring at each other for what seemed like minutes before Sean finally uttered, "When did you know?"

Billy held up the wood plane in front of him and turned it in the light. "It's pretty faint from wear, but did you know you can just about make out the engravin' of two letters if you hold it the right way?"

Sean leaned forward to see a worn etched RH on the bottom side of the tool.

"The hammer left at the museum after the 'robbery' had the same etchings, just a little clearer. It took me a little bit to find the house that had the garage sale. Randall Hayes—no. Robert Hiller—nope. But Richie Henderson, the old guy two streets over, remembered bein' happy his tools found an enthusiastic owner who looked a lot like you."

"You know, I wasn't the only one to buy tools from him."

"Good point. It was really odd that you asked Kenny Green about his blood type when he was shot. I've never heard you do that before, and he just happened to have the same rare blood type as your partner. The log shows that you took out his file several months back, and that file contained a lot of information, including his blood type. I'm curious why you picked him in the first place?"

"Billy, I look at a lot of files. It's just a coincidence."

Billy put the planer down. "Remember, I don't believe in coincidences."

"Yeah, that doesn't mean they don't happen."

"I know it happens, but it stops being a coincidence when it happens a lot. When we went to Reggie and Dougie's place, you seemed to deflect some of the questions toward him, but it was when I found something there that I became most concerned."

"Found what?"

Billy pulled a folded piece of paper from his pocket. "Nothin' too informative, just a note to meet someone behind St. Katharine Drexel's Church. Like I said, nothin' too unusual, except maybe the handwritin'." Billy unfolded the note and placed it down on the workbench. "Looks sort of familiar, especially that hook on every *s*."

Sean stared down at the handwriting but didn't say a word.

Billy stared at Sean. "You know, I spent two entire days at the Gardner lookin' at archived videotapes goin' back quite a few months. I almost gave up until I saw an interesting couple visit the museum on a rainy morning in June. Was that Jennifer? What was she? An art history major?"

Sean sat down on the folding metal chair next to the bench and stared at the floor.

"Was it a coincidence that we just happened to be right around the corner from the museum when the 'robbery' was occurin'? That you were the last one chasin' the decoy and stopped in the Dutch Room where the 'thief' was? How's that nasty bump of yours doin'?"

Sean continued to sit quietly.

"I never took you for the art museum type, but there you were sitting in the courtyard with the pretty young woman and her sketch pad. She was pointing out pieces of art, and there you were, gazing only at her. Then she took you around the museum and spent quite a bit of time in the Dutch Room, pointing out the empty frames and then showing you the Rembrandt self-portrait. It was the first time you stopped looking at her and studied one of the paintings. Is that when it came to you?"

Sean didn't respond or even glance up at him.

"Do you know what other coincidence I found out? Do you know who your friend, Kenny Green, just happened to spend time with in the same prison? Oddly enough, Reginald Hope and Douglas Jones. And guess what else Kenny Green happened to do out of the sudden goodness of his heart? He called me while you were at Sunday dinner and said he wanted to give me five hundred thousand dollars to pay for Mary's operation. Isn't that amazing? I don't think I ever even told him that she was sick."

Sean propped his elbows on his knees as he clasped his head in the palms of his hands. "We have to do something for her!" He lifted his head, fear in his eyes. "We can't just let her die!"

Now Billy didn't know what to say.

"Yes, I went to the Gardner with Jen, and she explained the artwork to me. She loved it, but when she started telling me about the reward money for the return of the paintings, it made me think about Mary and the possibility of getting the money she needed to live.

"A few weeks later, I picked up Kenny for possession one night when you were off duty. He was on parole from Walpole, and he pleaded with me to let it go. He said he'd do anything if I'd let it go—promised to not get into any more trouble. I told him he owed me one, and then I checked out his file. When I saw his blood type, I remembered you telling me about how rare yours was when we donated a few years ago. I saw him again, and he desperately wanted to repay me somehow, so I started to think about options that could do some good. The thought of the reward money kept creeping into my mind. No one would have to steal anything or hurt anyone, and insurance company profits never seemed more important than the life of the best woman I have ever known."

"It's not right," said Billy, his eyes burning with tears.

"It's not right for her to die, and for what? It'd be no worse than a rounding error for the insurance company. They'll still make plenty of profit. I started playing with the idea. How could we do this so that no one got hurt? Kenny needed a bulletproof alibi if he was going to claim the reward."

Billy said, "That's a bad pun. You mean he was willing to take a bullet for this scheme?"

"He knew a guy who was a good shot, and we studied what kind of bullet and location would be the safest. It took some convincing, but the remaining reward money seemed worth it to Kenny, who had little opportunity to get out of the hole he was in. When Kenny was in Walpole, he had talked over some different schemes with Reggie and Dougie, and he thought they'd be good candidates for the robbery in exchange for a healthy cut of the money. They didn't have to steal anything or get involved with disposing of any stolen goods. They just needed to study the plan repeatedly, practice each step, get the timing down, and be as athletic as hell to avoid getting caught."

"What about Tobey?"

"Tobey Hope was Reggie's nephew and already getting dirty. They told him nothing about the plans and gave him strict instructions to be ready in the park, ride like hell, burn the evidence, return the bike, and then shut his mouth. I guess he did as well as expected for a thirteen-year-old kid."

"That kid needs steering in the right direction, not more bad influences."

"I know."

Billy paced the cement floor. His mind raced as he rubbed the side of his head. "How did they do it? What was the plan?"

"Reggie and Dougie were to visit the museum several times in different outfits to get familiar with the layout. I had a diagram of each floor, the staircase, the camera locations, who the guards were, and their general habits. We went over the script, the timing, the escape plan, and the alibi so many times that they could teach them to me. We planned the timing of Kenny being shot. I knew you would offer to donate blood. I timed the route so that we would be close to the museum when the call came in and be the first on the scene. Reggie and Dougie would generally stay out of sight until it was time to go to work. Dougie was the decoy as he ran to the third floor Gothic Room to grab the small painting and then encourage every guard to leave their post in pursuit to stop him."

"Huh. But why did he take everyone through the Dutch Room where Reggie would be working?"

"How else would I end up in that room?"

"Why did you need to end up in that room?"

"Reggie had already taken care of the guard in the Dutch Room, spray painted the ceiling cameras with the extension sprayer, removed the painting from the wall and the frame. Then hid in a dark corner as Dougie sprinted through the room, lifting as many pieces as he could to trigger more alarms as he waved the smaller painting while he exited the room. I made sure I was the last one in pursuit and stopped to help the guard until everyone was out. Reggie and I had just a minute to place the painting in a large cloth pouch with clips on the open ends. We had to move the chairs, lift the draped silk wall covering under the frame of one of the Rembrandts stolen in 1990, clip the painting to the back of the fabric, and gently let the wall covering down and put the chairs back."

Billy smirked. "Brooks was good to notice one of those chairs slightly out of place. So you could explain your time delay by helping the guard and then bein' whacked on the head before you exited the room behind Reggie, who ran by Dougie and out the door. Dougie handed me the smaller painting and followed him out the door and into the park?"

"Yeah, so far, so good. They were fast and had a head start as we pursued them down the dark path."

"And they had dumped their stuff in Bubblegum Bob's bike baskets, where Tobey stood ready, and you almost hit him on the way out," said Billy.

"I would have run right into him if I hadn't been ready for him. Sully was behind me, and I pushed him aside. Giving chase, we lost them as we ended up at the basketball courts."

"With a ready alibi for two sweaty athletes and no sign of their black sweats or a very large painting in tow. Wait a minute—"

Sean smiled. "I know you saw Reggie carrying the large Rembrandt painting down the stairs and out of the museum."

"Yeah. I thought you said you left it, but we saw it in his grasp."

"Small trick I learned from Jen—and no, she doesn't know anything about this. Remember when we made a homemade kite when I was a kid? I bought a poster-sized photo of the Rembrandt painting on a thick vinyl-type material. I took two long pieces of thin wood sticks on a metal clip that held the painting tight. It looked very authentic. When they got to Tobey, they twisted the clipped sticks and rolled up the picture, stuffing it in the basket with their sweats. I guess one of the sweats missed. I managed to toss it deep under a tree when I retraced the path."

Billy leaned on the workbench. "So, Reggie and Dougie are safely playin' basketball. Tobey is busy racin' down Ruggles, losin' one of the ski masks as he clipped a bush, stops in the secluded spot behind the church to burn the evidence, and returns the bike to Bubblegum Bob early the next mornin'. And Kenny is sittin' in the hospital with a perfect alibi—and a reason to be generous."

Sean stood up and put his hand on Billy's shoulder. "I'm sorry if you think this was wrong, but we have to do something for her. I think saving her is far more important than anything else. You've said that yourself a thousand times. How can we let her down after all she has done for us?"

Billy stared down, shaking his head. "She wouldn't want it this way. I know her."

"Billy, why does she need to know?"

Chapter 21

Billy felt conflicted as he left Sean's garage. *What do I do?* he asked himself over and over. *What do I do? I can't turn Sean in, and I can't let Mary down. I can't let her die. I can't!* The mounting stress and anxiety made him feel dizzy.

He took a series of deep breaths and exhaled slowly to calm himself, but it didn't help. In fact, his chest felt tight and painful as he attempted to clear his thoughts. Finally, he entered the apartment to find Mary sitting in the living room. She seemed tired and frail as he watched her.

"Another walk, Mr. Quinn? You must be getting in really good shape," she said with apprehension.

Still, he stared at her in the doorway, feeling nothing but protective concern. What would he do to save her?

"Too tired to even talk, are we?"

He stepped toward her and then bent down to kiss the top of her head. "How are we feelin' today, Mrs. Quinn?"

"I'm doing all right. I've been a little worried about you lately. Should I be?"

"Nothin' to worry about with me. You didn't get to Mass this mornin'?"

Mary sighed. "I did want to, but I'm feeling a bit more tired these days. I'll be okay. Not to worry about me either."

He sat down next to her and held her hand. "We both know why you are feeling more tired. Do you ever pray for yourself?"

The question brought a tear to Mary's eye. She almost seemed surprised as she quickly wiped it away. She nodded. "I have started to, and I pray for you too."

"Well, I've been prayin' for you night and day, every day, waitin' for some answer. Sometimes I think nothin' will happen if I don't, and sometimes I'm not sure it'll make any difference at all. I hate to say that 'cause I don't want to lose hope..." He clasped her hand tighter. "And I don't want to lose you."

Mary clasped her hand in his. "I know. I know you love me more than you have loved anyone else, which means everything to me."

Billy turned and gazed deeply into her eyes. "If we could raise the money, would you be willing to have that operation? Would you be with me for a very long time?"

"Of course. I don't want to leave you. I never want to leave you, but we can't be robbing any banks either," replied Mary, raising her gaze to Billy.

He knelt down and put his arms around her, closing his eyes to focus on the feeling of holding her close. He thought about the first time he held her on a dance floor and knew she was the girl he was meant to spend his life with. "I'm not givin' up on you, so don't give up on me—or yourself."

After lunch, Billy made his way over to St. Francis. He knew Tom would be hearing confessions on Friday afternoon. Normally Billy would receive the sacrament of reconciliation face-to-face, but today he felt more comfortable talking to Tom in the anonymity of the confessional booth. Billy sat in a pew waiting for the woman who was in the wooden confessional box for quite some time before finally leaving to say her penance. Billy opened the door and knelt as he said, "Bless me, Father, for I have sinned. It has been three weeks since my last confession."

The voice came from the other side of the screen panel. "I'm glad you came. What would you like to confess today?"

Billy thought as he stared at the wood-carved screen. The small dark space felt safe somehow, but he hadn't come to confess anything in particular. "I don't know—I mean, I'm strugglin' with somethin' I need to understand."

"Are you struggling to know the right action to take with something but don't know the right thing to do?"

"Yeah. How do you always know what is right when both choices seem wrong?"

"That's a very good question. Sometimes we think there are only two choices, but there are often others. God tells us the actions that are harmful to us—lying, stealing, killing, coveting, not loving or honoring others, and not loving God with all your heart, soul, mind, and strength. If you look at the two choices you think you have, how does each one follow that guidance?"

Billy sighed. "Neither choice does well. Individually, they both feel wrong, but it seems clear which one serves the greater good—more than clear."

"That certainly seems like a tough dilemma. We should never justify sinning because we think it will serve an end we would like."

"I know. The end doesn't justify the means."

"Right. I think you need to look honestly at each option and follow your conscience, follow your heart. God has written his laws out of love on our hearts. We often know the right answer, even if we struggle greatly with the consequences."

"Much easier to say."

"I know it is. I really do. Did you have any sins you wanted to confess today as well?"

"Ah, yeah. I haven't been fully honest with some people, myself, and God.

I think that's it right now."

"Remember that God wants the best for us and loves us with unconditional mercy. You are forgiven and I absolve you of all your sins, in the name of the Father, and of the Son, and of the Holy Spirit. May you experience the peace and love of being closer to God. Take a few minutes when you leave to say the Hail Mary slowly. Bless you."

Sean picked up Billy at the usual time for their evening shift. He eased himself into the passenger seat. Nothing was said as Sean pulled away to begin their patrol route.

Finally, Sean broke the silence. "Don't leave me hanging here. What are you thinking?"

"I don't know."

"What does that mean? You don't know if we are going to get Mary that operation she needs, or you don't know if you're going to turn me in? What don't you know?"

"Sean, I need to figure this out. It hasn't even been a day, and I'm feeling pretty stressed about knowing what to do here. I just don't know, okay?"

They drove their rounds with little conversation for the next several hours until they received a dispatch call on the radio. "Attention, all cars in the vicinity of 950 Tremont. We have reports of a 10-62. Armed robbery at Hollywood Liquors at 950 Tremont and Roxbury Crossing."

Sean grabbed the radio mic and pressed the transmit button. "316, just around the corner and will respond. Request for backup."

"Three-sixteen, we receive you. Be careful out there."

Sean turned on the flashers and sped around one corner and then the next until he pulled in front of the plain brick building with a blue awning and the name Hollywood Liquors in large white letters. This was a no-frills liquor store that sold a lot of beer, wine, hard liquor, and lottery tickets. Nothing fancy and a high-risk target for robbery due to the amount of cash they transacted on Friday nights.

Sean and Billy got out of their parole car and drew their guns as they edged toward the door. All remained quiet for a full minute, but then they heard a loud blast. Billy could see a man at the counter holding a shotgun and aiming it down one of the aisles. Billy waved to Sean as they quietly opened the glass front door, triggering an electronic doorbell.

The man at the counter kept his aim on the aisle but turned his head to see who was at the doorway. Realizing it was the police, the man motioned toward the back of the store's rows of glass liquor bottles. Billy raised his hand in acknowledgment as Sean moved to one side of the store, his gaze sweeping left to right. Billy pointed to the round mirror reflecting two men crouched down behind a rack of shelves.

Billy yelled out, "Boston Police! Drop your guns and put your hands up. There's no way out. Be smart and put your weapons down!"

Sean started down the last aisle to cover Billy. Tension mounted as the armed men made no response. There was a quick motion, Sean fired, a quick retort, and suddenly, Sean slumped to the floor, clutching his chest.

Despite a narrow miss, Billy made it to the aisle and returned fire, taking down his target, a man wearing a red hat and sweatshirt.

Billy kept his gun aimed while he checked on Sean. Blood covered the front of his blue shirt, but his glazed eyes were still open. Billy grabbed his walkie-talkie. "We have two men down at 950 Tremont. Repeat, we have two men down and another still armed and dangerous."

As he finished, the backup team arrived at the door, and the other suspect put his hands in the air, dropping his pistol to the ground. One of the officers grabbed and handcuffed the suspect.

Billy shouted, "There's a man down in that back corner, and we have an officer down here."

The tears flowed from Billy's eyes as he saw the look of fear in Sean's eyes. Billy pressed on the wound to stop the flow of blood. "Sean, stay with us! We have EMTs on the way, and we're gonna take care of you. You're gonna be all right. Just hold on!"

Sean tried to lift his head, blinked, and then stared straight into Billy's eyes.

Billy put his gun down and placed his other hand tenderly on Sean's cheek. "Stay with us, Sean."

The seconds that passed seemed like hours until Billy could finally see the flash of the red EMT lights. Two sets of EMTs rushed in with medical bags and stretchers. Billy lifted his blood-covered hand from Sean as the medical team worked to stabilize the bleeding.

Billy rode in the ambulance with Sean to the hospital, a few streets away. Sean's eyes closed as Billy stayed by his side.

Ready to explode with pent-up emotion, Billy's mind flashed back to his son's room and seeing him lying in a pool of crimson blood with a gun by his side. The bullet entered under his chin, exited through his brain, and was a sight of horror to Billy, despite having seen hundreds of men killed brutally in the war. His only son's life had been over before it had really begun. Billy hadn't acted like a police officer entering a crime scene but a father torn apart by the shock of an image he couldn't comprehend. He remembered dropping to the ground and trying to hold his lifeless son's head as he hugged him, screaming, "Paddie! No. Paddie. No!"

After pounding up the stairs, Mary started screaming as soon as she entered the room. No amount of screaming would bring back their beloved son.

A blood-speckled note lay on Patrick's desk.

Dear Mom and Dad

I want you to know how much I love you. I have been struggling with something for a long time, and I'm so sorry that this is the only way out. I would never want to see you hurt, and you mean more to me than my own life. I can't tell you how painful this is and how much I will miss you, but know that I had no other choice. I know this is a Cardinal Sin. I'm so sorry.

All my love,

Paddie

Billy sat in the back of the ambulance feeling a rush of helplessness and deep loss. He had grieved the loss of Patrick for many years, but it never seemed as if it was ever complete. He thought he could hold onto Patrick in some way if he didn't let go of the pain, the loss, and the guilt.

Seeing Sean unconscious and bleeding in front of him brought Patrick onto the ambulance with them in a way that frightened and angered Billy. He couldn't do anything then, and he couldn't do anything now.

Sean was in the operating room for almost three hours before he was brought, unconscious, into ICU, where Billy could sit with him. Billy had called Tom and asked if he would bring Mary to the hospital to see Sean as well. When they arrived, Billy had his head on the edge of the bed and was holding Sean's hand.

Mary went to Billy and hugged him. "What happened? Is he going to be okay? Tell me he's going to be all right."

Billy sat up and returned the hug, grimacing as he glanced at Tom. "Thank you." He paused. "He lost a lot of blood, and they worked on him in the operatin' room for quite some time. They said he was lucky. The bullet hit an artery that caused the blood loss, but it didn't hit any organs. Barring any infections or setbacks, he'll need time to heal, but he'll be up and around in a week or so."

Relief flooded Mary's face as she embraced Billy again.

Tom said, "That's good news then? I mean, getting shot is never good news, but it sounds like he'll be okay."

Billy nodded. His throat too tight to respond, his body shook as he sobbed. "I couldn't help thinkin' of Paddie. I couldn't stop. I was holdin' him in all that blood, and I couldn't—"

Mary squeezed him tighter, tears running down her cheeks.

"He didn't have to die! I should have been there for him."

Tom pulled up a chair and sat down beside him. "Present suffering touches past suffering, making everything worse."

Billy turned. "You don't know. You just don't know!"

Mary glanced at Tom and then back at Billy. "Billy?"

Overwhelmed, Billy pulled away and rushed out of the room, seeking some way to keep his emotions in check...from exploding.

Chapter 22

As he visited Sean each day, the reward money dilemma haunted Billy.

Mary held his hand as they sat for lunch that following Friday. "Billy, you can't keep blaming yourself for Patrick."

Billy didn't lift his head as he spooned his stew and then let it drop back into the bowl. "I have to deal with reality. I can't keep running from it."

His guilt and unrest grew each day.

Mary pleaded with him. "Father Tom is a trained psychologist. Why don't you talk to him about it?"

Billy closed his eyes. "I've talked to him many times. It does no good. Can he absolve me from being the reason for our son's depression and suicide?! Can he?"

Mary leaned forward to touch his hand.

He pulled it back.

She sighed. "It's not your fault. You need to stop blaming yourself for everything."

A black shroud of depression suffocated him. He had tried to describe it to her once after one of his nightmares, but he had stopped as his fear had taken over. That same fear crawled over him. "I don't want to talk to Father Tom, okay?"

Mary nodded. "Okay, but we've got to deal with this, or it will destroy you."

He shrugged his shoulders.

Mary stretched further until she touched him. "I need you."

For the first time, he saw the frightened look in her eyes. He constantly worried about her death but didn't bother to think about how his own pain was affecting her. She had lost her son too, and Sean was the closest thing either of them had now. He never bothered to notice how she was feeling or asked her if she suffered from anger and sadness, knowing her end may be near. He reached out and held her hand and looked into her eyes in silent recognition of her feelings. They finished their lunch without any further discussion; then, she let him know she needed to take a nap.

Billy had planned on visiting Sean at the hospital. His partner had been there a week now, and he was anxious to be released. Billy drove the squad car to Boston Medical Center, known as the Boston City Hospital in previous years, a few blocks up from the police station. When he arrived at the doorway of Sean's room, he could see Tony Brooks and Jan Mullen at his bedside.

Sean was sitting up, appearing antsy, ready to get dressed and check out.

Brooks nodded to Billy as he entered. "Well, Officer Quinn, it looks like you won't have to find a new partner after all."

Sean scoffed. "It will be another week or so before I can get back on patrol, but I'm ready to get out of this prison. As a matter of fact, I think the food is worse than prison food."

Everyone laughed.

Brooks said, "We're still trying to get to the bottom of the Gardner mystery. There's no proof of that guy, Green, colluding with anyone involved with the robbery—or non-robbery if you want to be technical, but something still stinks with this one."

Billy made a point of not glancing over at Sean.

"We've got nothing more from that kid, Tobey, or from the guys playing basketball, and they're certainly sticking to their story more than ever. No stores in the area can confirm anyone buying the paint sprayer, ski masks, or sweats, and no one has seen Hope or Jones working with anyone different lately. We've got nothing, and I can't tell how that painting got back into the museum."

Despite his struggle, Billy glanced at Sean.

Brooks seemed to pick up the exchange. "Do you guys know something you're not telling me?"

Sean winced as he tried to stand. "If we did, we'd be detectives with cushy desk jobs instead of bullet holes in our chests."

Brooks smirked. "I get it. Come on, Mullen. We'll leave the men in blue to their fantasies."

Mullen patted Sean's shoulder and said goodbye.

Billy turned to Sean. "Are you honestly feeling ready to go?"

"Absolutely. Energy is back, healing well, no serious damage. I just need to keep this arm in a sling to avoid pulling on the wound. Otherwise, I'm feeling really good. I might need you to help me dress, though."

"You need a wife." After completing the discharge formalities, Billy was surprised at how well Sean was moving as they made their way to the car. Billy hesitated for a moment before he put the car in gear and pulled away from the curb. Instead of heading directly to Sean's house, Billy started driving east, down Dorchester Avenue, past his old neighborhood, and then finally to the Carson Beach near Boston College High. It was a brisk day outside, but the sky was blue, and the sun shone brightly. He pulled the car into a spot overlooking Speckle Island across the bay. They watched several seagulls fight over a hamburger roll before Sean finally spoke. "It's a little early for the L Street Brownies New Year's dip, isn't it?"

"I wanted a good spot." He turned toward Sean and looked directly at him. "Sean, I was really scared of losing you last week."

"No need to worry. I'm okay."

"I wanted you to know that we don't want to lose you or see you hurt. Somethin' like that brings it home."

They watched a father with his young son running on the beach. They were laughing and just enjoying each other, bringing a gleam to Sean's face. The man tried to make his son run with a kite string as he held it up, encouraging the boy to run faster.

"I appreciate that. I know you sat with me for a long time, and I heard you helped to keep pressure on the wound as I was trying to paint that liquor store floor red."

"Nothin' you wouldn't have done for me and then some. Sometimes I wonder if you wouldn't do almost anythin' for Mary and me."

"Not almost," said Sean as he watched the young boy now in his father's arms, hugging him tightly.

Billy ran his hand along the top of the steering wheel, searching for his next words.

"What is it?"

"I guess I've been thinkin' about the money for Mary's operation."

Sean winced as he faced Billy.

Billy sighed. "I wanted to ask you somethin'."

"You know you can ask me anything."

"Tell me about Kenny Green."

"Like what? You know his rap sheet, but I think being shot shook him up, and he wants to do some good with his life."

"I need you to be honest with me. He wasn't shot before he agreed to your plan. Why did he agree to do this? And why did you pick him?"

Sean shoulders slumped. "I told you. I picked him up, and he wanted to avoid breaking parole. The last thing he wants is to go back to Walpole."

"Something is missin' here. Why was he so willin' to risk bein' shot, committin' a felony that would put him in prison for a long time, and give up half a million to someone he doesn't know? Somethin' doesn't click for me here."

Sean ran the palm of his free hand across his lips. "I don't know what to tell you, Billy. He liked the idea of clearing a million to split and give Mary the money for the operation. That was my condition. Foolproof alibi and no theft. Why wouldn't he go for it?"

Billy opened the door and got out of the car. Leaning against the hood, he looked out over the sun shining on the rippling waves as seagulls circled and cawed above.

Finally, Sean reached over, opened the door, and got out. "What did you get out for?"

"You are a good man, Sean, but I could always tell when you weren't tellin' me everything. I know in my gut there's somethin' more to this Kenny guy. I could tell when I talked to him. It was too scripted."

They leaned against the car for over five minutes without exchanging a word. Billy was going to wait Sean out.

"You don't want to know this," said Sean as he slid his foot across the sand-covered asphalt.

"I need to know."

"You have to trust me on this one. You don't want to know. You don't."

A million thoughts ran through Billy's mind. *What wouldn't I want to know? I can't help Mary if I don't know the deal here, and I can't find it out afterward.* "I need to know, or we can't do this."

Sean let out a long sigh as he held his face up to catch the sun's warming rays on his closed eyelids. He started but couldn't get the words out. "I can't."

Billy straightened and started heading to the driver-side door. "Okay. It's off."

"Wait," said Sean as Billy clutched the door handle. "I'm telling you that you don't want to go here, but we can't let Mary down. We have to save her. You've told me a thousand times that you can't let her down."

Returning, Billy leaned on the car hood again. "Tell me everything."

"Okay. Okay. When I picked up Kenny, we talked for quite a while. I didn't want to report him and send him back, but I wanted him to take me seriously. He started telling me about his struggles in life. His father was in prison for robbery when he was little, and he never knew him. That caught my attention and my sympathy. When he got to high school, he talked about a boy on the basketball team he became friends with. His name was Patrick. Patrick Quinn."

Billy turned abruptly toward Sean. "He went to school with Paddie?" He started thinking about Patrick's friends. *Kenny? Kenny Green?* "KG? He was KG?"

"You knew him?"

"Sure. Paddie would go to his house and, I think, came over a few times after school, but I was always at work. I watched their basketball games, so I must've seen him. Yeah, they worked well as a team on the court. Why wouldn't you want to tell me that he knew Paddie?"

Sean took a deep breath of the salt air and then sighed again. "He spoke about Patrick with a great deal of fondness. He smiled as memories of becoming friends and playing ball came up. Patrick would go over to his apartment and work with Kenny on his studies, which got him interested in doing well in school for the first time in his life. And then—" Sean's voice began to crack a bit.

"And then, what?"

"He broke down crying."

"He missed him?"

Sean paused for a moment. "Kenny's older brother, Kyle, was part of the Orchard Park gang and would have gang members over to the house. Kenny said they would give him and Patrick a hard time for studying instead of enjoying life. They had taken Kenny and Patrick out for rides several times and got mixed up in some bad stuff, a few robberies and some drug deals. Kenny would get into fights with his brother about trying to get them in trouble. He told him that Patrick's father was a cop, but that only seemed to encourage Kyle. One night, they drove over to Lenox Street. While those gangs were allies, Kyle had had a run-in with the leader of the Cardinals a few weeks before and wanted to teach him a lesson. They rode slowly down the street on a warm June night, when everyone was out. Kyle suddenly pulled out a shotgun and aimed it at the crowd on the steps of the project. Kenny said that Patrick reached for the gun to stop him, but it went off and killed the Cardinal's gang leader."

Billy felt his whole body tighten. "No way. Not Patrick. Why do you believe this Kenny guy?"

"I checked out his story from the robberies to the shooting. They all checked. Why don't we stop here?"

"No. No. We can't stop. I need to know what happened."

"You don't need to know. You shouldn't know. I know Patrick wouldn't want this. I know it."

"What are you talkin' about? How would you know what Patrick would want?"

"You talked about how depressed and anxious he seemed that summer?"

"Yeah. I wasn't there for him. I was never around enough to give him what he deserved, and he didn't think his life was worth anything."

"Who said so?"

"I read some of his journal entries. He talked about my not bein' around, missin' his night games and other events because of my shift. He seemed angry and wished he had a dad who had a normal job and wanted to be with him. When he started getting depressed and withdrawn, he wouldn't talk to me or let me into his life. Lookin' back, it was obvious—" Billy exhaled, and his voice cracked. "It was obvious he was hurt and I was to blame. I wasn't there. I let him down! How could I not have known what he needed?"

As Billy broke down crying, he stepped over the curb and started pacing across the beach, which was now at mid-tide.

Sean left him alone for a bit but then caught up with him. "Billy, what can I do?"

"You can't fix it when someone is gone forever. I've tried. I need to know the rest of the story."

"I don't know. It won't help you."

"Tell me. I can't feel anythin' worse than what I'm feelin' now."

"Yes, you can. I beg you to let it go."

Gazing down at the wet grains of sand, Billy said, "I'll never let him go. Tell me."

Letting out a deep sigh, Sean said, "Kenny said that Patrick became stressed over getting caught up with this gang and didn't want to disappoint you, but Kenny's brother kept taunting Patrick about turning him in and shaming this family. The level of stress and depression began to overcome Patrick. He wrote a suicide note and got your gun out from your bureau. He asked Kenny to come to your house when he was alone when you and Mary wouldn't be home."

Billy squeezed his eyes tight and tried to soothe himself by running his hands down his face. "I can't go here. I can't."

Sean put his arm around Billy, who was now shaking. "I think we should stop. I really think we should. Let's leave it in the past."

He stepped back. "Nothin' is in the past. It's always here with me every second of the day. Don't you understand? Patrick is always with me, and his pain haunts me constantly." Tears continued streaming down his cheeks.

Clutching Billy's shoulder, Sean said, "You and Mary lost your only son. Kenny lost his best friend. He felt like it was his fault, and when he heard about Mary's medical condition, he thought it would be a tribute to Patrick's memory to help save her—to finally do something right and good."

They made their way back to the car and sat in silence as they watched the tide continue to go out.

"Okay," murmured Billy.

"Okay?"

"She's been getting noticeably worse, and I can't bear to watch it happen. She deserves better, and so does Paddie."

Sean breathed a deep sigh of relief. "I'm so glad."

Back at home, Billy sat with Mary at the kitchen table to share a cup of tea. Mary leaned in. "How was Sean doing today? Was he actually ready to go home?"

Billy took a sip and then replied, "He was more than ready. He also had some news that may be very good news."

Mary's eyes widened as she sat up and asked, "Is he engaged to that girl already?"

"No, no, no. Much better news than that. We may be able to afford your operation and get you back to bein' healthy again."

Mary put down her tea with a clang. "What? You didn't go and cash in your retirement, did you? I told you that we weren't going to do that. Neither one of us could survive."

"I wouldn't do that without talkin' to you. It has to do with a painter."

Mary laughed. "What kind of riddles are you telling me tonight?"

"Rembrandt may be helpin' out with the expenses. I think it's fitting since you like him so much."

"Mr. Quinn! I know you like playing games, but this is way too confusing."

Billy touched her hand. "The man who is claimin' the reward for helpin' to find the painting wants to offer to pay for your operating expenses."

Mary leaned forward and squinted as if checking to see if Billy was being straight with her. "That would be a very generous offer, but why would he be doing that for us?"

"Do you remember a friend of Paddies's called KG?"

Mary thought for a second. "Oh, sure. He seemed like a nice boy and came over here a few times. They were good friends and played basketball together. I think Patrick studied with him. I do remember that name now."

"Well, KG is Kenny Green, the man who is looking at a one-point-five million dollar reward. The same man who was shot and you asked if I could help find him a job. He is insisting that he be allowed to help us for saving his life but more as a tribute to Paddie's memory."

"That was KG? Patrick's friend from high school?"

"Yes. He said he's felt guilty all this time and wants to do something good. Aren't you happy?"

Staring down into her tea, Mary paused. "I think I have to let it sink in. I guess I've been so resigned to the reality of this thing; this doesn't seem real. He might change his mind too. That's a lot of money to give away to people you don't know very well."

"Mary, I don't think he'll change his mind on this. The insurance company just needs to confirm that he is eligible, and our prayers will be answered. I can't believe it myself. Are you okay if we start talking to the doctors about getting you on a list for transplant donations?"

"It's a lot to think about. I'm sorry—I guess I feel stunned more than anything."

"You're cryin'. I thought you'd be happy."

She wiped the tears from her face with her napkin. "Sorry. I guess I've never felt afraid of dying, not yet anyway, but I've felt frightened about leaving you alone. It just hit me that you might not have to be alone. I know, I'm talking crazy."

After his shift, Billy had trouble sleeping that night. He thought of everything that could go wrong; the insurance company might not award Kenny the money, the doctors might not find a donor match, and on and on. He tossed and turned and couldn't calm his mind, but one thing he didn't think of was not going through with the plan to save his bride. He walked to St. Francis for morning Mass with Mary. He wanted to thank God in person for the opportunity. After Mass, Billy told Mary he wanted to give the good news to Father Tom. Mary said that she felt a little tired and would meet him at home afterward.

After saying goodbye to the last parishioner leaving after morning Mass, Tom greeted Billy outside the church entrance. "Billy, good to see you and Mary this morning. Is she still inside?"

"No, she went home, but I wanted to give you some great news."

"Mary's getting that operation?"

Billy's shoulders sank with disappointment. "Now, who told you about that?"

"Mary dropped by around five last night to talk. Come on back in with me so I can change." They entered the church and made their way to the sacristy, where Tom took off his vestments. "She gave me the good news but didn't seem as happy as I would have expected, so we talked."

Billy helped to hold his vestments as Tom folded some for the drawer and hung others in the vestry closet. "I know. Her response was kinda subdued, but I figured she was more shocked than anythin'."

"That's what I thought too, but she told me she felt like something seemed off."

"Off. Like what?"

Tom chuckled. "You know that women's intuition thing? It's real. She wanted to feel happy, but something didn't feel right. She didn't know what, but it was just a feeling."

"Like what?"

"I don't know. She said you always talk about not believing in coincidences, and it seemed like a long shot that the man reclaiming the reward would just happen to be a boy that was Patrick's best friend when he died. How would he have found out where the robbers hid the painting unless he was connected to them? Things like that."

"But that's her and not you, right?"

"Right," replied Tom. "I would have a heck of a lot more questions than that, but you do this for a living, so you probably have all those same questions and even more, right?"

"No disrespect in God's house, but what are you drivin' at?"

"Billy, Mary wants to live, but she wants to do it honestly, above board. Does that make sense?"

Billy nodded but avoided eye contact.

"You have to admit; there are a lot of strange things about this case. Angelo thinks it would have taken two people to get that painting hooked onto the backside of that wall covering in that short amount of time. The second suspect's partner was never in that room long enough, and unless it was the security guard in on it, it does raise some interesting possibilities. Of course, it's possible someone brought the painting back into the museum and placed it there later, but the chief security officer would have to have been involved to make that happen—and that wouldn't explain where the painting went in the park if it had been stolen that night. Angelo wonders if the second suspect was carrying something that looked like the painting and was easier to dispose of."

Pacing, Billy replied, "Sure, there are always unanswered questions and possibilities."

"You said the first suspect seemed like he presented you with the Giotto painting. Any thoughts on why he would do that?"

Billy shrugged.

"Angelo discovered that this Kenny Green spent time in Walpole, overlapping with Reggie Hope and Dougie Jones. I know you don't believe in coincidences."

"I never said there are no coincidences."

"Like the police officers who were first at the scene when Kenny Green happened to be shot the night of the robbery also happened to be the first officers on the scene of the museum robbery?"

"I think that's enough, and I don't appreciate the veiled accusation." Billy shot an angry glance at Tom.

Tom said, "You're right. I know you love Mary more than anything and would do anything to keep her safe, but no part of me believes you planned or were part of anything dishonest. I really don't. I was just listing coincidences and questions."

There was a depth of sincerity in Tom's eyes that did not escape Billy's notice. "I'm sorry. It's been a tough run here, and I've been a bit tired and testy."

"I can understand that, and I know how much you love Mary and how much being a good cop means to you as well. I also know you're still feeling the painful loss of your son, even after all this time. You've been through a lot. It would take a toll on any man."

"After all this time. Honestly, it feels like time hasn't moved since that day." Billy sighed and closed his eyes. "When I saw Sean shot and all that blood, I couldn't help but think of Paddie—holdin' him—" He couldn't control his emotions as he choked up. "All that blood. He was only a boy."

Putting his arm around Billy's shoulder, Tom said, "He was a good boy."

"I know! And I wasn't there for him! He didn't have to die. If I had been there instead of on my shift. I should have been where he needed me. I wasn't there, night after night and even on many weekends. He needed a father."

He gripped Billy's shoulder tighter. "I have talked to Mary many times about this, and she says you were a very good father. She said you loved your boy."

"I love him more now than ever. I think of him more now than I ever did back then, but he needed me then. Don't you understand? He needed me when he was alive, not dead!" Billy pulled away from Tom. "You don't get it."

Tom took a deep breath. "Billy, I do know the pain of losing the person you love most in life to suicide. I know it personally, and I know it today because I still hold on to her despite that pain."

Heaving ragged breaths, Billy kept his eyes shut tight, trying to calm himself but to no avail. The room seemed to grow tighter, and the walls closed in around him. Billy felt trapped by the presence of something, someone he couldn't hide himself from. Suffocating pressure bore down on his chest, making it hard to breath. Panic set in.

Tom put his hand firmly on Billy's back. "Take it slowly. You're going to be okay. You don't have anything to fear with God. Nothing to fear. He's with you."

Billy covered his face with his hands as the watershed of tears fell. "I can't—I can't—you don't understand—no one does!"

Tom turned Billy to face him, putting his hands on each of Billy's shoulders. "You will not be judged here. You have to lay this burden down sometime and rest. The risk is never as big as we think."

His head snapped up in anger, fear, and panic. "No! You can't understand. I'm a fraud!"

"You're not a fraud to me or Mary or Patrick—or God."

Limp in Tom's embrace, his head shook vigorously from side to side. Billy peered into Tom's eyes. "You may be smart, but this is somethin' you are dead wrong about. Can't you hear me?"

"I'm here to listen, but I can't hear you if you don't trust me."

"Everything about me is a lie. Everything! From the time I was a boy—my mother desperately needed me when my father died, and I wasn't there. I gave her nothin' but trouble and grief. It was all about me. I was not a good son."

"I can imagine that weighs on you with regret, but you were a boy, Billy, a young boy without a father. None of us are perfect, but you can't judge yourself now based on things you wish you had done differently as a boy. Every one of us has deep regrets about our failings as a child, but they were there to learn and grow from. Did your mother still love you?"

Billy nodded. "But she asked me to take care of my younger brother, Jimmy. He looked up to me and joined the Marines right after I did, serving in the same battalion as I did in Viet—" Choking sobs racked Billy as he closed his eyes in agony, seeing only the battlefield of bodies, the explosions, and chaos. His face contorted as the painful memories reached the surface. "He is the one who should have that Silver Star, not me!"

Tom listened intently, bracing Billy's shoulders in support.

"We were chargin' down this hill, and he went first."

"You can't blame yourself for that, Billy."

Billy bit his lip. He could see himself watching his brother race ahead on the field through the barrage of bullets and mortar fire. "I froze. I couldn't move and just watched him charge into that gunfire. I watched the blood and bullets exit his back. I watched him die! And I did nothin' to stop it!"

Tom pulled Billy into a brother's hug.

"Jimmy," Billy moaned through the muffled tears and pulled back from Tom. He didn't feel as if he deserved comfort. He deserved judgment and condemnation. "I watched Jimmy die. I was a coward, not a hero. Now, do you believe me?"

Tom hadn't let go of his grip on Billy's shoulders. "I don't see a coward or a fraud. I see a human being who loved this brother through the years. Would he want you doing this to yourself? How would Jimmy want you to be living your life with your family now?"

Billy reached up and pushed Tom's hands away. "Redemption through those in our lives we've failed, is that what you mean? I had a chance with Paddie. He was a blessing to Mary and me, my son, and what did I do with that opportunity? I sat back and watched him die. I was too self-absorbed, too selfish to make him the priority he deserved to be. To be a real father to him. Oh, I've had my chances, over and over again, and I have failed those in my life every single time! Every single time." The last line was said softly as Billy hung his head in shame.

Stepping back, Billy took a deep breath. He stared at Tom, now with serious determination. "Now you know the real me, but this man isn't goin' to stand back and watch the only person left in his life die. I am not goin' to let Mary down and watch her die a painful death too! I can't do that. Do you understand?"

Tom nodded in understanding, his eyes expressing deep compassion.

Billy left Tom in the sacristy and exited from the side door. Cool air soothed his face.

While standing on a ladder, replacing a rotten piece of molding, Angelo called down, "Officer Quinn. Are you okay?"

Refusing to face Angelo, Billy merely called over his shoulder. "Mary's goin' to be okay. That's all that matters."

Chapter 23

Shaken, Billy walked the streets for several hours. By the time he reached Sean's house, he had regained his composure and cleared his eyes. He felt a certain peace in the resolve that, for the first time in his life, he was going to save someone dear to him, to be the man everyone thought he was.

When Sean answered his door and welcomed Billy in, he said, "Hey, I've been worried about you. I called the house, and Mary didn't know what happened to you."

"I'm fine. We're goin' to talk to the doctor on Monday about preparin' for the transplant operation. Hopefully, it will get the ball rollin' before the reward money becomes available to help save her." Billy projected resolve in his voice. No more hesitation or questions about what they were going to do.

"That makes me happy. I couldn't bear to think of what she would be facing without the surgery. And you're good?"

Billy nodded. "I'm good. As a matter of fact, I feel better than I've felt in a long time, thanks to you. Were you able to sleep last night with those wounds still healing?"

Sean shrugged. "Not really, but it's still better than the hospital. Jenny brought over some groceries and coffee this morning, so all is good."

Billy smirked. "Oh, Jenny, huh? So this relationship is goin' well then? I haven't known you to date anyone seriously for any period. You like her?"

"Yeah, I like her," replied Sean with a blush.

"Okay, here's the real question—"

"Oh, boy. Here it comes."

Billy scanned the apartment. "No, not that question. One much bigger than that—does she like you?"

Sean laughed out loud. "Oh, I see. How could anyone like Sean O'Donnell? Yes, she seems to like me. She tells me often enough."

"Mary will love hearing that. Tell you what. Thanksgiving is next week. Can we invite her over as your guest? Mary already asked, and if you really want to make her happy, that will do more than a free kidney any day."

"Okay, I'll ask her. She just told me her parents had to travel to see a sick aunt and wouldn't be home for Thanksgiving, so it might work out."

Billy loved ribbing Sean about things like this whenever he had a chance. "That's great, but I thought you couldn't ask a girl over until it was pretty serious. So, what is the actual story here? You know Mary will ask, so you better have your own story straight."

"I know you love embarrassing me. Jenny is—how do I say it? She's incredible. She's kind, generous, adventurous, fun, and very deep, honest, and loving."

"Loving, huh?"

"Yes, loving. She took me by surprise when we were cooking dinner together once and told me she loved me. The way she looked into my eyes, I knew she meant it."

Billy patted Sean's healthy shoulder. "That's really nice. And what did Mr. Wonderful say to her?"

"Oh, I fumbled that one. I was scrabbling to know what to say. My 'I love you too' was as insincere sounding as it could be. She said she didn't expect me to feel the same way that early on; she just couldn't hold it in anymore."

"Well, how do you feel about her now?"

"Oh, that one's easy now. I'm head over heels in love, and I know in my heart that she's the one, but—"

Billy interrupted, "But nothin'—when you know you've got the right one, there are no buts or hesitations allowed."

"Billy, I love her enough to want the best for her. I don't want to marry her just because I want her in my life, but because I'm the best person to share her life with."

Billy felt his forehead tighten with confusion. "Why wouldn't you be the best person for her?"

"I just don't know it in here," replied Sean as he hit his chest with his fist; he winced with pain.

Billy nodded gently. "Join the club, but if it means anything to you, I think she'd be a very lucky girl to have you."

Sean said, "I'll ask her—"

Billy lifted his head in surprise.

"To dinner. I'll ask her to dinner."

"Oh. Gotcha. I'll let Mary know. She'll be excited."

"I know she will, but we need to make sure she takes it slow."

There was a rap at the door, and Billy answered it. "Brooks, I didn't know you did house calls?"

Brooks replied, "Funny guy. I went to your house, and your wife said you were out somewhere wandering around the city, so I thought I'd check here to see how O'Donnell was progressing."

Sean asked, "Since yesterday? I'm doing fine. But you were looking for Billy too. What's up?"

Brooks glanced around Sean's apartment. "Nice. Very homey. I'm in one of those brick apartments on Dudley. No character at all."

Sean laughed. "So it's a perfect fit, then?"

Brooks grinned. "Good one. I guess you are healing fine. We've been trying to push on those two suspects, but they've been squeaky clean lately. No odd meetings or illegal activities. No one is changing their stories, so I think we're stuck."

Billy said, "What would you charge them with since they didn't technically steal something?"

"Nothing. But I'd work the connections with this Green guy a little harder. I don't think the insurance company inspectors are going to be able to prove anything. It's almost like the perfect crime—perfect alibis, no actual robbery, no evidence tying anyone to the incident, and no way of telling how Green knew about the location. It's almost as if there was a master planner that thought it all through cause I know none of the people we're checking out could plan all those pieces so perfectly. I'm not sure I could have planned it so well. Maybe Myles Connor or that Buck guy were involved."

"Maybe," said Billy.

Sean asked, "How long do those insurance inspections go on?"

"Not sure they will take very long." Brooks frowned. "There's no hard evidence of mischief, and they can't hold off paying based on just a feeling. Why?"

"Curious, more than anything. That's a lot of money. A lot of incentive for a greedy man," replied Sean.

Brooks nodded. "I guess if you were a greedy man, you'd be a crooked cop. By the looks of your spartan furnishings, you're anything but."

Sean laughed. "Well, thanks, Detective—I think."

"You take care of yourself, O'Donnell," Brooks said as he left Sean's apartment.

Sean turned to Billy. "He's a curious type."

Billy tilted his head. "In more ways than one."

Chapter 24

Billy woke up early that crisp fall morning. It was still dark, and the apartment was chilly as he arose to get the turkey ready for its long roast in the oven. He shivered as he worked but realized that felt good. He hadn't been freed from the personal guilt he'd carried for so many years, but he did feel somewhat lighter. He tried to put his finger on why as he rinsed the outside and inside of the carcass, patted it dry, and began rubbing the golden yellow stick of butter along the skinned body. He thought about the emotional breakdown he'd had with Tom in the sacristy on Saturday, revealing thoughts and facts about himself that no other living soul knew, not even Mary. At no time had Fr. Tom seemed to judge him or respect him less. He hadn't thought less of him at all and had only focused on his well-being. Billy was surprised he had survived revealing the darkest secrets he'd hidden in the deep recesses of this soul out of fear and shame—and it had made no difference to Tom. He'd cared. Tom had also let him know that it didn't make God love him less either. "Of course not. You can't hide anything from God," he found himself saying aloud and then looking around to see if Mary was behind him.

Mary had mixed the stuffing the night before and already had the large pan out on the counter with a rack on top of two sheets of aluminum foil. There was a small note on the rack that read: *Thanks to my hero, the man I admire, for getting up so early every Thanksgiving to let me sleep in.* Suddenly, his constant companion, anxiety, returned like a punch in the gut. Mary could never see him as her hero and still admire the man she thought she'd married if she knew the truth. He'd have to retreat to his prison of avoidance, or he would lose her.

After putting the stuffed and basted turkey into the hot oven, Billy slipped back into the warm bed next to his bride. Mary shifted over to be closer, and he put his arm around her and held her close.

"Thanks, Mr. Quinn," she whispered as she drifted off for another hour of sleep.

Billy wanted to rest, but his mind was racing again, thinking of all the pitfalls that could trip him today.

Most of what they needed to do had been readied the night before; the table was set, pies and breads baked, eggnog and cider were cooled. And vegetables were ready to be heated closer to mealtime, so when they finally got up, they were free to dress and attend Mass to give thanks to the Giver of all.

Billy was always surprised at how many families attended the nine o'clock Thanksgiving Day Mass, even though he knew the purpose of the day was to thank the Lord for all our blessings. The music was uplifting and lively, and Tom's homily was entertaining and moving. He explained that God had only made us and the universe out of His generous, self-giving love and that the point of life was not to accumulate those gifts but to generously offer ourselves as Christ had taught us. The only place we could truly experience love, mercy, and the meaning of life, was in that self-gift to others.

After Mass, the parishioners stopped to talk with Tom outside of the entrance and wished him a good Thanksgiving. When Mary found out that Tom and Angelo were planning on eating alone after serving a meal to the homeless at Rosie's place, she invited them to come and join the Quinns for a Thanksgiving feast. Tom seemed delighted, but Billy's hidden anxiety grew within him, wondering what would happen if he accidentally said the wrong thing. Instead of worrying about keeping his secret to himself, now, he had to worry about two people doing so. It suddenly seemed worse than ever.

On the way home, Mary turned to him. "Are you okay?"

He knew his dismissal of her observations never satisfied her instincts, but she let it go after a few attempts.

At home, they worked together to finalize the preparations. Mary always enjoyed it when they did the little things together, such as making a meal or taking a stroll.

Sean's familiar rap sounded on the door, soon followed by a woman who could only be Jennifer and Sean himself. "Happy Thanksgiving, everyone!" he shouted, holding a heavy bag in each hand.

Billy approached the door. "Thankful you are alive and well. And very thankful for your guest. You must be Jennifer." Billy said as he reached out his hand.

Jenny started to take it but then she hugged him instead. "I hope you don't mind. Sean has told me *so much* about you both; I feel like you're family."

"I never mind hugs from a beautiful woman. Sean didn't tell us that."

Mary came into the living room, wiping her hands on her apron. "Oh, never mind him. He's a pushover for attention. It's so good to finally meet you, Jennifer." Mary hugged her and looked her in the eyes with instant fondness.

"You can call me Jenny, Mrs. Quinn."

"And you can call me Mary. Well, it's nice to finally know that Sean has good taste. He's never brought a girl around in all the time we've been together," said Mary glancing at Sean.

Sean blushed.

Jennifer patted his arm. "Well, I feel comfortable already and really appreciate your kind invitation. Thanksgiving wouldn't be the same without family to share it with."

Mary waved her to a seat on the couch. "Sean said your folks needed to visit your aunt? I hope she's going to be okay?"

"I talked to them this morning, and she seems to be regaining strength. You're so kind to ask."

Billy turned to Sean. "Heads up, Mary invited a lonely priest and a handyman over for Thanksgiving dinner today. We hope you don't mind?"

Sean laughed. "Father Tom and Angelo are coming? The more, the merrier."

Jenny took Sean's arm. "You mentioned them to me. Are they the ones who were involved with investigating the Gardner heist?"

Before anyone could answer, there was another knock on the door. With a laugh, Billy opened it. "Speak of the devil himself."

Tom chuckled as he handed a bottle of wine to Billy. "That wasn't the welcome I was expecting.

Jenny approached. "Are you Father Tom? You're a lot taller and more handsome than Sean described you. He said you were short, bald, and gruff-looking."

Just then, Angelo showed up in the doorway holding a bag of bread and goodies from Boccaccio's bakery. "Did someone call me?"

Jenny laughed.

Mary took the food from Angelo and waved them inside. "Come in, Father and Angelo. I'm so glad you could come. This is Sean's girlfriend, Jenny."

Her face turned beet red as she extended her hand to Tom and Angelo. "Jenny O'Leary. Very pleased to meet you, Father and Angelo."

Tom said, "That's funny. I just saw a Jenny O'Leary on the volunteer's list at Rosie's Place. Angelo and I were there today helping to serve turkey dinner."

"I've been going there for a few years now," said Jenny. I heard an ethics lecture by Kip Tiernan, Rosie's founder, and started volunteering. I love the women there. I just can't imagine being homeless myself and having no place to go."

Tom grinned at Sean. "I like her already," he said, and everyone chuckled. "Kip believed that enough people working together could change the world if they were only willing to care enough, to take—"

"To take the risk of being human," finished Jenny.

"As I said, I like you already."

During dinner, the conversation and laughter flowed, and everyone commented on how tasty the food was.

Billy asked Jenny and Sean, "So how do a night patrol cop and an art history major slash teacher meet in today's dating world?"

Sean blushed. "Well, the normal way a beautiful woman meets a cop."

"Ah, a traffic violation, huh." Tom laughed.

Jenny blushed. "How did you know?"

"What?" Billy asked. "When was this?"

Sean exhaled. "Back in April. She kind of slid through that stop sign on Tremont, and I got out to give her a ticket."

Angelo nudged him. "But you didn't give her the ticket, did you?"

Jenny blushed. "No. He asked for my number."

Mary asked, "Did you give it to him?"

"No, of course not," Jenny replied.

Mary set down her glass. "Then how did you start dating?"

"Well, this sly one looked up my license plate and address and showed up at my door for several days in a row until he finally caught me coming out of my apartment. We went for coffee and then lunch, and I realized he was a pretty special kind of guy."

Angelo winked at Sean. "Aren't you glad you didn't give her that ticket?"

"So things are good?" Mary asked.

Jenny put her hand on Sean's arm. "Very good."

"So," Mary asked. "What happens these days when things are going *very good*?"

Billy turned to her. "Mary!"

Sean laughed. "Well, I know one thing that won't be happening with this one. No moving in together. She's a bit old-fashioned about relationships."

Jenny arched back a bit. "I believe in marriage and commitment. I see too many friends today being used and broken-hearted with these uncommitted 'mini-marriages.' I don't think it's natural or healthy."

Tom nodded. "You have a very wise girl there, Sean."

"I agree, but isn't it better to be sure you know someone, everything about them before you get married, so you don't get surprised and then split up?"

Tom shook his head. "I get the logic, but there is a fallacy in it."

"What fallacy?"

"People who live together and are intimate together aren't really committed. It's kind of a lie, in a way. The fallacy is that you will learn everything about a person during that time, so you're sure they're the one with no surprises. Well, life has many surprises, good and bad, healthy and not so healthy, rich and not so rich. The commitment isn't about feelings but about actively loving each other, no matter what. When you aren't committed, you're not going to reveal all of yourself—because they can leave if they see the ugly parts that everyone has. When most people marry, they don't even know or accept themselves fully, so—"

"So," Jenny added, "when you have really made a commitment to stay through thick and thin, and you can completely trust each other, it becomes the beginning of fully revealing yourselves to each other, accepting everything, and offering unconditional love."

Tom raised his eyebrow. "That is rare and insightful wisdom these days. She's definitely a keeper. Life is about trusting God. Knowing our self-worth comes only from God and knowing we are made wonderfully by Him. Marriage is the closest we get to seeing that kind of trust and then love in another for us and us for them. It can be a scary proposition to reveal everything about yourself to another person, but knowing that they won't abandon you in the process frees you to take that risk and to see yourself for the first time. When you start working it backward, you can fool yourself—and the current results in today's culture are pretty concerning."

Sean sat back. "Huh. I would never have thought of that if I had a hundred years. I would like to make a toast to Billy and Mary for a true commitment to each other, and Mary's health and long life."

Jenny's eyes widened. "I heard you have some wonderful news, Mrs. Quinn?" There was silence in the room for a few seconds. "Sorry, was that okay?"

Mary passed down some bread as Billy placed some more turkey on Sean's plate. Mary said, "You are fine. Thank you, but nothing is set in stone yet, so I'm trying not to get my hopes up too high."

"I'm sorry."

Mary said, "It has been a fascinating case to watch, though. I'm just so glad that the Rembrandt portrait is back where it belongs. Have you been to the Isabella Stewart Gardner Museum? Of course, you have. Sean said you were an art history major."

"Been there? I want to live there! I took Sean there on one of our first dates. I'm not sure he was all that interested at first, but he seemed to get into it as we went along. He certainly asked a lot of questions. It's so weird that we spent so much time with that painting, and then it's part of a heist—or non-heist, I guess."

Mary glanced at Billy. "There are a lot of weird things with it, to be sure."

Angelo said, "Yeah, I think the suspect in the Dutch Room would have needed some help, and it seems weird for the thieves to go through all that only to leave everything in the museum."

Tom was chewing some turkey as he added, "Maybe they planned on removing it later. It's easier to steal something everyone thinks is gone."

Angelo said, "Then how does Green find out the information to claim the reward? He has to be connected in some way unless you believe in coincidences—and lots of them."

Billy caught Tom watching Mary becoming increasingly uncomfortable. "Mary, are you okay?"

She sighed. "I don't feel right about it. I know it's just an instinct or a strange feeling I'm having, but I don't think I can do it."

There was silence at the table until Billy asked, "Mary, what is it? You can't do what?"

"I don't think I can accept that money for the operation." She shook her head. "I just feel confused about it—my conscience feels unsettled. Father Tom, isn't it wrong to do something against your conscience?"

Everyone turned to Tom, waiting for his perspective.

Tom replied, "Well, our conscience is a natural gift, but it can be misleading if it's not well-formed and doesn't carefully reason clearly and objectively from true moral principles. However, when it is right, yes, you must follow the reasoned judgment of your conscience. Mary, I've known you for a long time, and you take the moral teachings of Christ and the Church seriously. You have a well-developed sense of right and wrong based on that and solid reasoning."

Sean cocked an eyebrow at him. "So, what does that mean?"

Tom sat back. "Only Mary can really answer that. We can't base our morals on feelings, but a combination of a well-formed understanding of right and wrong guided by our natural conscience that speaks to us about the right path to take versus the one we may prefer to take. If we only have feelings or are confused, we should seek reliable guidance to help."

"That's why this one is so confusing," said Mary. "A man is trying to be generous, and I certainly don't want to leave Billy alone. I don't have any hard evidence—just a gut feeling about a lot of unanswered questions. Oh, I'm sorry to ruin the party here. It was such a nice Thanksgiving conversation."

Billy put his arm around her. "No apologies necessary, Mrs. Quinn. How about if we heat up that nice-looking apple pie Jennifer baked?"

Jenny stood up. "And we have some Brigham's vanilla ice cream to go with it."

Mary helped Jenny to get the desserts ready as everyone else cleared the table and rinsed the dishes. Angelo made some fresh Italian coffee he had brought. The mood and conversation quickly changed and became enjoyable for the remainder of the afternoon.

Stuffed and satisfied, Tom and Angelo left first, thanking everyone for a great time. As Billy and Sean watched the end of the Packers/Lions football game, Jenny helped dry the remaining dishes while Mary washed.

Even though Jenny whispered, Billy could hear the conversation from his chair.

"Do you really think there's something sketchy about the reward claim?"

"I don't know," said Mary. "It just seems like too many questions and coincidences. Something doesn't feel right."

"Sean said that Kenny Green had been shot on the night of the robbery. That doesn't seem planned."

Mary said softly, "I know, but how would he have found out about the location of the painting, and why in the world would the robbers go through all that trouble and not take anything? It just seems like it was part of the plan to get the reward money instead of stealing the art. What do you think?"

"I guess I'm curious about the same questions, and Angelo said that he thought it would take two people to hook that painting behind that wallcovering and get everything back in place. I guess the guard could have been in on it and then let the thief knock her out with the ether. But that doesn't explain why Kenny Green is claiming the money unless he is part of the plan."

"And why would they all agree to hand over a third of the reward money to me? Kenny says he has a reason because of our son, Patrick, but why would the others agree to something like that? They don't even know us."

Sean turned and yelled out, "What's all the whispering going on in there about? I hope it's not anything about me."

Jenny shouted back, "Everything isn't about you, Mr. Sean."

Sean laughed. "That's not what you told me the other day."

Jenny blushed. "Well, I do have to feed that male ego once in a while."

Sean replied, "That would be true."

After everyone left, Billy could tell Mary was exhausted. But he was also really tired. Neither said anything about the conversation concerning Mary's operation and the reward money.

Chapter 25

On Friday morning, Billy woke up late. The sunlight through the bedroom window rested on his pillow where his head remained comfortably placed and his eyes shut. Mary was already up, but he heard no sounds from her. As he dressed, he called out, "Good morning, Mrs. Quinn!"

No return response.

He entered the living room, then passed through the kitchen and checked the bathroom. There was no sign of her. *Maybe she decided to go to morning Mass and didn't want to wake me.* He made his coffee and cooked up some eggs and toast for breakfast, and then read the morning paper at the kitchen table, peering up several times at the front door in anticipation of her turning the doorknob, but no sign of her. As it got to be ten and then eleven o'clock, he began to worry and called the rectory. "Father Tom, good morning. Did Mary happen to come to St. Francis today?"

"She did come by early. Hey, thanks again for inviting us to Thanksgiving. That was very nice, and I liked that girl, Jenny, a lot."

"Sure. Sure. Did she stay long? Did she say anything? She hasn't come home, so I was just checkin'."

"She wanted to talk, but I can't talk about it."

Billy huffed. "Did she tell you not to say something to me?"

"No. No. You know any talks I have are confidential. I would never share the conversations I have with anyone."

Relief filled Billy. He knew he could trust Fr. Tom to keep his secrets as well.

Tom said, "Are you worried, Billy? I can help look for her."

"She's probably fine. She doesn't have a phone, but I'll check around at places she might go. No worry, and thanks for offering."

Billy hung up and began pacing the apartment. He called around to friends, but no one had seen her. Another hour passed, and none of the friends he called had seen her, so he decided to go out searching. He was a police officer, so he should search for a missing person. He tried to think of where she would go. He worried that she didn't have the energy she may have thought and collapsed somewhere. He went to Sean's to let him know he was looking for Mary. Sean joined him and together they searched the local shops and coffee houses. Maybe she was simply Black Friday shopping? They finally went to the Gardner Museum and were told that she did indeed drop by and talked with Dr. DuBois.

DuBois was in his office, and he rolled his eyes at the sight of them in the doorway. "'ow can I be expected to accomplish anything today if your entire family drops in without an invitation? Tell me this?"

"So Mary was here?" asked Billy.

"Of course. Do you 'ave other family members who will be dropping by?"

"No. Do you know what she wanted?"

DuBois made an exaggerated sigh. "Why don't you ask 'er? She wanted to know what I thought about the thieves leaving the painting behind instead of stealing it." DuBois crumpled his face. "'ow would I know that? I said I was just glad to have our Rembrandt back. Then she asked what I thought about Mr. Green and the reward money." DuBois stood up and said, "I said I was 'appy to have found him so quickly. So many other paintings are still missing—" DuBois clenched his hands together. "I would have paid anything to get this masterpiece back."

"Did she ask anything else?" inquired Sean.

"She asked if the reward money would be paid soon. I don't know why she wanted to know, but I told 'er it looked like the insurance company was wrapping up its investigation. Oh, she asked if there was any way that Mattie Everett or Bob Touhey could have been involved with the robbery. I told her that I am certain they were not and 'ave thoroughly checked them out. Is there something I should know or be concerned with? Do the police suspect something?"

Billy and Sean exchanged glances. "No, nothing you should know. I was just looking for my wife, and I heard she came to the Gardner. She loves it here."

To that, DuBois straightened up and, curling his mustache, said, "Well, of course, she does. And we are grateful for the many times she has volunteered here. Now, I would like to get back to my work, if we are finished?"

"Absolutely," Billy said, and they left the museum.

"Where would she go next?" Billy asked Sean as they made their way to the entrance.

They searched through the Back Bay Fens park and around the entire neighborhood until they ended up back at Billy's apartment. Still no sign of her as they called in and requested patrol cars to be on the lookout for her. Finally, at a quarter after two, the door opened and in strode Mary.

"Where have you been? Are you all right?"

She put her hat and coat in the closet without a response and then turned toward the kitchen to ask, "Would anyone like some tea with me?"

They nodded as Sean opened the cabinet and lifted out the cups. Mary heated the well-used red kettle on the stove. Billy and Sean sat on one side of the small kitchen table and Mary on the other as she poured the steaming water over the tea bag in each cup. There was anticipation in the room as the silence continued, until Mary put down her cup.

"Well, I guess we should talk."

Billy glanced at Sean and then back to Mary. "Okay, but first, are you okay?"

"I'm fine, but I'm not okay."

"What is it?"

Mary squinted her eyes and hesitated before replying. "I don't think I can do it."

Billy frowned. "Do what? You don't think you can do what, Mary?"

"I've thought a lot about the operation and the money. I don't want to die, and I don't want to put you through this, but I have to do what I think is right. I couldn't live with anything less—and I wouldn't want you to."

Sean said, "What wouldn't be right? Kenny Green wants to do something good in life, and he wants to do it in honor of Patrick."

Mary said, "I know. I've had a funny feeling that something isn't right with this. Somehow, this seems too uncomfortably coincidental."

Billy felt disappointed. "You're gonna give up the answer to our prayers based on a feelin'?"

Mary peered over her glasses at Billy. "No, not a feeling. The feeling just got me wondering...and wondering and wondering. I've talked to Father Tom several times, and he has a lot of the same unanswered questions I have. I talked some to Angelo, and he was trying to piece together the possibilities. He's been checking this out for some time, trying to put the puzzle pieces together where they fit versus trying to jamb them in place."

"Angelo told us everything he knows. What did he tell you?" asked Billy as he nervously eyed Sean.

Mary sat up and slowly sipped her piping-hot tea. "He spent some time checking out Mr. Green. For someone who wants to take the right path, he sure hadn't been heading in that direction after doing jail time. Job opportunities aren't great for an ex-convict, true, but he's been dealing a little and involved in some thefts."

"How does Angelo know this?"

Mary smiled. "I guess he has a lot of connections. Well, also, he thought the shooting alibi seemed a little too convenient."

Sean spluttered. "He thinks he got himself shot as an alibi? Seems kind of extreme."

"Yes, it does, but one-point-five million is an extreme incentive too. Well,

Angelo located the guy responsible for shooting Mr. Green. He was a marksman in the army and has been doing—what do they call it—'contract work' since he's been home. His name is Frank Gala."

"Frank Gala? Who's he?"

"I just told you. He's the contract man who shot Mr. Green. Angelo said he's a deadly shot and knows how to place a bullet to do the most or least amount of harm. He wouldn't give up the name, but he said it could have been a paid job. I guess they have a vow of confidentiality, like priests do."

"Mary, this is crazy. What does this have to do with the reward money?"

"Well, this Mr. Gala said the oddest part about the job was that it had to be precisely at a particular time and that Mr. Green would be waiting for him."

Sean tapped his spoon nervously on the napkin.

"Angelo helped me find that boy, Tobey, and he said that he didn't know much about the robbery but got fifty dollars to take the evidence out of the park and destroy it. He did confirm who those two men were."

Billy said, "Well, I think we've got a good idea about who those two probably were."

"Hmmm. Well, I went to talk to them."

"What?"

Mary answered, "I had a nice visit with Mr. Hope's mom, Rozzy. She said that Reggie kept telling her that things would be getting a whole lot better soon. She didn't know what that meant. When I saw Reggie, he was too smooth to answer any questions, but when I told him the woman who was knocked out with ether was still in critical condition, he seemed to panic and asked about her."

"Mary! Mattie Everett isn't in critical condition?"

"I know, but I wanted to see his reaction."

Sean laughed uneasily. "She's a sly one."

Mary nodded. "I asked Rozzy if Kenny Green ever came over, but she couldn't think of ever seeing him talking with Reggie. When I saw Mr. Jones, he seemed too nervous to talk but relaxed when I said I wasn't there to turn him in. When I said he seemed physically fit, he perked up and started telling me the shape he kept himself in. When I asked if it was hard running up and down those marble stairs in the museum, he slipped and said, 'Nay, not too hard at all.' When I asked why he presented the Giotto to you on the way out, he just shrugged and said he was done talking."

Billy asked, "What are you trying to do here?"

"I needed to see if I could get answers to these questions that have been bothering me and a few other people. Don't they bother you two?"

Neither Sean nor Billy responded.

"Not to leave anyone out, I was able to find Kenny Green." She glanced back and forth as if to see if there was any reaction. "He seemed a bit anxious when he saw me, but when I told him I wanted to thank him in person for his incredible generosity, he was more relaxed. We went to his apartment, and I met his mother, Melina. She was very nice, very Christian, and welcoming. She made me some tea while Kenny and I talked. He wouldn't give up the name, but it seemed obvious that someone had given him the location and plan. When I started to talk about his friendship with Patrick, he beamed at the memories, but when we touched on things closer to the end, he got emotional. He was respectful but wanted to end the conversation."

"So, I don't understand how any of this leads you to not takin' care of your health. If the insurance company has investigated and is okay with payin' the reward money, why are the findin's of those professionals not worth trustin'?

Mary put her cup down on the table. "Well, I'm not done yet. It doesn't bother me as much that dishonest people would be dishonest, but if honest people are dishonest, then there's no one I can trust. I can't be the reason for that, and I couldn't live with that."

Sean squinted at her. "What do you mean?"

Mary raised her head. "One person knew all the players, was in the Gardner prior to the robbery plan, had the perfect timing to be at the alibi scene, then at the robbery, and then in the room when the painting was being hooked to the back of that fabric wallcovering. One person was motivated enough to do anything to save me from dying and leaving my husband alone."

Heavy silence pervaded the room.

Frustration shook Billy's voice. "What is it, Mary? You need that operation, and we have prayed for years now for some hope—an answer. Why can't we accept it when it comes?"

He watched Mary fix her eyes on Sean, and he slowly turned until his eyes met hers. She seemed to be waiting for him, but he remained silent. "Sean, you know I love you, right?"

Sean dropped his head and shrugged half-heartedly.

"And I would never give up on you either?"

He made no gesture in response.

"I know you'd do anything for me. I know you'd sacrifice your very life, and in some ways, I think you have. I know you love me."

A tear made its way down his cheek.

"I know you love me."

More tears started to fall.

"Sean, be honest with me. Did this plan begin to come to you when you visited the Gardner with Jenny and because you were afraid I'd die?"

Sean exhaled a long breath.

"Then, when you picked up Kenny Green, the wheels started to click, and you only focused on finding a way to pay for my operation without technically breaking the law—because you believe in the law?"

Sean shuddered through a sigh and closed his eyes as if trying to escape. "I—I—"

"Sean, you planned this so that no one would steal anything and no one would lie. Reggie and Dougie just did what they were told, with a promise of a high return for no crime committed. Tobey simply ran an errand for fifty dollars, no questions asked. Frank Gala performed a service that Kenny reluctantly agreed to for the money and for Patrick. Kenny would get the instructions, destroy them, and show them the location—the only requirement for claiming the reward. He wasn't connected to the robbery and only knew his piece of the plan, like everyone else. Only one person knew the entire plan and how to make it happen."

Sean blinked his eyes open and stared down at the table.

"And this person was you?"

After a long hesitation, Sean nodded.

Billy leaned back in his chair and stared at the ceiling.

"Why did you do it?" asked Mary.

Tears began to flow again. "Why?" choked Sean.

"Yes, why did you do this?"

He looked up, his eyes red and his voice tight as he responded, "Because I love you—both."

"I know you do, but why something like this?"

Sean wiped away his tears with the back of his hand. His guise was one of distress. "You need this, and I wanted to do something real for you."

Billy patted Sean's arm. "Sean, you've always been there for us; from the day you came to stay with us, everything you've done has been real."

Sean clearly struggled to find the words as he squeezed his eyelids closed and continued to breathe in short breaths. "I've always tried so hard to please you—to never disappoint you."

Mary held his other hand. "Sean, you never have. You've been a joy and a blessing to have after—"

Sean's forehead tightened as he opened his eyes to look at her. "After Patrick?"

She nodded.

"After Patrick. I never experienced a dad or mom—being wanted. I felt as if I really had a chance to have a home and parents who loved me."

Billy said, "We do. This is your home."

Sean shook his head. "I know you gave me more than I deserved, and I expected too much. I was a placeholder for Patrick, but I would never be a replacement. I could never be your son. I was here to fill a void that couldn't be filled. I tried hard to fill it—I tried so hard! I just couldn't do it."

Mary took his hand. "Sean, we love you. We always have. You've been a blessing to us."

"I've always thought of you as my mother and father, but I'm not your son—I can never be Patrick or fill his place. I was never good enough, and I know that deep down. I know I'm not good enough to be wanted and loved, and that's why I'll never be good enough for someone like Jenny either," replied Sean, his voice high with strain.

Billy put his arm around Sean's shoulder. "Don't say that. You're more than good enough. You are a gift to us, and a man like I've never known."

Sean strained against Billy's hold and tried to pull away. "No. I can try all my life, and I'll never be the man you are. You're not only my hero but a true hero and a great man. Mary knows this, and I know it. Everyone knows this, so why not be honest about it? I'm not the man you say I am."

Billy stood up and paced, staring at Mary for some guidance. He didn't want to go here, but Sean was slipping into the abyss of self-rejection and lack of self-worth. He looked for it through the approval of others his entire life. "Sean, no one is as great as they seem on the outside. I've come to realize that I'm a flawed and imperfect man in so many ways that I hide it from everyone. Paddie needed me as a father. He needed me to be there for him, and I let him down, not once but every day and night. I was never there when he needed me, never the father and mentor he craved, and—" Billy breathed in deeply as he ran his hand across his mouth. "And probably the reason he felt hopeless and took his own life." He put his hand on Mary's shoulder and squeezed it tightly.

Sean turned his head toward Billy. "No, you're not."

"It's kind of you to say, but it's true. I've known it for such a long time. He deserved to live and be loved by his father, and I let him down. He is dead! Because of me! I'm the cause of his death!" Billy shouted.

"No, you're not."

"You weren't there!"

"But someone was."

Chapter 26

Billy fell back into his chair. Mentally, he couldn't go back into that room with Patrick, but what did Sean mean? What did he know? Billy rubbed his temples and tried not to get sucked in.

Mary turned to Sean. "What are you trying to tell us?"

Fear filled Billy's eyes as he lifted his head. "He's trying to save me from the truth, but he knows in his heart that I let Paddie down. He knows Paddie would still be with us if I had been there. He only wants to save me from my shame."

Mary lifted her hand. "Let him tell us what he has to say. Sean, what is it?"

Sean rubbed his mouth as he seemed to search for the words. "I know how much you both loved and adored Patrick. I wish I'd have had that. I know it's painful to think about him and how he died, but—"

"Sean, don't worry, just tell us what you know," pleaded Mary.

"Kenny was there."

"Kenny was where?"

"Kenny was in the room when Patrick died."

Billy's head shot up. "What?"

"I started to tell you this at Carson Beach, but it was too much. I didn't want you to go through that pain again, but you have to stop blaming and torturing yourself. You have to stop."

"Stop? This isn't somethin' you can wish away!" shouted Billy.

"I'm not asking you to wish away the truth. I'm asking you to listen to it!"

Mary put her hand on Sean's shoulder and said to Billy, "Please, let him talk. Listen to what he has to say."

Sean leaned forward, pressing his lip to his hands, and closed his eyes a moment before taking several deep breaths. "Patrick asked Kenny to come to the house that day when you were both out. Patrick didn't die because you let him down or because he thought you didn't love him—very much the opposite. He loved and admired both of you. You were more important to him than his own life. He didn't die because he was depressed or because of anything you did. It was just the opposite. I can't watch you blame yourself any longer."

Billy ran his hand through his graying hair. "What do you mean? How do you know any of this?"

"Kenny told me the whole story. He broke down telling it because he feels responsible."

"Why would he tell you this?"

Sean replied, "When I stopped Kenny and threatened to bring him in, he pleaded for me not to. I told you that we talked for quite a while about his problems in life and then how he met Patrick at school, played basketball with him, studied with him, and they became best friends. I think he knew who I was and needed to show a connection to avoid being arrested during parole. When he started getting into the stuff his brother Kyle was involving them in, I pushed back a bit. I couldn't imagine the Patrick you described getting caught up in any gang-related stuff. When he talked about the day he and Patrick were in the car during that drive-by shooting, I didn't know where he was going, and I pressed him some more."

"What are you trying to say?" pleaded Billy.

"Patrick was under a lot of pressure after the shooting, but he didn't kill himself. He couldn't."

Billy furrowed his brow. "Sean, he left a note. He held my gun. Why are you doin' this?"

Sean turned to Billy. "He didn't do it."

Mary interrupted, "Who are you saying did it?"

Billy was silent. He was taking in the cryptic information Sean was relaying. *If Paddie didn't pull the trigger, who did? Kenny was there.* Anger rushed through him. Anxiety turned to panic as he tried to process what Sean was saying.

Mary eyed him. "Billy, what are you thinking?"

Billy stood up. He didn't respond to her but walked directly into the bedroom. For some reason, he had kept the gun that took his son's life and pulled it out of a box. He loaded it. He came out of the bedroom and grabbed his jacket.

"Billy! Where are you going?"

The door slammed shut.

* * * *

Sean shot up, wincing as the dressings pulled. He peered out the window and saw his partner driving away in the squad car. "I shouldn't have said anything. I'm so sorry. I've never seen him like this."

Mary paced in agitation. "We've got to stop him from doing anything stupid."

"Oh, no. Have you seen this side of him?"

Glaring, Mary replied, "This is not good."

Sean tried to think.

Mary said, "Father Tom is just around the corner. He has a car. Let me call him."

Within minutes, Tom was in front of their apartment with Angelo. Sean slid into the back seat.

"Where are we going?"

Sean gave the address, and they headed to Kenny Green's apartment next to Orchard Park.

"What is going on, exactly?" asked Tom.

Sean moved up in his seat. "I tried to tell Billy that he wasn't at fault for Patrick's death. He wouldn't believe me; he forced me to tell him that Kenny knew the truth and was there. When I told him that Patrick didn't pull the trigger to kill himself, Billy's entire demeanor changed—I've never seen him looking that angry before."

"Oh, boy," said Tom as he rounded the corner to Kenny's street and pulled in front.

They all got out and started into the apartment building, as two girls jump roping in front said, "You lookin' for Kenny too?"

Sean stopped and turned to them. "You saw him?"

"He left with a white guy. They didn't look happy."

"Which way did they go?" asked Tom.

Both girls pointed down the street.

Tom turned to Sean. "Where would he go?"

Sean replied, "I don't know." He thought for a few seconds. "There's only one place I can think of."

They jumped back into the car and drove over a mile to an overgrown field that held a handful of abandoned metal buildings known to be used as a site for drug transactions and contract killings. Sean remembered going here with Billy one time and finding the bullet-riddled body of a young man tied to a chair. He had obviously been tortured for information by one of the gangs and then left for dead. Sean never knew if they had killed him because they got what they needed or because he wouldn't cooperate. Billy had said it reminded him of men they found in Vietnam in similar circumstances, brutally tortured and then killed.

Sean's hand shot out as he pointed to the squad car, and Tom slowed down, pulling alongside it. No sign of Billy or Kenny. On foot, they approached the first of several buildings and found no sign, the same with the next and the next. They stopped at the smallest of the buildings with faded blue paint and years of rust on the roof and corners. They heard voices behind a corrugated metal door. "You don't want to know this," sounded one voice.

Sean pictured Kenny cuffed to the rusted metal chair they had found the dead man chained to and Billy holding the loaded gun to Kenny's head.

Sean tried to pull open the door, but it was locked in place. Tom and Angelo searched for another opening or a window, but none existed.

Billy's voice rose. "I want to know every single thing!"

Sean yelled through the opening. "Billy, don't do anything you'll regret!"

"Stay out of this, Sean!" bellowed back Billy.

"Father Tom and Angelo are here as well."

"Why don't the three of you get back in the car and let me take care of this?" Billy turned to Kenny. "Tell me what happened, and don't lie."

Kenny's voice was shaking. "Mr. Quinn, I loved your son. He was the best thing to ever happen to me—ever. I'm sorry for everything that happened. Please don't shoot me."

"I don't care how sorry you are. I want to know the truth, or this goes off!" snapped Billy.

Kenny stammered, "Okay, okay. My brother Kyle didn't want me hanging around with Patrick. He ragged on us constantly and even got us involved with things that we didn't want to take part in—robbery, drugs. Patrick never did any of that stuff. He was more than a good kid and friend. I didn't know my brother was going to be involved in a drive-by with the Cardinals that night. Patrick and I were in the back of the car when we drove up to Lenox Street, and Kyle pulled out a shotgun. I never saw it, but Patrick realized what was happening, and he reached forward to pull the gun from Kyle's hands as it went off, killing the Cardinal's gang leader. I panicked and dropped down. The other Cardinals saw Patrick's white face in the car with his hand on the gun."

Sean heard no response from Billy as Kenny pleaded with pain, "I'm so sorry! From that night on, Patrick was a marked man. The Cardinals wanted retribution."

"Oh, my Lord."

"I can stop. I'm sorry," Kenny cried.

Sean, Tom, and Angelo continued banging on the metal door and shouting.

"No. I need to hear everything," demanded Billy.

"They put a bounty out for my brother Kyle—and Patrick. They wanted them dead. Patrick didn't want you and Mrs. Quinn to know he'd been hanging out with the Blazer's gang and mixed up with their activities, never mind a drive-by shooting. He was frightened and depressed that there was no way out. Patrick did a good job of avoiding being seen by anyone from the gang. He went to school early and stayed late to avoid being vulnerable. He didn't want to be caught going home. When the Cardinals finally took out my brother by knifing him in a game at the Ramsay Park courts, Patrick became even more frightened and felt hopeless. He thought it was time to go to you, but I told him I was picked up by some of the Cardinals, including their new leader. I had never been so frightened in my life. They told me I was a dead man if I didn't bring Patrick in."

Billy yelled, "What? Is that what this is? Don't tell me you took him to them?"

"No. Patrick was my best friend, my brother. He stayed out of sight and didn't go home where they could find him. I was picked up again, and they convinced me more than ever that they would kill me if I didn't take out Patrick—and they upped the ante."

"What did that mean?"

"If I didn't kill Patrick, then they would kill my mother, and—" Kenny paused for several seconds.

"And what?" asked Billy as he held the gun up a little higher.

"They told me to tell Patrick that both you and Mary would be taken out in the most brutal way if he didn't submit to me killing him and delivering this retribution. The Cardinals said there were no other options."

"What did you tell Patrick?"

"I told him everything. If Patrick informed the police, you and Mary would be dead. If I didn't take him out, you, Mary, and my mother would be killed. There was no negotiating. This is when Patrick began to feel the most hopeless and felt he had literally no way out. He couldn't bear the thought of losing you and being the cause of your deaths. He told me that everything could be solved only with suicide."

"He killed himself to save Mary and me? Why didn't he come to me? Why didn't *you* come to us? Why?" stuttered Billy.

"I wanted to, but then, no matter what, someone would then kill you. He didn't feel like you were safe if he came to you. He thought the only possible way you and Mrs. Quinn would be safe was if he was dead, and it had to be at my hand."

"What?"

"That was the condition. I told Patrick that I couldn't do it. He had a note on the bureau, and Patrick sat in his room with me. I didn't know that Patrick even had a gun. He sat and held it under his own chin for the longest time. He said he couldn't do it. He couldn't pull the trigger, and I'd have to do it to save his parents. I told him I couldn't do it, and then Patrick said they would kill my mother if I didn't."

Sean stared at the closed door, frozen with tension as he listened to Billy pacing back and forth. They all felt as if they were in the room with Patrick and Kenny, getting closer to the moment that had terrified and haunted Billy for years. Finding Patrick's lifeless body in a pool of blood had been traumatic enough with no way of comprehending what had happened—

only the note. Sean, Tom, and Angelo continued to bang on the metal doors from the outside, pleading with Billy to open the door.

Billy yelled at Kenny, "What are you sayin'? I don't understand what you're tellin' me!"

"I felt panicked. I told him I could never kill him. He screamed at me, 'You have to save your mother and my parents! You have to do it!"

Billy screamed, "You're not tellin' me what happened!"

Sean, Tom, and Angelo hollered desperately through the metal door, "Billy, don't do anything stupid! Let us in! Let us in!"

Through the small opening of the door, Sean could see Billy place the same gun that had ended Patrick's life under Kenny's chin, pressing it painfully against it.

Billy screamed, "This is loaded. If you don't tell me the truth, I swear to God I'll pull this trigger. Patrick held this gun to his head just like this, and what happened?!"

Kenny's body twisted as he tried to wiggle free.

Sean banged his fists on the metal door. "Billy!"

Billy pushed him down and pressed the gun harder. "Tell me!"

"You don't want to know!" screamed Kenny.

"Did he pull this trigger?"

Kenny shook his head.

"If you don't tell me what happened, it will be the last bad decision you'll ever make."

Just then, he cocked back the gun hammer, making a loud *chak-chak* sound, and Kenny screamed, "I don't know! Something snapped. There was a loud blast, and Patrick collapsed to the floor." Tears were rolling down his cheeks.

Sean was screaming a the top of his lungs. "Billy! Don't do this!"

Billy kept his eyes on Kenny, squeezing on the back of his neck. "Who pulled the trigger?!"

Sean, Tom, and Angelo could hear Kenny yell out loud, "I did!" and immediately, there was the piercing sound of a loud gun blast and a thud. An eerie silence followed.

Angelo had disappeared moments before and then waved to Sean and Tom from the corner. He found a side access they were able to pry open, letting the late afternoon sunlight into this dark and deserted tin can of an abandoned garage.

The rays of the sun almost reached Kenny's body as he lay on the ground, handcuffed to the tipped-over chair. Billy sat motionless on the ground next to him, barely holding onto the gun that had just been discharged. Painfully, they stood in horror at the sight, the man in shock who had been through so much and the young man now laying on the dirt floor.

Sean stepped toward Billy and put his hand on his shoulder as he leaned down to pull the warm gun from his loose grasp.

Chapter 27

Strong arms helped Billy to his feet and out the opening into the sunlight. Billy felt dazed as he ambled in with Sean holding his arm.

"It was never your fault," said Sean. "Patrick loved you so much; he was willing to die for you, not because of you."

Billy was still letting his pounding heart settle and his breathing ease as he remained distant and silent. His feelings of anger and rage were now more of numbness and confusion. All these years of his self-imposed prison cell of guilt and shame should've been more about mourning and honoring his only son, who sacrificed himself for love alone. Patrick had never lost the meaning of life; he had cherished it. He hadn't killed himself, but he had been willing to do whatever it took to safeguard the lives of his parents. Billy didn't know which apostle wrote it, but all he could think of was what Jesus said: *This is my commandment, that you love one another as I have loved you. Greater love has no one than this, that one lay down his life for his friends.*

Tears rolled down his cheeks as he said softly, "That was my son."

"Billy, what did you say?"

Before Billy could respond, Tom came running out of the building and reached Sean's side. "He didn't shoot him."

"Patrick?"

"No, Billy didn't shoot Kenny. He must have pulled the gun away at the last minute, thank God. Kenny probably fainted or hit his head as he fell, but he's okay. Angelo is taking care of him."

Sean closed his eyes, and tears rolled out. "Thank you. Can you watch Billy?"

Sean disappeared into the building as Tom put his arm around Billy. "Are you okay, Billy?"

Billy gazed up, his body shaking. "He didn't commit suicide."

"I know."

The inside of his chest filled with the sensation of grief and loss. "I miss him." Tears came streaming faster. "I miss him so much."

Tom nodded, grief in his eyes. "I know you do. Maybe you can let him rest now in your heart, knowing he has always loved you."

"I don't know what to do. I wanted to kill that man in there. I wanted him to pay for what he did to Paddie—and Mary—and me. I almost did. What do I do now?"

"I couldn't hear everything, but from what I did, I didn't hear someone who hated your son. I think he loved him. I think he's been suffering with the pain of this for a long time."

Billy turned to Tom. "You want me to forgive him?"

Tom shrugged. "God wants you to forgive him, and my guess is that Patrick already has. They were friends in an impossible situation. I think the intense emotions of the moment were overwhelming. I don't think he meant to do anything but end your son's painful dilemma and panicked. I can't tell you what to do, but I don't believe hate will help you, Mary, or Patrick."

They both turned as Angelo held back the opening to the metal garage, and Sean came out with Kenny by his side. As they approached, thoughts ran through Billy's head faster than he could process them. Was this man the killer of his son? Or was he a true friend that got caught up in an impossible situation? Kenny had said he was sorry over and over and wanted to make amends for Patrick's death. Billy could see the dirt from the fall on one side of Kenny's face. One part of him wanted to reach up to wipe it off, and the other part wanted to belt him with his clenched fist.

The five of them stood in the abandoned parking area with spotted brown grass and weeds growing through the cracks of the broken tar. No one was talking.

Tom's eyes moved from one person to another. "So, what's going to happen next?"

All eyes turned to Billy. He took a few steps toward Kenny, thinking for several moments, and then reached out for Kenny's arm. With fear in his eyes, Kenny jerked away, but Billy turned him and started to unlock the handcuffs that had torn his skin during his struggle. Once Kenny's hands were free, Billy held the cuffs and the key by his side. No one knew what was going to happen next, not even Billy. They stood in a semi-circle, each wondering about the possible directions this could play out.

Finally, Billy said, "Angelo, can you take Sean and Kenny back? I need to talk to Mary."

Angelo nodded. "Sure. I love the idea of taking a police officer for a ride instead of the other way around."

Back at the house, it was obvious that Mary had been frantic, not knowing what was transpiring. She approached Billy and offered him an embrace. "Are you okay?"

"I'm workin' on it."

Billy and Tom sat in the living room and told Mary the story Kenny had shared. As it did for Billy, it brought up an avalanche of buried feelings and emotions—relief on one hand and the emotional pain of Patrick's gruesome death on the other.

"What are we going to do?" asked Mary. "What do we do?"

Tom said, "Tom said, "This is no small thing you've just found out. It would be almost impossible to sort it out emotionally and mentally against what you have believed or wondered all these years. Patrick was so young and faced with something that seemed like an impossible situation. I think he knew it wasn't right to take any life—including his own, but he must have honestly believed there was no alternative. Even if the answer was wrong, I think his resolve to love and honor his parents, to put the lives of the two people he loved most ahead of his own, was more than admirable. I'd be very proud to have a son like him, and I'm sure he remains very proud of both of you."

Mary nodded, but Billy's face tightened as he held in the tears. He stared at the floor.

Mary reached over to hug him. "We have to let him be with God."

Billy continued to shake. "I know that, but I know he can't be proud of me. You can't be proud of me!"

"What are you talking about? I have every reason to be proud of my husband. Everyone is," responded Mary as she rubbed his back.

Tom shifted on the sofa. "Everyone except for Billy."

Mary sat up. "What?" She turned to Billy. "What does he mean?"

Billy remained silent.

Mary turned to Tom. "What do you mean by that?"

Tom replied, "Mary, do you feel as if you see all of Billy? Or have you felt as if there were walls up? Places you weren't let into?"

"I'll admit there are places where he seems more sensitive. I think we all have that, though—we want to protect ourselves."

Tom asked, "From what? Protect ourselves from what?"

Mary placed her palms on the table and thought. "I don't know. I guess from things we're afraid of."

"What would we be afraid of?" asked Tom.

"In the end, I guess being rejected," replied Mary. "Who would reject Billy?"

Billy lifted his head. "You would have to reject me! Patrick would reject a fraud! Everyone would reject a fraud, a phony, a coward, an absent father, and a selfish son!"

"What? You are none of those things. Billy, how long have you felt this way?"

Billy didn't respond.

Tom spoke up. "I think he has been feeling this way his entire life, fearing that love is not greater than his faults, that he has been disappointing the people closest to him."

"Billy, is this true? Don't you trust how much I love you? You've never disappointed me."

Tom patted Billy's shoulder in affirmation.

Billy tensed, even though he knew that Tom had never shown any negative judgment or change in affection after Billy had emotionally opened up all of his darkest secrets. Billy wanted to express his thoughts but couldn't get any words out.

"You do trust me, don't you?" asked Mary.

"It's not about me trustin' you."

"Of course it is. You should be able to share anything with me and know that I'll love you."

"Mary, you love the man you think I am. I'm not him. How can you love a fraud?"

"What are you talking about?"

Billy glanced at Tom, who simply nodded with encouragement. Then he looked directly into Mary's eyes. She didn't look as if she would run away, nor did it look as if she would let him do that either. "Mary, you've always called me your hero. I'm no hero."

"You are to me."

"You know how much my mom struggled and needed me to step up. She told me she needed me, and I did nothin' but let her down. I was a selfish and constant burden to her."

Mary tilted her head and gave Billy a gaze of compassion. "And you were a young boy with no father and no mentor to help you be that man. You can regret that you weren't perfect, but all we can ever do is love those we are with now."

Billy replied, "I know. I would have said the same to Patrick, but that isn't all. I was never a hero in the war. I hesitated and let Jimmy die. I didn't protect him. I froze and was a coward. He ran ahead, and I watched him die. My little brother."

Mary let out a compassionate sigh and hugged Billy. "I know it was so tough to lose your brother during that horrible war. I talked with two of the men who were there with you. Sam Bickel and Rizzo something—oh, Russo. Tony Russo. They told me how torn up you were and how you blamed yourself. They said it was nothing like that. Tony told me that Jimmy had jumped the orders, and Sam had held you back as you tried to pull away. Once the orders were shouted out, you had charged ahead, but Jimmy was too exposed and had gotten shot. There was nothing you could have done. They all said how courageous you were. Even if you weren't, I wouldn't love you any less. You are my hero. I wish I had met and known your brother. You always kept his memory with honor and dignity."

Tom nodded. "And you have blamed yourself for Patrick's death all these years. It was never your fault. You were a good dad to a proud son. What happened was wrong, but he loved others more than his own life. We're not perfect people. We fail at times, but we have to forgive ourselves so that we can love others and give them ourselves as God sees us, not in our harsh self-judgment and rejection. We cheat our loved ones when we do that. We hold back and give them less. Mary loves you—all of you, the real Billy Quinn. No shame, no guilt, no fraud—you. That is the gift you have to give, so don't short-change her."

Billy turned to Mary, who was now crying enough to flood the Charles River. He stood up and took her hand, helping her to stand, and gave her a long embrace with all of his being. "I don't know if I can process all of this. I think he's sayin' that I've been cheatin' you all these years. You don't deserve to be cheated."

Mary wiped her eyes as she continued to hug him. "I want all of you. Warts and all. No holding back. I married all of William Patrick Quinn, and I want all of him to have and to hold, for better or worse, for richer or poorer, in sickness and in health, all—"

"All the days of my life," finished Billy as he gazed into her eyes as he had on their wedding day. He pressed his lips against hers and gave her a long and passionate kiss.

"Now that's what I've been missing. Somehow I feel closer and more proud of you than ever."

For the first time in his life, Billy felt a sense of freedom to let down his guard. Right in this room, three people knew his darkest and most feared secrets, secrets that had robbed him of peace of mind, joy, intimate relationships, and much of life itself. Suddenly, all the pressure of hiding himself and avoiding dealing with it began to melt away. He felt a sense of freedom. For the first time in his life, he felt love—because he knew it was him they were loving and not a false notion of him. If Patrick were here with them, Billy thought maybe he would have even looked up to him and admired him, but, at the moment, knowing that Mary's love was enough.

Tom cleared his throat. "Should I be leaving?"

Mary laughed. "No, Father Tom. It's just nice knowing I might have my whole husband with me now."

Billy fell silent.

"Billy, is there more? What is going on in there?"

"Mary, now is good, but I want you for many years to come. You still need that operation."

"I know, and that is what I want too, but I've thought a lot about it, and I don't think I can do it." She glanced at Billy and then Tom.

Billy sighed. "He knows about Kenny and Sean."

"Okay, then, Father Tom. You know why I can't take that money. It wouldn't be right, and I don't want to make believe it would."

Billy riveted on his friend. "Father Tom, this is her life. Her life has to be worth more than money. Right?"

Tom replied, "There are a lot of very difficult things that happen in life. It's never right to do something wrong to achieve what we think is a higher end. The ends can't justify the means. I know this is an awful answer for you to hear, but Mary's soul and your soul are more important."

"More important than Mary's life?" shot back Billy.

"More important than all our lives," said Mary. "I think we need to trust and pray."

"We've been doin' that for years now. What has it gotten us?"

"Years together. This moment. Being together for eternity and seeing Paddie again."

Tom approached Billy. "Mary knows how much you care, how difficult this is. We talked for hours, and she doesn't take your feelings lightly. She struggles to be fair to you, knowing how she feels about it. She knows how *you* feel. It's important to know how *she* feels too."

Billy sat and contemplated his wife. "I don't understand it. I can't bear to see you suffer, to lose you, or to see you die. I couldn't bear to see you not doin' what you know is right, either. I get it, but I don't have to like it—" He glanced up at Tom. "I don't like it—at all."

Mary hugged him. "That means more to me than you could ever know. It really does. I have a question, though."

Tom and Billy eyed each other, not knowing what to expect. "What is that?"

"What happens to Sean? And what happens to Kenny Green?"

Billy sighed. "Sean was only trying to save you, to help. He hasn't technically done anything criminal yet."

Mary rolled her eyes. "Is that true? Coordinating insurance fraud, having a man shot, falsifying a crime? None of that sounds good."

Tom said, "If I may. You are right that what's been done was wrong, but Kenny Green could withdraw his claim for the money, telling the Gardner that he feels uncomfortable now with the source of the information. Kenny agreed to be shot, and the painting was never stolen, so there were no actual crimes. There may be a way to end up doing the right thing here."

Mary raised a brow. "You are very sly, Father. Are you sure you are in the right profession?"

Tom sighed. "I guess there's the larger question: What are you going to do about Kenny?"

Billy exhaled a long sigh. "I've been thinkin' about what you said. Part of me thinks he could never suffer enough for Paddie, but part of me thinks he's suffered enough already, including what I did to him today."

Mary's head cocked back. "What did you do to him today?"

Tom replied, "Some secrets are okay not to share. It's rare, but I think this one's okay."

Billy nodded.

Mary frowned. "I'll have to trust you two on this."

Chapter 28

Billy tossed and turned the entire night, struggling with conflicting emotions and what path he wanted to take. Mary reached over repeatedly to gently rub his back and shoulders.

He showed up early at Kenny Green's apartment door with Sean the next morning.

Kenny opened the door warily, his eyes wide with anxiety.

Billy told him to get dressed and come with them.

Kenny's knees and hands were shaking as he followed them down the worn and stale-smelling stairs to the bottom floor and out the main entrance. Although the sun had barely peeked over the horizon, people were out and watched Kenny being placed into the back of the police squad car. Heading eastbound toward the harbor and turning off on Morrissey Boulevard, Billy drove without saying a word. Kenny fidgeted as he stared out the window. Billy finally pulled off the road to an open park, got out, and opened the door for Kenny.

He pointed toward the paved path leading through the open grassed area. In the middle was a stone sculpture with two large arches and a tall stone at the center. As they got closer, they could see the letters over a gold star carved into the granite: Dorchester Vietnam Veteran's Memorial. Billy had never brought Sean here. Billy approached and ran his hand over the stone where the name *James G. Quinn, USMC,* was etched.

Billy contemplated the name. "I was shipped to Vietnam in the sixties, and my little brother followed right behind me. When I came back after two years of hell, he never did. He was the same age as you, Kenny, when you knew Paddie. There was no fanfare for me when I came home, and it took decades before we could even get his name back into his hometown. Jimmy was the most courageous, honest, and self-sacrificing man I've ever known."

A cold breeze blew off the ocean and Kenny shivered, his gaze bouncing uneasily off Billy.

Billy continued, "I don't know if he can hear me, but I still talk to him. He had a tough ride without a dad. Our mom struggled to make ends meet, and I was not the big brother I should've been." Billy finally turned to Kenny. "You've had a tough ride too, haven't ya?"

His shoulders hunched against the cold wind, Kenny attempted a shrug. "Paddie, well, Patrick, meant somethin' to you at seventeen, didn't he?"

Kenny stopped shuffling and nodded.

"I think he meant a *lot* to you, didn't he?"

Kenny said, "Yes, he did."

"You were both pretty panicked about the death threats from the Lenox Street gang, weren't you?"

"The Cardinals, yeah. They were a tough gang and had to revenge their main man. It's code, no exceptions."

Billy nodded. "Cardinals, yeah. That's what Paddie meant by 'Cardinal Sin' in his note. You told me the truth yesterday, didn't ya?"

Kenny hesitated as he ran his hand across his face.

"Patrick didn't pull that trigger."

Kenny shook his head.

"You did?" asked Billy.

Kenny's gaze jumped to the gun in Billy's holster. He closed his eyes and straightened as if readying himself for execution, hauntingly like something out of Vietnam.

"It took a lot of courage to tell me the truth, and I think you've been livin' with the pain of it for a long time now."

Kenny lifted his head, and tears were in his eyes.

"I brought you here for one reason."

Kenny squeezed his eyes shut.

Billy sighed. "I forgive you."

Kenny dropped to his knees, his body shaking, tears streaming freely. "Why?" asked Kenny.

"Because I believe you. Because my brother would want me to. Because Paddie would want me to. And because God wants me to. I forgive you." Billy stepped forward and helped Kenny to his feet.

"Your son would still be alive if he didn't hang around with me." Kenny wiped his dripping nose with the back of hand, like a kid trying to calm himself.

"I know that, but he wouldn't have been livin' his life. It was so much shorter than it should have been, but he lived it to the fullest, unselfishly, and with honesty. My brother died with honor, and so did Paddie, even if what happened was wrong. You were an important part of the life he did have. You didn't want that nightmare to happen any more than he did."

Kenny dropped his head against Billy's chest.

Billy wrapped his arm around Kenny.

They walked further down the path and sat on the beach overlooking the harbor, letting the breeze brush their faces. Weak November rays of light shone upon them. They sat in silence until Billy said, "We've got another problem to solve."

Sean asked, "What's that?"

"We ain't claiming that reward."

Kenny's eyes shut. "How can we do that? I already put in the claim and swore it was legit, totally above board. I got prison time guaranteed if I pull back now."

Billy said, "That's why I said we've got a problem to solve. Mary won't accept the money, and I agree with her."

Sean stared at him. "You didn't agree with her before."

"Yeah, well, things change. Men get smarter and more honest."

Kenny stared out at the water. "What are we going to do? We've got some other hands involved too. It's a lot of money to walk away from without a fight from them."

Sean said, "It definitely is, but if Billy says it's not happening, we've got to figure out something else."

Billy sighed. "I think you need to go to Dr. DuBois at the Gardner and tell him that you think the information you received is suspect, and you don't feel comfortable with the claim, so you're withdrawin' it."

Sean paused a moment before responding. "I'm sure that works fine for the museum and insurance company, but we still have to worry about the other guys. 'Sorry' won't work after the risk they took."

Kenny stood up. "When I told you I wanted to do something good by giving your wife the money for her operation, that was the plan, and I meant it—I want to do something good in honor of Patrick."

Sean turned toward Kenny and tilted his head to shield his eyes from the sun. "What does that mean?"

"I've got to take the hit for this," Kenny replied. "We'll tell them that the police squeezed me on another job and used it to pressure me on the insurance money. There was some rumors floating around about Reggie and Dougie coming into some money and about me getting ready to buy some new wheels. Something like that. You've got to pull them in for questioning and press them hard, stressing the point that I wouldn't rat on them but thought the source of information was suspicious. You've got to make them real nervous that they will be fingered, but it wouldn't be by me."

Sean nodded. "We could definitely do that."

Kenny continued. "I don't want to be doing any inside time, but if I can be charged and receive a suspended sentence and some community work, it might make it more believable—otherwise, those jacks will have my neck on a rope for giving up this payday."

Billy got up and extended his hand to Kenny. They shook hands and walked back to the patrol car. They drove to the station in silence.

That afternoon, Billy and Sean had Reggie and Dougie back in for intense questioning. They tramped into the interrogation room, fury in their eyes.

"What's this all about?" demanded Reggie as he shot Sean and Billy a glaring stare.

Sean tried to signal back that he was trying to help them but had his hands tied.

"We've been hearin' lots of things around town about people coming into some money," said Billy. "Did you two get big promotions lately? Funny, I don't see anythin' in your records about even bein' employed."

Reggie sneered at him. "That's crap. You gonna book us for gossip now?"

Glaring back, Billy said, "Nope. We got much more than that, but it does raise some serious concerns, don't you think?"

"We didn't do nothin', Dougie yelled. "We didn't steal nothin'. We didn't do nothin'."

Billy moved forward. "You know, they're doin' a whole lot these days with DNA from skin and sweat on things like ski masks and sweats that never made it into the fire. We got street cameras that tell us a lot about when people entered the park to play ball. And we've got the orchestrator of this caper on the ropes. I think we can get Mr. Green to talk. I guess the question is, how hard do you two want to land on this one?"

Reggie peered over at Sean. "You know, sometimes forced confessions have a way of backfiring. We didn't do anything, so we can't help you out. Is there anything else?"

Maintaining his look of confidence, Billy replied, "It's your life. You can go—for now."

* * * *

That evening Sean received a call from Kenny.

Kenny said, "Reggie and Dougie paid me a visit today. They were pretty rough with me, threatening to have me killed if I ratted them out. I told them I was under a lot of pressure to 'fess up to my role, but I would never rat out anyone from the neighborhood, even if it meant another stint in Walpole. They seemed relieved that I'd make it a condition to drop all other suspects if I pleaded guilty to attempted insurance fraud and they dropped the drug charge."

"Do you think they bought it?" Sean asked.

"So far," replied Kenny before hanging up.

Kenny showed up at the Isabella Gardner Museum with Billy the next day. Billy asked to speak with DuBois.

DuBois came out to the desk. "What is this all about? I am very busy, and we don't have your money yet, Monsieur Green."

"Dr. DuBois. Would you mind if we meet in your office?" Billy asked. "It should only take a few minutes of your time. Promise."

DuBois pursed his lips, spun on his heel, and stepped around the corner. "Follow me."

"So," he said with brow raised, "what is so urgent that it would justify interrupting my busy day?"

Billy motioned to Kenny to proceed.

Kenny said, "Doctor D."

DuBois rolled his eyes and held his breath.

"I have something to tell you."

DuBois raised his eyebrows. "The painting is not authentic! No!"

Kenny replied, "No."

"No, it is not, or no, it is? I must know which 'no.'"

"I don't know nothing about paintings. I've come to withdraw my claim for the reward."

"But if the painting is real, why?"

Kenny sighed. "I don't deserve it. I was not totally honest. You have your painting, and you should keep your money."

DuBois stood up. "You are a fraud?"

Kenny nodded. "But an honest one."

Billy smirked as DuBois paced his office. Billy stood beside Kenny and said, "Dr. DuBois, we thank you for your patience, and we will take care of everything from here. Hopefully, everything can return to normal for you."

DuBois plopped back down in his chair. "What is normal?"

As Billy and Kenny exited the museum, Kenny said, "I like that place. I might actually go to visit it someday." He glanced at Billy. "As a museum. I should take a closer look at a painting worth one-point-five million."

Billy laughed. "That was only the insurance reward. The painting itself might be worth two hundred million!"

Kenny stopped in his tracks. "What?!"

Billy took his arm to pull him along. "Don't get any ideas, Monsieur Green." He chuckled as they headed back.

Chapter 29

Sunday morning dawned sunny and warm. Billy got up and dressed before Mary.

When she got up, she hugged him. "You seem in a good mood this morning."

"Yeah? I guess I slept last night. It seems like it's been a while, doesn't it?"

Mary placed her head on his shoulder. "Yes, quite a while, indeed. Did you want to go to early Mass?"

"If you're my date, Mrs.—" Billy stopped to gaze into her eyes. "Mary. Not Mrs. Quinn, but Mary. I feel like we can get to know each other again."

"I like that, Billy. I really like that idea."

As they walked to St. Francis, footsteps trotted beside them. They turned to see Sean, one arm still in a sling.

"Out for a jog, Sean O'Donnell?"

"Hey, I didn't want to be late for Mass. Can I treat you two young lovebirds to breakfast at the Eastside afterward?"

Billy patted Sean on the back. "If you're buyin', you can take us anywhere you like."

Tom grinned at the three of them sitting in the second pew.

Billy had grabbed Tom earlier for confession. But it was obvious when Tom's brows lifted that he seemed surprised to see Sean sitting with him and Mary.

Billy absorbed the beauty of the church, seeing things he hadn't noticed before. He attended Mass every week, but he knew God was the one person from whom he couldn't hide the truth—he couldn't hide himself. He realized that he'd been going to Mass feeling a sense of shame and guilt because his true self wasn't a secret to God. Billy hadn't accepted himself, and he couldn't forgive himself. How could he? His mother, his brother, Jimmy, and his son, Paddie, couldn't forgive him. How could he forgive himself? How could God ever forgive him?

That morning he felt differently. Billy was thinking about how much energy he had spent keeping his secrets concealed to avoid being rejected. Now, others knew his secrets, and they hadn't rejected him. Surprisingly, they loved him more, not because he finally told the truth, but because they could now know and love the real him. He let them in. He trusted them, and they loved him back unconditionally, something Tom always preached that God did for us—no matter what. The truth of that love gave him a sense of great peace now that he allowed himself to finally feel it.

As he sat, he wondered if he felt better because he no longer carried the burden of his guarded secrets. Still, maybe it was because what he believed to be the unforgivable truth was not the actual truth and never unforgivable. "That's it," he inadvertently said aloud.

Mary turned from her prayers and leaned over, whispering, "What is it?"

"Oh, nothing," replied Billy, feeling surprisingly unburdened. His head felt cleared, and his heart opened. He didn't gaze up at God in shame but instead realized how loved he was.

Tom offered a special prayer intention for Mary at the Mass, which Billy nodded to.

After Mass, Tom greeted the parishioners as they exited the main entrance. As Billy, Mary, and Sean approached him, he said, "My favorite family. Good morning!"

Sean asked, "I know this is your busy day, Father Tom, but do you have a break before your next Mass? There's a free breakfast in it for you."

Tom lifted his head toward the bright blue sky. "Someone's always looking out for us. It just so happens I have a visiting priest taking the next Mass, and I would be happy to take advantage of that offer."

Sean grabbed Tom's sleeve. "Uhm, I know we undid the false report and insurance fraud, but is that still something I should go to confession with?"

Tom raised his gaze to Sean. "That is a great question. Come see me sometime, and we can talk about it if you are open to it."

Sean returned a half-smile and a nod. "Thanks. I will."

The waitress, hurried as ever, scurried past them and pointed to an open booth as they entered the Eastside Diner. She yelled out from the kitchen, "It's yours if you tip well!"

The four of them slid into the sunny booth, and soon, Linda brought over hot coffees and dropped the menus on the table. "No time for chit-chat on Sunday mornings."

Everyone laughed as they settled in and sipped their almost passable cups of coffee. "Good thing there's entertainment," said Tom as he put his cup down. "So, how is everyone today?"

They glanced at each other until Billy said, "We're good. Your guidance along the way has been appreciated."

Sean put his hand up. "Father Tom, Billy has been the man I have most admired in life. He tried to convince me that he didn't deserve my admiration, but—" Sean glanced over at Billy, a question in his eyes. Billy only shrugged in acceptance. "I don't know if Mary even knows this, but Billy looked Kenny Green in the eye and forgave him, really forgave him."

Tom nodded.

"I didn't know I was goin' to do that," Billy said after a sip of coffee. "It just seemed like the right thing to do."

Mary put her arm around him. "That couldn't have been easy."

Billy said, "You know, I asked Paddie what he wanted. It felt much more natural than all the fear, anger, and resentment I've been holding onto, mostly against myself—and I felt it was what he wanted me to do."

Tom lifted his cup in the gesture of a toast. "And you've forgiven yourself?"

Billy tapped his cup against Tom's. "Workin' on it. And you?"

Tom nodded. "Working on it."

Billy and Sean shared all the things that happened during the past few days that Tom and Mary didn't know. Afterward, Tom said, "You know what the greatest gift is here?"

"What?" asked Billy.

"You."

Billy laughed. "Me? What are you talkin' about?"

"All these years, you've been cheating every one of *you*. You believed things about yourself that weren't true and hid yourself in shame. You never let Mary or Sean or your friends have access to all of you, the wonderfully made Billy Quinn. God gives us something special, and we give it away in our self-gift to others. In that act is where you find love, joy, and freedom."

"Hey, I might feel a little freer, but I'm not conceited enough to think of myself as a gift."

Tom pointed to Mary and Sean. "Do you think they're worth it? Don't you think I'm worth it?"

Billy gave a lighthearted laugh. "Maybe them. You need to step up your prayers for Mary to earn your spot."

Tom gazed fondly upon Mary. "That's a deal. I have lots of hope."

"Thanks. We appreciate your friendship and prayers, too," said Billy.

Mary set down her mug. "Well, I, for one, am looking forward to getting to know my husband better. I do have one request, though. I'd like to do something we should've done a long time ago."

Sean said, "What is it, Mary?"

Mary took Billy's hand. "Billy and I didn't have to talk about this very long to both agree. We're just hoping you'll agree. You've never been a placeholder for Patrick, and you have been a blessing to us every single day. I'm not sure we would have survived without you, but we loved you for you."

Billy added, "You've been our son since the day you walked into our home and our hearts. I'm so sorry for being so caught up in myself that I didn't make that clear, but you're our family. What we're asking is, would you let us adopt you as our son?"

Mary brushed away a tear. "If you want to, it would mean a great deal to me and Billy."

Sean sat, stunned and silent.

Tom patted him on the back. "You didn't see that coming, did you?"

"Are you serious? Of course, I would. Can I call you Mom?"

Mary nodded as they slid out of the booth and hugged. She kissed him on the cheek and said, "I love you, Sean. Thank you so much."

Billy hugged Sean next as Linda returned with their plates of eggs, crispy bacon, pumpkin pancakes, and home fries. "This huggin' stuff is a fire hazard, you know," she said as she rolled her eyes and covered the table with the hot plates.

Tom stood in front of her with his arms open.

"Go hug a tree or somethin'. Can't you see how busy I am?"

Everyone in the café laughed as Tom slid back into his booth, and they returned to eating their breakfast and engaged in a fun conversation.

When Billy glanced over at Mary, he could tell that she seemed happier than he had seen her in a long time. He smiled back as she caught his loving glance.

Chapter 30

Over the next several weeks, life seemed to take on a comfortable rhythm for Billy and Mary. They felt closer as friends and more in love as a married couple. They shared the ups and downs of each day, residual, sometimes haunting, memories, and their concerns about her future health.

Jenny started coming over regularly for Sunday dinner with Sean, who felt proud to share his adopted family, expressing his greater self-confidence.

While Kenny awaited the court's decision, Billy and Sean kept in touch with him and tried to find him a job so he could take a better path. On one of their visits to Kenny's apartment, they noticed drawings out on the kitchen table.

"Did you do these?" asked Billy.

Kenny nodded.

"I'm no expert, but these are really good. Did you always have this talent?"

"I don't know. I've always liked doing it. It takes me out of here while I'm doing it. Patrick was *really* good," replied Kenny.

Billy said, "I remember. If you could use this talent in a job, would you be interested?"

"I guess."

"I know a company that does art and graphic design work for customers lookin' for advertisement, logos, and other design work. I was talkin' with one of the owners a few weeks back, and she said they're always lookin' for people with natural talent and imagination. It's worth a try."

Kenny laughed nervously. "I don't know if I'm good enough for that."

Sean said, "I'm learning to give myself a chance. Nothing to lose, right?"

Kenny shrugged. "Rejection can be rough when we don't have enough cookies to give up."

"I get it," Sean replied, "but sometimes I think we're way too hard on ourselves to avoid risking rejection and then life itself. At least, that's what I hear."

Kenny nodded with a look that showed wheels turning in his mind. "Huh."

A week later, Billy had set up an interview for Kenny. Impressed with his skill, the company said they would take a chance on him at the start of the new year.

Billy could hardly believe Christmas was only four days away. Billy and Mary had been invited to a neighborhood party the Saturday night before Christmas. The house was a few doors down and festively decked out for the holiday. When they arrived, it was already filled with friends and neighbors, most of whom they had known for years. The atmosphere was packed with energy and cheer as lively conversation and laughter filled every room.

Raising his glass, Tom made his way to the front door. "Merry Christmas, Quinns! It's good to see you both. How have you been?"

The two shook each other's hands. Billy said, "Merry Christmas, Father Tom. We've been doin' more than well. I wanted to thank you for all your listening and wisdom. I don't know if I would've figured things out or had the sense to take a chance."

Tom leaned in. "I don't think I heard but every other word, but I got the gist. I'm very happy for you. How has Mary been feeling?"

Billy reached out for Mary's hand as she was saying hello to friends. He tugged, and she extracted herself. "Father Tom, Happy Christmas. It's so nice to see you out having a good time."

Tom hugged her and glanced at Billy, sensing something wasn't completely right. "How are you feeling, Mary?"

"A little more tired lately, but it's been a busy time. I'll be fine," replied Mary.

After chatting for a bit, Billy and Mary excused themselves to thank the Clearys for inviting them. As they strolled home with Tom, Mary stumbled, ready to collapse. Billy was holding her arm and kept her from falling. He turned and shot a concerned look to Tom.

With gentle concern, Tom assisted Billy and Mary the rest of the way home.

On Monday morning, Mary got up later than usual.

In the kitchen, Billy said, "You've been getting more tired lately, Mary."

"I know. It comes and goes. My system's been off, and I've been feeling a bit cold and dizzy," replied Mary as she lowered herself into her soft reading chair.

Billy crouched down next to her. "Tell me the truth, have you had any coloration in your pee?"

Wincing, Mary nodded.

"I'm taking you in for a check."

Mary shook her head, but Billy held up his hand. Then he called the doctor and arranged to go to Boston Medical for specialized tests.

As Billy sat in the waiting room, Sean showed up and sat next to him. "How is Mom?"

Billy shrugged. "I don't know. It's been hours, and she's sleeping now. They said to go home and come back in three or four hours. I don't want to lose any time with her."

Sean rested his hand on Billy's arm. "Why don't we get some fresh air while we're waiting. Maybe it'll help pass the time, and we can find out what they know. I'll give them your number in case anything comes up. What do you say?"

Billy thought for several seconds. He felt disoriented, and maybe Sean was right about getting some air. As they stepped into the brisk wind and walked, Billy grew more panicky. "I think I need to go back."

"I know how you feel, but sitting in the waiting room will drive you crazy."

Billy sighed. He didn't know what to do with his anxious energy. If he couldn't be with Mary, he suddenly felt as if he needed to be somewhere. "Do you have your car?"

Sean looked confused. "Sure, why?"

When they got in the car, Billy said, "Head down to Blue Hill Ave and take Legion Road."

Following Billy's directions, Sean stopped the car at the entrance to the Mount Calvary Cemetery. "Why are we here?"

Billy got out of the car, made his way down the path, and stopped in front of one stone. Sean approached him from behind, seeing, for the first time, the stone for Patrick's grave. The stone was an attractive granite with the Celtic cross engraved above the inscription: *Patrick William Quinn, Born: June 17, 1975, Died: August 15, 1992.*

They stood in silence for several minutes before Sean said, "I've never seen where he was buried."

"I've tried to come here, but I couldn't get myself to do it. For some reason, I needed to see him today. Mary and I always intended to put an inscription below his name, but we could never agree on what to say."

Sean said, "Maybe you weren't supposed to put one on until you knew the truth about his story?"

Billy nodded. "Maybe."

"I think what Father Tom said might be the right thing to add. *Greater love has no one than this—that someone lay down his life for his friends.*"

A tear rolled down Billy's cheek. "Yes. I've been so afraid of losing Mary too." There were no stones, but the plots next to Patrick's grave were for Billy and Mary.

"Me too. I think about it every day. I'm glad you brought me here, though. I feel more of a connection to him."

Billy continued staring down. "Sean, think of Paddie as the brother you never met. I lost my brother, and so did you."

"I like that. We've got to stick together and do what we can for Mom."

Billy knelt down and touched Partick's name, and slowly stood up. "Thanks. I think I'm ready to go back."

When they returned to the hospital, Billy asked the nurse at the desk if there were any updates and when he could see Mary. The nurse waved at the doctor coming down the hallway. "Dr. Hanson was asking for you, Mr. Quinn."

Dr. Hank Hanson had been caring for Mary for several years and approached Billy. "Mr. Quinn, how have you been holding up?" The doctor was tall and thin as a rail but very good at his job and always thoughtful in his interactions.

"I'm not worried about me."

"You never are. Why don't we go into the visitor's room to talk? Is this Sean?"

Sean extended his hand. "Sean O'Donnell. How did you know?"

"Mary's been talking about her family. Good to meet you. Let's sit in here," replied Dr. Hanson.

Billy sat nervously on the orange cloth-covered couch with Sean. The doctor sat across the coffee table from them. "Mary is feeling better now. We did more tests, and her kidney and liver aren't doing well. I was dismayed at the progression."

Billy started shaking his head. "So, what do we do?"

"I know we discussed dialysis treatment some time ago, but I feel we are in a different place now."

"What are you saying?"

Dr. Hanson sat forward in his chair. "We are in a tough place. I think the best answer would be for a double transplant. While there can be complications, she's actually in strong health if it weren't for issues with these particular organs."

Billy said, "Even if we could find a half-million to pay for the cost of the transplant, you said it would take a long time on the waiting list to even be eligible."

Dr. Hanson said, "Well, I put her on the list a while ago, so hopefully, that will improve her place. We would just need a donor match over the next six months and—"

Dr. Hanson turned to the door to see someone standing at the entrance.

"Sorry to interrupt," said Tom. "I wanted to see how Mary was doing. I couldn't help overhearing."

Billy waved Tom in. "No apologies. You're family too. Dr. Hanson is tellin' us that Mary needs that transplant operation. I think we're goin' to need more than prayers at this point."

Dr. Hanson stood up to shake Tom's hand. "We still have more tests to run, but you can all go in and see her. Her spirits are good."

When Mary saw her three favorite men at the door, she grinned. "This is quite a sight. The three musketeers are coming to save me."

"Better than The Three Stooges." Tom laughed. "How are you?"

Mary sat up. "Room service is pretty good, but I miss my man here."

She took Billy's hand.

He kissed her cheek. "This is no place to spend your Christmas Eve either. The doctor said you can go home after a few more tests if you take it easy."

Mary frowned. "I'd so like to go to Mass on Christmas Eve."

Tom said, "It would be nice, but you'll be there in spirit."

Mary nodded.

The apartment was adorned for a cozy Christmas evening. Mary always took the time to decorate for each holiday, but Christmas was her favorite. She agreed to take it easy on the couch as Billy checked the roast, lit the pine-scented candles, and put the angel on the tree before flipping the switch to light to tree. Sean and Jenny arrived early to help out, and they sat together in the living room, drinking mulled cider and sharing memories of favorite Christmas traditions and events.

She raised her mug. "To Sean and Jenny. May you enjoy each other's company for years to come and share a wonderful Christmas."

Jenny grinned and raised her glass. "I already am, and here's to you, Mary, the most wonderful, sincere, and beautiful woman I know—and many years of life and love to come."

Everyone quietly drank to that. After a tasty dinner fit for a Christmas celebration, they sat around the tree and exchanged a few gifts, laughs, and a feeling of family. Billy could tell that Mary was happy with the evening and the small gathering—then there was a knock at the door.

When Billy opened the door, Tom and Angelo were standing behind several singers from the children's choir, caroling, "Hark! The Herald Angels Sing." After a rousing finale, the kids tromped inside for some cookies, sang a few more songs that Mary loved, and headed back to their homes as everyone thanked them.

Tom lifted a case he'd brought in. "Since Mary couldn't come to Christmas Eve Mass, I thought I'd offer to celebrate Mass here."

Mary's eyes brightened, and everyone nodded. Angelo set up a small table, and Tom put out a candle, water, wine, and a metal container with the Communion hosts. He hung a white-and-gold stole around his neck.

* * * *

Billy caught Mary's smile as she spotted the Christmas stable that she had stitched onto the stole and presented as a gift to Tom when he first arrived at St. Francis years ago. The intimacy of the Mass readings, prayers, homily, and sharing of Holy Communion in their living room lit only by the glow of the Christmas tree was moving.

Afterward, Billy watched Jenny approach Tom. "I liked that very much. I've felt like something's been missing in my faith, and I felt it tonight. Thank you."

Tom smiled. "My honor to share Christ himself with some of the nicest people I know. What better night for it?"

Tom and Angelo stayed for several more hours as everyone enjoyed the spirit of the night and the warmth of the company. As large snowflakes began to fall outside the window in the light of old street lamps, Tom said, "I think that's our cue, Angelo. Let's load up the sled and deliver those gifts."

Jenny asked Angelo, "Is he serious?"

Angelo shrugged. "Sort of. We are taking some presents over to the sisters and then heading to bed for early morning Masses and a whole lot of people that only seem to find their way to church on Christmas and Easter."

By the time everyone left, Billy was exhausted.

"Billy, leave everything till the morning."

Billy picked up the mistletoe and held it over his head. "Only if my Christmas girl gives her man a kiss."

In bed, they pulled the soft comforter up to be warm and cozy as they lay side by side, looking up at the ceiling. "You know what I think?"

Billy said, "You think this is the nicest Christmas we've had in a long time, and you love me?"

"Sure. That too, but I think we need to paint this ceiling. It's starting to peel in a few places." Then she laughed. "Yes, this was a special Christmas Eve. I'm so lucky to be able to share it with the best guy in Boston." She leaned over and kissed him on the cheek.

"So, only Boston, huh."

"Hey, I didn't know your self-esteem had improved that much already."

Billy reached down to tickle her feet, knowing it was her most sensitive spot, and she returned the favor. They laughed like children, and then she tucked her head into his shoulder as he pulled her closer, feeling grateful to be sharing life and this precious, fragile moment with her.

Chapter 31

Christmas Day was quiet and peaceful as they watched the snow blanket the street below, opened gifts, and enjoyed their time together. In the evening, they enjoyed watching their traditional movie, *It's a Wonderful Life*, as Mary dozed on and off during segments of it. The phone rang several times from friends wishing them well, but then came an unexpected call. "Hello," whispered Billy as he took the phone into the kitchen.

"It's Father Tom."

"Merry Christmas. Did you forget something?"

"I think I stole the last of those cookies, so no, but I do have a request."

"Sure, what it is?" responded Billy.

"What are you doing on New Year's Eve? Are you off duty? Can you get off from work?"

"New Year's Eve?" Billy sighed. "You know, we're not really your New Year's Eve party types."

"Can you be free? Just trust me—oh, and you'll need a tux and a nice dress for Mary. I saw one in the window as Filene's. It will probably be half-priced tomorrow." *Click!*

Billy stood bewildered, holding the phone. "Are you okay?" asked Mary as she wandered into the kitchen. "Who was that?"

"Wrong number."

On New Year's Eve, Billy was dressed to the nines and ready for anything, but he still didn't know what was going on at 6:45. Mary had napped during the day to have the energy to go out for the evening. She told Billy that she was even looking forward to it. The doorbell rang exactly on time, and Billy opened the door to see Tom in his traditional back attire and Angelo obviously less than comfortable in a suit and tie. Billy grinned at Angelo. "You too, huh?"

When they reached the street, there was a long black limo with a driver outside waiting to take them to their mystery destination. They drove around the city, looking at all the holiday decorations and lights still illuminating the city, skaters on Frog Pond in the Common, people flocking to one event or another, and glistening ice sculptures being completed for the city's celebration for First Night. After the city tour, the limo pulled up in front of the Isabella Stewart Gardner Museum, which was lit up for the evening. Mary gave Billy a curious glance as he helped her from the car.

"Don't ask me," said Billy as they watched men and women dressed for a gala celebration filing into the museum entrance.

"Father Tom?"

He shrugged.

"Angelo?" asked Mary.

The man merely offered an exaggerated, bewildered expression.

As they entered through security and checked their coats, Mary anticipated seeing her favorite space in Boston decorated for New Year's, but when she turned the corner, she was not expecting the grandeur of the sight: the enormous Christmas tree at the center, the strings of lights reaching the high arched gothic window three stories up, the sculptured figures, and the enormous display of festive flowers.

As Mary took in the scene, she turned toward DuBois, who seemed more than pleased by her expression of wonder and awe.

"Isn't it incredibly splendid, Mrs. Quinn?"

"Dr. DuBois, did you arrange all of this? Splendid is the perfect word."

DuBois offered his hand for a dance, and she accepted it. He slowly twirled her around. "Ahh, but not quite as exquisite as you are beautiful."

Mary blushed. "I'm sure there are many more beautiful women here tonight."

Wrinkling his nose, DuBois twirled the tip of his mustache. "I don't believe that any of them is the woman of honor as you are tonight."

Billy glanced around with Mary, noticing not only Tom and Angelo grinning at her, but now they saw Sean and Jenny, Dr. Hanson, many of the police officers and spouses they had come to know over the years, Sister Helen and other teachers at St. Francis School where she had volunteered, and many people they didn't recognize.

"What is happening here?" she asked.

The wait staff began passing out champagne-filled glasses to the hundreds of people who filled the courtyard area, all dressed for a special occasion. DuBois held up his glass as high as he could reach. "Everyone. Thank you so much for coming and being so very generous. Tonight is a very special night. This is our first annual Isabella Stewart Gardner's Annual James Gerard Quinn and Patrick William Quinn Fundraiser. Tonight zis gathering is in honor of two very special men who put the lives of the ones they loved over their own in the ultimate gift of love—their own lives. Each year we will gather to honor them in this fundraiser that has been traditionally held to raise funds to enhance this vision of Madam Isabella Stewart Gardner herself. Beginning this year, we will be donating fifty percent of those generous donations from each one of you to a very worthy purpose. This year, a very important person in this community will be given the chance to receive critical medical treatment to ensure a long and happy life."

DuBois clasped Mary's hand as he continued. "Mrs. Mary Quinn is one of the most wonderful women I know. She loves zis museum and 'as volunteered here many times. She loves children and volunteers her time to work at neighborhood schools, even after tragically losing her own son. She has given countless numbers of hours of 'er time to 'omeless shelters, food drives, neighborhood relief for victims of fires and other tragedies. As ze wife of a Boston Police officer, you can imagine her nights of worry. I am more than pleased to announce that we have collected over one million dollars in donations this evening, and one-half of this amount will be donated to support medical expenses for this precious member of our community, Mrs. Quinn. I am sorry to surprise 'er in this fashion, but"—he turned to Mary—"Mrs. Quinn, I don't believe you would have shown up otherwise."

Everyone clinked their glasses together and drank a toast to Mary, yelling out, "Here, here!"

Mary's mouth opened, and she bawled.

She tried to speak, but words would not come. Finally, Billy hugged her, and she grew composed enough to offer her thanks. "You are all so wonderful. I really don't know what to say. I can't believe this generosity. It's been an odd several weeks. I haven't seen my husband cry for years, and now he's crying all over his rented tux."

Everyone laughed while many wiped the tears from their own eyes.

"I, um, I'm so grateful that this event is being held in honor of my son and my dear brother-in-law. They both died as teenagers, but they gave their lives for others. I hope they serve as an inspiration to many other young men in this city."

The policemen, firefighters, and veterans in the audience yelled out, "Hooyah! Hooyah!"

Tears streamed down her cheeks as she held up her hand. "Thank you all. Really, thank you so much."

DuBois leaned over to Mary, "I'll 'ave you know, zis was all Father Tom's fault. He was de one who organized this effort and 'elped to round up all these people on short notice."

As if trying to escape, Tom turned.

Mary grabbed his arm. "Oh, no, you don't," she exclaimed. "I should have known you were the one behind something like this." She gave his arm a squeeze. "I have a mind to—say, thank you. Thank you for everything." She gave him a big hug.

There were violins, cellos, horns playing and hundreds of people gathered. Mary and Billy enjoyed catching up with old friends in the grand setting. Billy was well aware that the funding for the operation was only one part of the challenge. Finding a donor match would now be a difficult wait.

At one point, Mary asked Billy, "While I have the energy, would it be okay to go upstairs and see Rembrandt back in its place?"

"Sure we can." Billy nodded.

Guests were moving from room to room, but when Billy and Mary reached the Dutch Room, they had it to themselves. It felt romantic in the warm glow of the candlelight, and Billy held Mary's hand as they approached the young man's image captured in paint almost four hundred years earlier.

Mary sighed. "Isn't it magnificent?"

Billy stood mesmerized. He felt as if he were viewing the painted image for the first time. Not the painting, not the distracting ostrich plume on his ostentatious beret or the jeweled chains hanging on his fancy costume, but the man that existed inside. He wasn't able to think about the young Rembrandt before because he couldn't even see himself before.

As he gazed at the painting, he found himself staring squarely into the eyes of the young Rembrandt, who was just starting to discover who he was. Billy didn't feel afraid to be seen for who he was, imperfect but good enough to be loved by Mary, Patrick, Sean, and God, who made him.

He squeezed Mary's hand.

Mary said, "You know what was interesting? He painted portraits of himself his whole life. It seems like he painted himself more and more realistically as he aged, not afraid to show who he was."

"I think you're right, but despite all the distractions, the eyes still let us in." Billy turned and gazed deeply into Mary's. "I want to know all of you, and you to know all of me."

"You're a brave man, Mr. Quinn," said Mary as she kissed him.

"More than before."

Behind them came an unexpected voice. "Mrs. Quinn?"

Mary and Billy turned.

"I don't know if you remember me—"

Mary stepped back. "Of course I do, Melina. Melina Green. Isn't that right? Your dress looks stunning."

Melina blushed and leaned forward. "I actually can't wait to get out of it. I heard about this fundraiser and wanted to help out. Your husband has done so much to help get Kenny a new start, and your son meant so much to him in high school. I am so grateful. Thank you both. Even more, I am so sorry about the loss of your son. He was a wonderful young man and a good influence on Kenny. His death was such a shame. And, well, you were so nice when you came over to visit the other day; I wanted very much to do something."

Mary took Melina's hand. "I am very touched, but it looks like we'll be able to manage our medical expenses now. Please don't feel that you need to do anything."

Tears trickled down her cheeks. "Mrs. Quinn, I know about your son. I know what it meant for your husband to forgive my son, and it was incredibly kind to help him find a good job. I love that boy, and I so liked your boy. It means everything to me to give something back. You have given life back to my son after him spending so many years buried in guilt and running from himself. He was not on a good path, but now he is. You must know what that means to a mother."

Billy could see the depth of love in Melina for Kenny that he and Mary had for Patrick. They stepped toward the corner of the room and away from the doorway next to the Rembrandt painting. Melina squeezed Mary's hands. "I want to be the donor for your kidney and liver."

Shaking his head, Billy said, "No, Melina. That is too risky for you and too much to ask."

"But you didn't ask." Melina grinned from ear to ear. "I've been thinking of this for a while now. I was able to get the full story from Kenny, and I couldn't believe your response to him, your love and mercy."

Billy said, "Mrs. Green, I almost killed your son that day he told me the truth."

"Oh, I know. I almost killed him myself, but neither one of us did. We showed him the love and forgiveness God offers us. I imagine that was harder than a little inconvenience of donating an organ."

Mary shook her head. "Little inconvenience? We don't even know if you're a match."

Melina laughed loudly. "I already checked that out and have been for several tests at the hospital. Your Dr. Hanson actually said I was a perfect match, and I think you'll be lookin' good as a woman of color. Don't you think so, Officer Quinn?" Melina turned back to Mary. "I want to do this— for both of us."

"I can't—"

"You can't say no. I'm glad we agree," said Melina.

Melina embraced Mary for several moments like one would hold a close sister whom she hadn't held in a long while.

Chapter 32

On a cold Friday morning in late January, the city was blanketed by a coat of fresh white snow. Billy sat inside the Mass General Hospital chapel with Sean, Angelo, Kenny, Father Tom, and Sister Helen. In silence, he prayed for a safe and healthy outcome to the double surgery for Mary and Melina. The chapel was simple but beautifully designed with arched openings and stain-glassed windows on each side, bright plastered walls, a wooden beamed ceiling, and a large rose window over the altar. Candles flickered in sconces along the walls, and a sense of peace pervaded the space.

After some time, Tom said, "Lord, we pray for your faithful servants, Mary Quinn and Melina Green, as they enter surgery today. We thank you for these two beautiful women and the life-giving gift from Melina to Mary today. Please guide the surgeons' hands, and take good care of them today and throughout the healing process. Amen."

Everyone repeated, "Amen."

Tom put his hand on Kenny's shoulder. "Your mom is a special kind of person. She sacrificed to give you the gift of life in one way, and now she's giving the gift of life in a very different way today—both out of love."

Kenny stood and walked toward one of the alcoves and a stain-glassed window.

Tom approached him. "I know you're worried about your mom, and I hope I didn't say anything to make it worse?"

Lowering his head, Kenny replied, "I've always admired my mother, and I've always let her down—made life tougher for her. She's doing a good thing here, but she wouldn't be doing it if it weren't for me. If she doesn't make it, it'll be my fault."

Tom said, "It will be a long day of surgery, and these are the best transplant doctors around. I have a feeling she will be all right."

"I know, but feelings aren't enough."

After ten hours of surgery, Mary and Melina were returned to their rooms for recovery. They would not be up for visitors, but knowing they were both out of surgery and doing well in this first critical stage was a huge relief for everyone.

Tom grabbed Kenny by the shoulder. "Your mom is a strong woman. I think she'll be okay."

Billy didn't go home that night and neither did Kenny as they paced from the waiting room to the chapel to the cafeteria and back to the waiting room, catching moments of sleep until morning finally came. His visits were short but enough to let him see that Mary would be okay. When he finally ventured outside the hospital with Kenny by his side, the fresh cool air felt good. They walked together in silence for several blocks as they headed back to the South End.

Finally, Kenny murmured something.

Billy stopped. "What's that?"

Kenny stood with his hands in his old jacket and stared at the ground. "What made you do it?"

"Do what?"

"Forgive me. How could you ever forgive me?"

Billy sighed. "Somehow I finally understood that you really loved Patrick too, you really missed him, and you'd been punishing yourself for years."

Kenny wiped the tear that was beginning to form in the corner of his eye, but it was no use. "Patrick and my mother were the only two people to ever see me and then come closer and love me. I never wanted to hurt him. I just don't know what happened. I'm so sorry. I'm so sorry."

Billy put his arm around him. "Kenny, I have three gifts today to celebrate."

Kenny asked, "What's that?"

"I finally have hope that Patrick is very happy in heaven right now. Your mom has given life to another, giving Mary and me a chance to be together for a good while."

"What's the third?"

"I think I'm goin' to have a good friend in you now. So, how is that job of yours goin'? I want to see some of your work."

As they started forward, a runner slammed into Billy with a thud against his chest. He put out his hands to keep her from falling backward. "Are you okay, miss?"

"I'm so sorry," she said as she picked up her hat from the sidewalk. She glanced up and smiled broadly. "I know you! Officer William Patrick Quinn, right?"

Billy stared at the pretty pink cheeks of the girl until he recalled that expression from that Halloween evening. "Um, Jen—no, Jess—Jessica. Do I have that right?"

She nodded as she continued breathing heavily.

"Still running, huh?"

"Hey, it's daylight this time, and I met a boyfriend, and he won't let me run at night without a running mate, so you and my dad don't have to worry."

"Well, I'm glad to hear that."

Jessica laughed. "He is too. Hey, I know it's daylight, and this will sound kind of weird, but you look different in some way, happier or something? You have such a great face; I'd love to paint your portrait."

Billy laughed. "Hey, I'm open to anything these days!"

The End

Acknowledgments

So many people dedicated to the mission of Catholic novels work behind the scenes on the writing and publication of these stories. Christ taught wisdom and truth through intriguing stories and relatable characters, so follow his model and realize how much support we need to make that happen. Ellen and James Hrkach work tirelessly to spread the good Word in so many ways, and I'm blessed to have them as dedicated publishers. Authors and editors such as Michelle Buckman, Theresa Linden, and Ann Frailey have been a joy and gift to work with as they have guided and helped me grow as a writer. I thank God for their loving and patient work to support these stories.

About the Author

Jim Sano grew up in an Irish/Italian family in Massachusetts. Jim is a husband, father, lifelong Catholic and has worked as a teacher, consultant, and businessman. He has degrees from Boston College and Bentley University and is currently attending Franciscan University for a master's degree in Catechetics and Evangelization. He has also attended certificate programs at The Theological Institute for the New Evangelization at St. John's Seminary and the Apologetics Academy. Jim is a member of the Catholic Writers Guild and has enjoyed growing in his faith and now sharing it through writing novels. *Self Portrait* is his fifth novel.

Jim resides in Medfield, Massachusetts, with his wife, Joanne, and has two daughters, Emily and Megan.

Published by Full Quiver Publishing
PO Box 244
Pakenham, ON K0A2X0
Canada
www.fullquiverpublishing.com